THE SUMMER HOUSE

KERI BEEVIS

Boldwood

First published in Great Britain in 2023 by Boldwood Books Ltd.

Copyright © Keri Beevis, 2023

Cover Design by 12 Orchards Ltd

Cover Photography: Shutterstock

The moral right of Keri Beevis to be identified as the author of this work has been asserted in accordance with the Copyright, Designs and Patents Act 1988.

A CIP catalogue record for this book is available from the British Library.

Paperback ISBN 978-1-80415-132-7

Large Print ISBN 978-1-80415-131-0

Hardback ISBN 978-1-80415-130-3

Ebook ISBN 978-1-80415-133-4

Kindle ISBN 978-1-80415-134-1

Audio CD ISBN 978-1-80415-125-9

MP3 CD ISBN 978-1-80415-126-6

Digital audio download ISBN 978-1-80415-127-3

Boldwood Books Ltd
23 Bowerdean Street
London SW6 3TN
www.boldwoodbooks.com

For Ellie and Lola,
Fluffy divas, purr monsters, and the best companions a writer can have.
(Yes, I just dedicated this one to my cats)

1

2005

We are playing one of our games.

Wait for me in the summer house, your note had instructed. *Midnight. Wear your red dress. And don't put on any underwear. G xxx.*

I know you like how the red dress looks on me, the way it dips between my breasts and skims my hips, but you have never made any specific request for me to wear it. Until tonight.

Well, it isn't exactly a request. I had smiled earlier as I pulled it from the hanger, knowing I will do whatever I am told. It is all part of the thrill, of the excitement, not knowing what will happen next or how far you will push me.

The summer house is our special place. This private part of the garden, far away from the main house, is a place of secrets. They are ours alone and no one will ever learn what truly goes on inside this pretty white wooden building with its vaulted roof and panelled door. Here, when the cacophony of daylight sounds have finally quietened under a cloak of darkness, and while everyone sleeps, we creatures of the night come alive. This is when I can truly be myself.

My blood had heated in anticipation as I made my way across the lawn, the grass dry between my toes and the fragrant scents of honeysuckle, lavender, and jasmine clinging to the air. My excited heart beating faster as I wondered what tonight's game would be.

The chair that had been positioned in the centre of the floor had drawn my attention as soon as I entered the summer house. The cushion had been removed and from the glow of the paraffin lamp, I could see a red silk scarf draped across the wooden seat. Behind it was a second note, which I opened with trembling fingers, reading your words.

> *Sit on the chair*
> > *Put the blindfold on*
> > *Wait*
> > *Do not move and do not disappoint me*

I recognised your scrawling handwriting. Could picture your long, nimble fingers holding the pen, and heat pooled inside me, knowing your hands would soon be touching me.

The blindfold is a first for our games but I covered my eyes willingly, knotting the scarf behind my head. Eagerness overriding the flicker of apprehension in my gut.

It is not uncomfortable, but the silk is thick, and as I sit here waiting for you, I can't see a thing. It heightens my other senses and I am aware of everything: the ticking of the wall clock, the hoot of a barn owl and the creak of the chair as I shuffle slightly, trying to find a more comfortable position. Without the cushion, the seat is hard beneath me, and after a while, I can feel the spindles digging into my back.

Although the temperature has dipped slightly, the humidity allows little respite. It is going to be a warm night, too hot for sleeping. I only showered an hour ago, but already the nape of my neck is damp, my legs are sticking to the chair through the thin fabric of my dress, and a trickle of sweat is running down my back.

When I finally hear the door open, I flinch. In truth, I have no idea how long I have been waiting, but it has felt like forever, and although I have known you were coming, the sudden noise of your arrival still catches me off guard.

The key twists in the lock, then I hear the curtains being drawn, shutting us away from the world. Your footsteps grow closer, then further away again, and it takes me a moment to realise you are moving around me. I resist the urge to fidget, knowing I am being studied.

I only realise you are behind me again when your hands touch my shoulders. They are warm, though the texture of them is different. And your touch is light as your fingers trail down my arms. Your familiar fragrance lingers in the air and I breathe it in, steadying myself as I resist the urge to speak. I am desperate to know what tonight's game will entail, but I also understand that the rules are I must never ask.

You are guiding my arms behind me now and for a moment I wonder what you are doing, then I am aware of something wrapping around my wrists. Rope, I think as it grazes over my skin, before you pull it securely, forcing my hands together.

The first flutter of fear drops in my stomach. This game is darker than we have played before. I want to speak, to say it hurts, that it's cutting into my flesh, but I don't because I'm afraid you will be angry with me.

You are anchoring the rope to something now and it forces my shoulders back so they are pressed uncomfortably into the chair. I give my hands an experimental tug, panic lodging in my dry throat as I realise I can't pull free, and a whimper escapes.

Although you don't respond to the sound, I am sure I can see you smiling through my darkness.

I am scared, but the idea of being touched while I am helpless like this heats something deep inside of me. My cheeks flush both in shame and anticipation, but then comes another lick of fear when your hands grab my ankles, binding them to the front legs of the chair.

I wince as the rope digs deep into my skin. It's too tight. 'Please stop, you're hurting me.'

'Shh.'

I hadn't meant to speak, but this game feels different to the others. You always command and sometimes you punish, but I have never felt unsafe with you until now.

Tonight I fear we are going to cross a line.

I tremble, my heart thumping, scared of what comes next, but then I hear the lock turning, the door opening and closing, and realise you have left.

Alone, tied to the chair in this unbearably hot room, I wait; my imagination running wild.

Where have you gone?

Are you coming back?

Is your plan to fuck me or just leave me here?

Are you going to hurt me?

Real panic kicks in with that last thought and I struggle to free myself. I am bound too tightly. My body is drenched in sweat, the red dress sticking to me and the blindfold damp against my eyes. My hands and feet are starting to tingle and there is pain in my shoulder blades from the way my arms are positioned.

I want you to come back and untie me.

Moments later, your hands touch my shoulders again and I yelp, jerking against the chair.

It was a trick. Knowing that this whole time you have been right here watching, unsettles me further.

'Please let me go.'

I know I am not supposed to speak, but things have gone too far. Again you silence me with a 'shh'. This time, your finger presses to my lips and it's then I smell rubber and understand why your touch feels different. You are wearing gloves. Why do you have them on?

I am scared now. 'I want to stop. I don't like this game.'

Ignoring me, you lean in close, your warm breath against my ear as finally you speak.

'This isn't a game.'

Realisation is followed by horror. Finally I understand just how much trouble I am in.

2

PRESENT DAY

The place was just the same.

Lana Hamilton jangled the keys in her hand, taking a moment to study the house: the arched windows, the three chimneys, the yellow roses trailing around the front door.

She didn't come back often these days, but on previous visits, Nana Kitty had always been waiting by the front door, a smile on her face to greet her.

Though not this time.

Kitty now resided in the family plot at St Andrew's Church in the charming North Norfolk market town of Holt. Lana had stopped by the graveyard on her way to the house to lay flowers and again try to justify the reasons for selling her grandmother's beloved home.

The place had been left to Lana and her twin brother, Ollie, but she knew they couldn't keep it. Her life was in Cambridge and Ollie lived in London. Even if they could make it work, neither of them wanted to live in the house. Not since what had happened to Camille.

It was seventeen years since their sister's murder, but it never became easier. Camille had been just nineteen when she'd died, the twins two years younger, and her death had changed everything, including their relationship with Mead House.

Ollie had only come home a couple of times since graduating university, while Lana kept her visits short and sweet, the memories painful, but unable to abandon their grandmother. She was only here now because the house needed clearing before it went on the market.

It irked her that Ollie had shunned his responsibilities, forcing her to do this alone, claiming he couldn't get time off from the bank where he worked, and yes, her ex-boyfriend, Matt, had offered to come with her, but given that their relationship had not long ended, she was wary of giving him the wrong signals.

In truth, Lana could really do with the time away. Her boss at the magazine had agreed to let her take an extended six-week break. As a graphic designer, she could have worked remotely, but getting the house market-ready was going to be a big job. It was easier just to take the time off. Money wasn't an issue. She had some savings, and once the house had sold, her bank balance would be very healthy. It was bittersweet though, as it came at the expense of her grandmother.

Kitty's death had been a huge shock. Even though she was in her eighties, she was still fit and active, so to lose her to a senseless accident where she had fallen down the stairs had been hard. And what made it worse was Lana had missed the chance to speak with her grandmother one last time.

She had tried to contact Lana the day of her death and the brief voicemail asking for a call back was still on Lana's phone. She had been in a meeting all afternoon, though, and by the time she had picked up the message, it was too late.

Thank goodness a few of her grandmother's friends had been going over for a bridge evening and had spotted her through the hall window, otherwise her body could have remained there for days.

If she could trade her inheritance for another year with Kitty, Lana would do so in a heartbeat. Instead she was left with a message containing what were possibly her grandmother's last words.

The memories were strong as she forced herself towards the house and unlocked the front door. Her luggage was still in the boot, but it could wait. Right now she wanted a few minutes to reminisce. Her mother had died of cancer when Lana had been little more than a toddler and her father, Kitty's only child, had drank himself into an early grave just a couple of years later. Nana Kitty had taken all three of her grandchildren in and Mead House had become their home.

Although Lana and her siblings had gone to boarding school, this was where they spent all of their holidays. The long, lazy days of summer, playing in the gardens or swimming in the outdoor pool, and Christmas, when their grandmother went to town with decorations, making the place into a winter wonderland.

The house was set on a generous plot of land just a couple of miles from Holt. A sprawling country manor built in the mid-nineteenth century and hidden away down a long driveway, it had been a place of happiness until what had happened to Camille, but Kitty hadn't ever considered moving. She had lived here ever since marrying Lana's grandad, when she had been in her early twenties. He had died before all three grandchildren were born and Kitty had never remarried.

Lana hated the idea of her grandmother rattling around in the big house alone, but she knew Kitty would never leave. This was her family home.

As she pushed open the front door, the bright and airy hall was just as she remembered. Painted in a cheerful daffodil yellow, the wide staircase straight ahead and the morning sunlight spilling through the wide window at the top of the stairs, bouncing off the crystals of the oversized chandelier and making them sparkle.

If her grandmother was still alive, the vase on the hall table would be filled with spring flowers, freshly picked from the garden, and the scent of pine furniture polish would cling to the air.

Instead there was a hint of mustiness and dust gathering around the vase. It was now June and nearly two months had passed since the funeral. It showed.

The lounge stood to the right. A large but welcoming space dominated by a huge fireplace.

Lana paused by the mantel, two pictures of the three siblings still taking pride of place. One of them as youngsters. Her and Ollie all dark hair and olive skin, while their older, flame-haired sister sat in the centre. The twins wore matching toothless grins, while Camille was poised and elegant, even though she was only about eight at the time. The only hint of family resemblance was in their identical, almost black eyes. In the other photo, they were older and Lana recalled the picture had been taken not long before Camille died.

It had been half of her lifetime since she had seen her sister, but she could picture her clearly that last summer. Camille had been slender, pale and pretty, with an almost ethereal beauty. And a look in her dark eyes that suggested she had secrets.

Lana had always felt clumsy beside her. The scruffy tomboy with the short cap of hair and crumpled clothes. While Camille wore pretty dresses and spent her free time reading or writing in her journal, Lana was climbing trees and play-fighting with Ollie and his best friend, Xav.

Her hair was longer now and she had overcome her aversion to dresses, even if she did often wear them with trainers, but she would never have the elegance of her sister.

Wandering through to the garden room, Lana looked over the main back garden; a generous patio and the pool were closer to the house, with a wide lawned area beyond, its borders awash with the bright colours of early June flowers. Behind the row of conifers at the end of the lawn was the rose garden and leading from that she could see the beginning of the pathway that cut through the orchard to the summer house beyond.

At some point, she would have to go down there. But not today.

She hadn't been inside the summer house since Camille's body had been found but knew enough from the things she had seen online to be able to picture the scene. Her naked sister bound to a chair; her body cut and bruised and graffitied with vile words.

Lana tried to shake the image. Camille's killer was in prison and she had helped put him there. Justice had been served, though it didn't bring her sister back or make it any easier

She needed water. Thinking about Camille and what had happened always made her nauseous. She would get a drink, then bring her bags in from the car.

The kitchen, with its slightly dated oak units, had been the heart of the home, but it felt empty now, which was probably why she spotted the coffee mug straight away.

The rest of the worktop was clear of clutter, so why was there a random mug on the counter?

Lana was curious but not alarmed until she picked it up, realising the dregs of coffee in the bottom were still warm.

Was someone in the house?

As that thought crossed her mind, the ceiling creaked above her, and the unmistakable sound of footsteps crossing the landing had her shoulders tensing.

Lana was considering her options, and whether she should call the police before or after leaving the house, when a loud scream pierced through the air.

3

Hearing the sound of a car engine approaching, tyres crunching against the gravel outside, Xavier Landry stepped over to the window, paintbrush still in his hand, his heart sinking when he spotted the Range Rover.

He wasn't in the mood for visitors, especially not this one, and didn't appreciate being interrupted when he was working. He stared at the naked woman on his canvas. One leg extended. Wisps of hair escaping from a messy knot. He never painted their faces. They were all anonymous to him.

'Xav? Are you upstairs?'

Christ. Had she even knocked? He needed to get better at locking his doors.

He ran a frustrated hand through his hair, set down the paintbrush with the other and headed to the door of his studio, colliding with Trudy Palmer just as she was about to enter.

She was peering over his shoulder as he guided her back out into the hallway.

'Is that a new piece for the shop? Can I see it?'

'It's not finished yet.' Xav closed the door. She knew he didn't like anyone seeing his work until it was complete. 'What are you doing here, Trudy?'

'I brought pastries and I thought we could discuss sales, and maybe doing another meet the artist evening. The last one was a big success.'

It had been and they had sold several paintings. Though he did wonder how many had been drawn to the tiny shop because of who his brother was.

Truthfully? Xav had always hated the publicity side of things. He understood it was part of the job and for a long time he had played the game, but he had moved back here for a quieter life. He was happiest when he could just lock himself away and paint.

'It was only a few months ago. We should probably leave it longer.'

'And miss out on potential sales? I could advertise in a different area, try to pull in a new crowd. And it helps people to connect with your work,' Trudy was pushing now, sounding more like she owned a gallery rather than a small art and craft shop in Holt. 'They love you, Xav. The brooding French artist.'

'Half-French,' he reminded her. 'And I've lived here longer than there.'

'Minor details.' Trudy waved his concerns away. 'You know the language, can charm them with your accent.'

'I don't have an accent.' Well, barely. Xav had moved to the UK with his mum and brother when he was nine, shortly after his father had died, and although he had lived in France for a couple of years in his late twenties, the North Norfolk coastline was the place where he felt most at home.

'You really shouldn't undersell yourself, hon. You're the full package.'

Trudy's gaze was fixated on his face now and she had a wistful look in her eyes. Shit!

If Xav was counting his faults, failure to read signals would be on the list. Trudy wasn't really here to talk sales and again he mentally kicked himself for sleeping with her. One stupid drunken decision he was coming to regret again and again and again.

Trudy wasn't an unattractive woman, but there was no spark. At least not on Xav's side. He had known her for a long time and she had been in the year below him at school. Xav had left town after his brother, Sebastian, had gone to prison, unable to deal with the gossip and the pointed stares, and for a long time he had stayed away. His mother was still here, though, refusing to leave her home, and knowing she wasn't getting any younger, he had returned a year ago. Trudy had been one of the first to welcome him back.

Being friends was fine, but he didn't want a relationship with her.

'You have a little paint.'

'Sorry?'

'On your cheek.'

Trudy had licked the pad of her thumb, was already reaching in to rub it when Xav caught her hand.

'I need you to leave.'

'What? But I bought pastries.' Trudy didn't bother to hide her disappointment at his bluntness.

Add lack of diplomacy to his list of faults.

'Take them with you. I've already eaten. Now isn't a good time. I really need to work.'

'We do need to discuss business, Xav. You can't just lock yourself away.'

She sounded a little annoyed and he didn't want to fall out with her. Although he didn't need her business, he liked working with her, and to her credit, Trudy Palmer had always gone above and beyond to sell his work since he had been back in Norfolk.

'I need to head into town tomorrow, so how about I call in and see you? The new painting should be ready and I can bring it with me.' He offered her a smile, relieved when her frown relaxed.

'You promise?'

'I promise.' *Now just go.*

'Perhaps we can go for a coffee.'

'Hmm, maybe.'

He managed to get her down the stairs and out of his house, closing the door as soon as she was back in her car, this time locking it.

Hector, his overweight tabby cat, who was lying on one of the kitchen chairs, glanced up, looking annoyed at the interruption. Judgement all over his stripey face.

'Yes, I know it's my own fault,' Xav muttered to him, going back upstairs.

In his studio, he picked up his brush again, dipped it in the paint, stroking the canvas with the confidence of a skilled hand.

It was all in the details and the painting needed a splash of colour.

The curve of the back, the elongated neck, and the red scarf she now wore in her hair.

4

For a moment, Lana froze in panic. Someone was being murdered in Nana Kitty's house.

Her eyes widened when the scream was followed by loud giggling and then another shriek, but this one was laced with amusement. And definitely female.

It was a Wednesday morning. Who the hell was in the house?

Perhaps she should still have called the police, but Lana had gone from frightened to angry, and armed with the old rounders bat she found in the cupboard in the games room, she marched up the stairs, ready to wage war. She knew she could do some damage with it, having broken Xavier Landry's nose when they were fourteen.

In fairness, it hadn't been her fault. Ollie and Xav had played a prank on her. The three of them were home alone and had been watching a scary movie and when Lana had gone to the loo, her darling brother and his best friend had decided to hide. She had already been on edge from the movie, so when Xav had jumped out at her, she hadn't hesitated before swinging. She had been grounded for a week, though it was kind of worth it, as Xav seemed to view her with a newfound respect afterwards.

Recalling how he had looked at her the last time their paths had crossed had Lana's gut tightening more than the threat of what was upstairs.

You're dead to me. Leave me the hell alone.

She could remember the hatred on his face, knew he meant every word, and all these years later it still cut deep.

Trying to push him from her thoughts, Lana focused on the sound she had heard. She was on the landing now and the doors to the rooms were all open. All but one.

Her old bedroom.

She hesitated. Was that where the woman was?

As if to confirm, she heard another giggle come from beyond the closed door, then the muffled sound of voices.

Lana pushed the handle of her bedroom door down slowly, easing it open. Through the visible crack, she could see her unmade bed and a naked woman sitting in it. Some Barbie doll with a lit cigarette in one hand and a phone to her ear in the other.

What the fuck?

Lana threw the door wide, charging into the room, her bat poised and ready to strike if necessary.

'What the hell do you think you're doing in my house?'

The woman's eyes went wide, her mouth dropping open. As she realised her bare breasts were on show, something had to give. Unfortunately, it was the lit cigarette as she sought to cover herself.

'My duvet!'

'Fuck!' Barbie finally dropped the phone, scrambling to retrieve her cigarette from the now smoking bedding. Her eyes were wild as she screeched, 'NOLLY! GET OUT HERE NOW!'

The en suite door opened and Lana tightened her grip on the bat, her mouth dropping open when her brother stepped out.

'Ollie? What the hell?'

'This crazy woman was attacking me.'

'Lana? What are you doing?' Ollie had a towel around his waist and a horrified expression on his face as he glanced between the pair of them.

'Nolly. Tell this woman, whoever she is, to get the fuck out of our room.'

'Nolly?' Lana dropped the bat to her side. Ignoring her brother, she turned to Barbie. 'His name is Ollie. There's no N in it. And, for the record, this is my room, not yours.'

Ollie had his hands on his head now, classic Ollie Hamilton panic mode. He decided to go for humour. 'So maybe this isn't the best time to introduce you two, but, Lana, this is my fiancée, Elise. Elise, meet my sister, Lana.' He followed it up with a laugh, as both women scowled at him.

'What are you doing here, Ollie?'

'There's a leak in the ceiling in my room and Elise preferred the view from yours. We can move if it's a problem.' He shot Elise a worried look and, seeing her scowl deepen, quickly added, 'Though you don't really mind, do you? It's not like we've lived here in years.'

Lana sighed. 'I meant, what are you doing *here*? In this house?'

'You told me to come.' Ollie's voice had taken on a petulant note now. 'Remember? You were quite snotty in your messages, telling me I had to take my share of responsibility.'

'I thought you couldn't get time off work?'

'Well, I sorted it.'

Lana glanced between her brother and Elise.

He was right; she had told him to come. Still, she hadn't expected him to show up, certainly hadn't anticipated he would bring company. It stung that her twin brother had failed to tell her he was engaged. She hadn't realised he was seeing anyone seriously. He had been alone at the funeral, which had only been two months ago. Lana had made most of the arrangements for that, communicating with Ollie mostly via WhatsApp. At no point had he mentioned anything about a fiancée.

Looking back, she supposed they hadn't really spoken much on the day, both of them still in shock and dealing with their grief as they thanked well-wishers.

Pushing her hurt to one side, Lana reminded herself that he was here now, and that counted for something. Maybe this was a chance to reconnect and start fresh.

That meant giving Elise a chance too. As first impressions went, Lana wasn't a fan, and she was pretty certain Kitty would have shared her opinion, but for Ollie's sake she would make an effort.

She found a smile for them both. 'You're right. I did and I'm glad you're both here. I'm sorry. I didn't mean to barge in here and scare you, Elise. I thought the house was empty and panicked.' She looked at her brother, 'I never saw your car.'

'I parked it in the garage,' he confirmed.

That would make sense. She offered Elise another smile. 'I'm honestly not some bat-wielding psycho. Can we start over? I'm Lana.'

Elise sniffed and for a moment Lana didn't think she was going to accept her hand, but then she gave it a brief shake. 'Elise,' she said stiffly.

'Where's Matt?' Ollie questioned, looking around.

This wasn't the time to get into her failed relationship. 'It's just me.'

Ollie's eyes narrowed. When they had been younger, the pair of them had had the whole twin thing going on, but these days Lana swore he was too self-absorbed to pick up on her vibes, so he surprised her when his expression softened. 'I never really liked him anyway.'

She shrugged. 'It's for the best.'

The moment was broken by Elise sighing loudly, suggesting she was bored, and a switch flipped in Ollie, the shutters going back down.

'So are you okay if we stay in this room?' he asked.

'Yeah, keep it. I'll go in Camille's.'

Lana was still a little annoyed that they had taken her old room without asking, but they were unpacked and it wasn't worth an argument.

Leaving Ollie and Elise to it, she went to fetch her bags from the car, lugging them back up the stairs and along the landing to her sister's old room. Opening the door was like stepping back in time and her heart hitched. She had forgotten just how much of a shrine it still was to her sister. The walls painted in cream, the double bed covered in a dusky-pink duvet and piled high with cushions. Lana knew that Kitty had never been able to bring herself to part with Camille's things. Her sister's clothes hung in the wardrobe, and her make-up and perfumes were still littered over the elegant dressing table with its big three-way mirror.

It looked and felt the same. The only thing different was the smell. Seventeen years of mustiness now clung to everything, overriding the once familiar floral scent.

Crossing to the window, Lana pushed it open, letting the warm summer air into the room.

Like her old bedroom, Camille's room overlooked the back of the house and up here there was a clearer view. The gardener had stayed on at Lana's request to maintain the grounds and look after the pool and directly below her, she could see the water shimmering in the June sun, while the top lawn was awash with colour. Pale-purple verbenas towered over lavender blues and primrose yellows, in front of a rainbow wall of well-cared for rhododendrons. Stone steps led through an archway in the bushes into her grandmother's beloved rose garden, then on to the orchard, and in the distance beyond the trees, she could see the roof of the summer house.

After the murder, Lana had suffered from troubled dreams where she had tried to warn Camille that last fateful night, listening to her sister's cries as she desperately tried to reach her. What had her last moments been like? Had she realised she was going to die?

For a long while, Lana had carried the guilt of believing she could have prevented Camille's death. That night, she had seen her crossing the lawn with Sebastian Landry, knowing they were going to the summer house. She remembered thinking it was romantic at the time.

Little did she know that as she drifted off to sleep, Sebastian had been choking the life out of her sister.

They had both returned to Mead House – Lana and Ollie Hamilton.

George Maddox had been expecting Lana, as he had spoken with her on the phone, but Ollie and his girlfriend had been a surprise and they had really caught him off guard, finding George in the house when they had arrived yesterday.

He had managed to deal with that little hiccup, claiming he did a sweep through of the place each visit, just to check everything was okay. Ollie hadn't questioned who had given him the keys. It was assumed Kitty had, and George didn't correct him. No one needed to know that he had borrowed one of her spare sets a long time ago and had a copy cut.

He had been caretaking Mead House for as long as he could remember, long before he had taken over officially as Kitty's gardener four years ago, just after his twenty-eighth birthday. This place had secrets and he needed to make sure they stayed buried. Especially now with the return of the twins.

They planned to put the house on the market once it had finished going through probate and that was a good thing, though they would need to clear it first, and that could be dangerous.

George had tried to make sure there was no trail to link back to him, but if they looked hard enough, who knew what they might unearth.

He would keep watch, play his role of the friendly and helpful gardener. Completely harmless and a bit of a goof. That persona worked for him best, as it encouraged people to drop their guard. They didn't perceive him to be a threat.

He worked at Mead House three days a week, usually taking on other projects on the side, but he would make sure that while the Hamiltons were in town, they had his undivided attention. Once the place had been sold, he could breathe a little easier that the secrets of Camille Hamilton's murder would remain hidden.

He thought of her now. The cool and beautiful redhead who had a dark and secret wild side. The last time he had seen her, she had begged him for her life.

It had been over for her too quickly, but he couldn't afford to dwell on that.

One fuck-up defined him. If any problems arose, he would deal with them.

George had a wife and kids now and he was happy. He would do whatever was necessary to ensure nothing disrupted the life he had built for himself.

Lana's resolve to get along with her brother's fiancée lasted less than twenty-four hours.

She had tried. She really had, but Elise was proving to be insufferable.

Lana had gone out to buy groceries, and she had then spent the afternoon giving the house a good clean. It was tidy, but dust had started to gather. Finally, when she was dead on her feet, she had cooked dinner for the three of them. A peace offering and a fresh start, she figured, ignoring the fact that while she had been working, Elise had been swanning about the house as if she owned it, more interested in Kitty's heirlooms than whether Lana needed any help.

Ollie had made a token effort, cleaning the bathrooms, before disappearing upstairs at Elise's command. Lana had hoped to have a catch-up with him, but that seemed unlikely while his fiancée was about.

She made sure to give them plenty of warning, shouting up the stairs a good half an hour before serving up the food, and her first thought when Elise walked into the kitchen fifteen minutes later was that she was a little overdressed for dinner, wearing a black chiffon dress and heels, her blonde hair in an updo, and big earrings glittering at her lobes.

Lana ignored the rumble of annoyance as Elise gave her jeans and T-shirt a disdainful look. Okay, so she was a mess, but she had been working.

'I hope you're hungry. I made way too much pasta.'

'Actually, we're going out.'

'You're what?'

Lana thought she had misheard, but then Ollie appeared, one of his dark-grey suits on, and the top two buttons of his shirt undone. He was freshly shaven and his expression was guilty as he glanced first at the set kitchen table, then at Lana's scowl.

'Sorry, I didn't realise you were going to all this trouble.'

'Are you ready?' Elise demanded, ignoring the awkwardness.

'You never said you were going out to eat.'

'We only decided an hour ago.' The rude woman couldn't even be bothered to look at Lana as she spoke.

'Ollie! You knew I was cooking.'

'I'm sorry, Lana. I thought you were just going to throw a pizza in the oven or something. Elise wanted to go out and...' He trailed off, flicking a quick glance at his fiancée. 'Maybe we should stay.'

'Nolly! You promised. Come on!'

Lana watched as Elise stomped across the kitchen, disappearing through the door into the garage.

Her brother was flustered. 'Maybe we can heat it up and have it tomorrow.'

'NOLLY!'

'I'm coming. Look, I really am sorry, Lana. We have to go.'

She watched him leave, the garage door closing, and moments later heard the sound of his engine.

Lana stared at the pasta dish she had made, fuming that she

had bothered to cook. She should have just ordered in a takeaway and left Ollie and Elise to their own devices.

Determined not to let them ruin her first night back in the house, she opened one of the bottles of wine she had bought and settled down to eat her meal for one with the radio for company.

She reminded herself that she hadn't expected Ollie to show at all, so it was good that he was here. It was just unfortunate he had brought Elise.

After she had eaten, she took her wine through to the garden room, opening the doors and stepping out onto the patio. It was still warm out and she had forgotten quite how silent it was in this little corner of the world. The house set back down a long driveway and far from any busy roads.

Tomorrow, she would start the arduous task of packing her grandmother's things. Camille's too. She had already spoken with a couple of estate agents who were chomping at the bit to get the listing. Despite the long-ago murder, they didn't think they would have any trouble selling the house. Sadness mingled with guilt and had her questioning if they were doing the right thing by selling.

No, they had to. They couldn't stay.

Dusk was settling, the water in the oblong pool now a black mass and the floral scents of gardenia, honeysuckle and rhododendron clinging to the air. At the end of the lawn, the entrance to the rose garden, her grandmother's favourite part of the grounds, was shrouded in darkness. and it was there that Lana spotted the beam of light.

She blinked, for a moment doubting herself.

The orchard lay beyond the rose garden, the path that snaked through it leading to the summer house, and beyond the high fences surrounding the property was woodland. The garden lamps that had once lit the way were no longer in use. Kitty not wanting the reminder of where her eldest granddaughter had died.

Lana must have imagined it. But even as she told herself that, she was certain she saw a flicker of movement, a figure stepping into the shadows.

A shiver of cold crept down her spine. Was she being paranoid or was there really someone out there? No one had any business being down by the orchard.

She told herself she was overreacting, but that didn't stop the uneasiness coiling in her gut.

Part of her wanted to find a weapon, to go and look and reassure herself everything was okay. She wasn't a coward, but she also wasn't stupid. Her sister had been killed in the summer house. A place where she should have been safe. And although Sebastian Landry was in prison, she shouldn't take foolish risks.

Instead, she stepped back inside the house, making sure all of the doors and windows were locked. Then, keeping her phone close, she went upstairs and stood in Camille's dark bedroom where she had a better view of the orchard. If anyone was down there, she would call the police.

She watched and waited, the only sound coming from the ticking of the alarm clock and her own steady breathing. Eventually, convincing herself it was her overactive imagination, she stepped away from the window.

It was being back in this house. She was sure of it. Her mind was simply playing tricks. She was tired and needed sleep.

Still, she made one last trip downstairs to recheck all of the locks, before having her well-earned shower. Eventually, she crawled into bed and was out like a light as soon as her head hit the pillow.

When she was awoken by shrieking, it took her a moment to realise where she was. Grabbing her phone, she saw it was after 1 a.m.

What the hell?

Not just shrieking. There was laughter too.

Lana threw back the duvet, rubbing at her tired eyes as she crossed the bedroom and threw open the door. She blinked against the harsh light, saw Ollie doing a bad job of creeping up the stairs, Elise hanging on to his back, a bottle of champagne in her hand.

'Ollie?'

They both turned to face her, Ollie raising a finger to his lips. 'Shh!'

That had Elise erupting in more laughter. 'I think we've already woken her.'

Lana stepped back into Camille's bedroom and slammed the door shut, crawling into bed and pulling the pillow over her head. It took forever to fall asleep again and when she did, her dreams were filled with her sister, dressed in red, her vibrant hair flowing, and of the stranger with the torch who was lurking in the orchard.

Lana spent Thursday morning packing up her grandmother's clothes. It wasn't the easiest of tasks. Kitty had liked to hoard, always reluctant to part with things, and some of the older outfits evoked strong memories that made the pain of losing her grandmother so much sharper.

Lana tried to be methodical, not letting her mind wander, and relieved when it was finally done, she loaded up her car.

'Are you heading into town?'

She glanced up, hearing Ollie's voice. He stood on the front porch, dressed, though looking a little worse for wear. It was the first she had seen of him all morning.

'Yes, why?'

'Can I grab a lift to get my car? I left it at the restaurant.'

Lana resisted the urge to say no, remembering how inconsiderate he had been the previous night. She hadn't had any chance to catch up with him, though, and was eager to find out what the deal was with him and Elise.

'If you're quick,' she told him. 'I need to get a move on.'

'I'm ready.'

Alone with him in the car, she steered the conversation round to his fiancée as she drove, trying to keep her views on Elise's rudeness to herself, not wanting to antagonise him. Instead, she focused on specifics, surprised to learn the woman originally came from Norfolk, mildly amused when Ollie described her as a model who was between jobs, and concerned when she found out they had only met a couple of months ago.

Ollie was being rash. It was too soon.

She gently tried to point that out, but he immediately went on the defensive.

'It's none of your business who I date or propose to, Lana.'

He was right, it wasn't. But it didn't stop her worrying about him.

She could see the stubborn set of his jaw, though, and knew him well enough to change the subject – at least for now. 'How long have work given you off?'

His answer came after some consideration. 'I can take as long as I need,' he told her, and Lana spotted the tic in his cheek and his steady focus on the road ahead as signs there was something he wasn't telling her.

'That's very generous of them,' she fished carefully. 'I thought your boss was always funny about you taking too much holiday.'

The tic continued, the dragging silence making her more suspicious.

'I quit, okay?'

'You what?' Was he crazy? Ollie had worked at the bank for years.

'I've been wanting to for a while and it's not like we need the money now.'

'Just because you get an inheritance doesn't mean you quit your job. Jesus, Ollie.' He had always had a reckless streak, but this was something else. 'And besides, we don't have the money yet.'

'I have enough to get by. And again, it's none of your business, Lana.'

His tone had turned sulky and seeing the restaurant coming up, she indicated, slowing down. Not wanting to leave things on a bad note between them, especially as they hadn't had a chance to talk about the house properly yet and form any real plans, she eased back. 'It's not any of my business, you're right, but I do care about you,' she said quietly. 'And I appreciate you coming back here. I know it wasn't easy for you.'

'I'm fine.' The easy-going grin was back in place as he leant over and kissed her on the cheek. 'You don't have to worry about me.'

With that, he was out of the car and Lana's shoulders sagged. She was certain things weren't fine, but what could she do? If she kept nagging, she would only push him further away. For now, she tried to put it to the back of her mind and after dropping the bags of clothes off at one of the local charity shops, she decided to try some of the art shops and studios in town to see if anyone was interested in buying her grandmother's paintings. Kitty had been a big art collector and had several pieces around the house. Lana didn't have room for them and the one thing she had managed to ascertain from her brother was that he didn't want to take them either.

It was yet another reluctant sale that she hoped would not have their grandmother turning in her grave, but it was better they went to someone who would appreciate them.

The first place she tried was the Little Picture Shop and it wasn't until the woman sitting at the counter called out to her that Lana realised she knew her. Trudy Palmer was the daughter of her grandmother's former doctor, who had also been one of Kitty's close friends.

'Lana Hamilton? I heard you were back. How are you?'

'I didn't know you worked here.'

'Own it, actually. It was a dream of mine to be able to work with local artists.' She paused. 'I'm so sorry about Kitty. Dad was too. They went back a lot of years.'

'Thank you. It was a shock to us all.'

As a teenager, Trudy had been quiet and studious, and there had been rumours that Dr Palmer had been a strict father. There was nothing quiet about her now and she was confident and articulate. Even the clothes she wore flattered rather than hid her tall, toned figure and her once dark hair was highlighted to a honey blonde.

'So what brings you into my shop, Lana?' she asked eventually. 'Are you looking to get some new pieces for the house?'

'We're not staying. Ollie and I are planning to sell.'

'Really?'

Was she imagining it or did Trudy sound a little critical, as well as surprised?

'The place is too big and I live in Cambridge. Ollie is in London.' She hated that she was trying to justify the decision, her tone defensive. 'We can't keep it.'

'Relax. I'm not judging you.' Trudy's face softened into a smile and Lana realised it was her own guilt making her read into things.

'Sorry, I know you weren't. It wasn't an easy decision. I hate that we are selling it,' she admitted.

'Perhaps it's for the best, though. Kitty's accident, and of course Camille. I know there are some bad memories for you.'

There were, but Lana didn't want to dwell on those. 'So how do you feel about buying my grandmother's art?' she asked, deciding to cut straight to the chase.

'Are you kidding me?' Trudy sounded excited. 'Yes, I would love to take a look.' The bell chimed at that moment and she excused herself as a customer entered the shop. 'Have a look around, okay? I'll be right back with you.'

Lana did as suggested, wandering over to view a selection of coastal prints. She recognised the beach at Wells-next-the-Sea, the marshland at Burnham Overy Staithe. Stunning sunrises and sunsets shot by local photographers, Gary Pearson and Lila Amberson, among others.

The next wall was dominated by a series of life studies. All naked women, though tastefully painted to show natural feminine beauty in the curve of a back or the crossing of ankles. There was only one splash of colour in each piece: emerald earrings, pink lipstick, a ruby pendant, or, in the case of one of the figures, orange brushstrokes slashing over her buttocks. Every painting was subtle, sexy and mesmerising.

Lana looked at the artist's name, her breath catching.

Xavier Landry.

Trudy stocked his work?

Lana knew Xav had found success as an artist, and she would be a liar if she pretended she had never Googled him over the years. But he kept his private life exactly that – private. And other than his paintings, there was little to tell about the man himself. He had moved away after Sebastian had gone to prison, but Lana knew his mother, Joanna, still lived locally. Did Xav ever return to Holt to visit her? Did Joanna hate Lana as much as her son did?

'He's a brilliant artist, isn't he?' Trudy's voice cut through Lana's thoughts and she guiltily stepped away from the display, as if she'd been caught looking at something she shouldn't.

Heat rushed to her face. 'They're very good,' she agreed, glad that she managed to sound praising but nonchalant at the same time.

Trudy knew the details. Everyone did. That the boy Lana had given her teenage heart to was the brother of the man who had killed her sister. But did she know that he now hated her passionately for telling the police about Sebastian?

Lana was glad when the subject returned to Kitty, and they
made arrangements for Trudy to drive out to Mead House the
following afternoon.

As she turned to leave, the door opened, and Lana collided with
the man who entered. Rushed apologies were exchanged before she
glanced up, freezing when she found herself caught in the gaze of
shocked, earthy-green eyes.

There was no mistaking Xav Landry, even though many years
had passed. The softness of youth was gone and what stood before
her was an older, but finer honed version, his jaw grazed with
stubble and fine lines fanning from his eyes. The dark waves of his
hair were more unruly than she remembered and the perfect
symmetry of his face was flawed by his slightly crooked nose. The
one Lana had broken years earlier.

For a moment, they simply stared at each other and Lana tried
to kick her startled brain into action.

Speak, for fuck's sake.

There were so many things she had wanted to say to him over
the years, but in this moment, the words were all gone from her
head. Instead, her mouth opened and closed like a goldfish.

Xav was the first one to react, his expression going from shocked
to horrified to disgusted, as he visibly flinched, stepping away.

It was then that Lana found her voice. 'Xav!'

He pushed past her, heading into the shop without a word.

'Xav. Please.'

She was wasting her breath. He didn't even hesitate, instead
speaking directly to Trudy as if Lana wasn't even there. It was only
then she realised he was carrying a canvas.

'I'll take this straight out back.'

His voice, with just the faintest hint of accent giving away his

French roots, conjured up a whirlwind of memories, many good, but others painfully bad, and she stood rooted to the spot as he disappeared through the doorway behind the counter, unsure whether she should follow after him and try to make him talk to her or if it was better to leave.

Why was he here? He was supposed to have moved away. Was he just visiting?

Eventually, her head won over her heart, something that might have been to do with the way Trudy was looking at her sympathetically.

Lana didn't need pity and, wanting the ground to swallow her, she muttered a quick goodbye and hastily left the shop. She slipped her sunglasses on as a layer of privacy before she crossed the street.

All of these years had passed and he still hated her. Still hadn't forgiven her. How pathetic that her first reaction when seeing him had been a kick of lust stirring in her gut? It was quickly turning to anger, though.

How dare he blame her? Yes, she had given evidence against his brother, but what was she supposed to have done: broken the law? And, okay, so he was annoyed she had played a part in Sebastian going to prison, but how dare he try to take the moral high ground when it was his brother who had choked the life out of her sister?

This was better. It was more productive turning her hurt into anger.

He had no right to judge her.

If she hadn't known him when Camille died, she would want nothing to do with him or his family. What had been between them had died the moment Sebastian was arrested and they could never go back to how things were before.

Lana refused to be cowed into returning to her car, keeping her head held high and trying to banish thoughts of Xav from her mind as she spent the next half-hour running errands and pausing to look in a couple of the town's boutique shops. He didn't matter and she no longer cared what he thought of her. But as she returned to her car, the hollow emptiness in her heart returned.

Caught up in her thoughts, she was oblivious to the eyes watching her from across the street.

She looks nothing like her sister, at least not physically, but it is there in the mannerisms, the way she holds herself, the confidence of her stride, the jut of her chin. She is a Hamilton and carries that same self-assured belief that she is something special.

Her waste-of-space brother is the same. Her grandmother was too. Sitting there in her big house away from the town, lauding her money and influence over everyone, as she judged from afar. And that bitch, Camille. She was the worst. A thief and a liar and a charlatan. It made me sick watching the town mourn for her. They had no idea that their adored princess was not all sweetness and light as she tried to portray. What would they have thought of her if they had known the truth? If they had learnt that really, she was a skanky ho with the morals of an alley cat? I made her confess, to repent her sins, to reveal her true self before I choked the life out of her.

The Hamiltons are a disease and they infect everyone they touch, and the sooner this town is rid of them, the better.

Xav had known she would come back here after her grandmother's death and he was aware of the rumours that they planned to sell the house.

That was good and it would be a chapter in his life he could finally close the door on. All he needed to do was lie low, focus on his work, and stay the hell away from Lana and Ollie Hamilton.

They had once been his best friends, but that was a lifetime ago when everything had been different. Now he had no desire to see either of them and the sooner they were gone, the better.

Damn fate for interfering and putting Lana in his path. He had gone out this morning because he needed to pick up some supplies and he had promised Trudy he would take in the stupid painting.

Of course, she hadn't missed the exchange and had been full of questions after Lana had left, poking her nose in where it wasn't wanted. Xav had made his excuses and left as soon as he could.

He mostly preferred his own company these days. And the small circle of friends and family he did have, he kept extremely tight.

His home was on the outskirts of Salthouse, a village built on the marshes and nestled between Cley-next-the-Sea and Kelling, and the converted barn where he lived and worked had spectacular views of the surrounding countryside down to the coastline, while being far enough from his neighbours to give him the privacy he craved. It was also close enough to his mother if she needed him.

Not that she claimed she ever would. Joanna Landry was independent and kept herself active, but at least Xav was there if things ever changed.

He let himself into the house, took a cold bottle of water from the oversized fridge in his kitchen, then headed upstairs to his studio, still trying to shake off the shock of seeing Lana.

Hector was sunbathing on the landing, in his favourite position in front of the floor-to-ceiling window at the top of the stairs, his view one of green fields down to the salt marshes, and his tawny brown stripes almost blond in the sunlight that was filtering through. He glanced up sleepily, hearing the creak of the step, and Xav stopped to make a fuss of him. It was hard to believe that just nine months ago this porker had been a skinny runt abandoned in a box on the edge of the woods.

Xav hadn't wanted a cat, but he hadn't been able to stop thinking about the pitiful creature he had rushed to the vets. When a week later, he had called for an update and found the cat wasn't chipped so would be put up for adoption, he had stepped in without thinking. Now they were roommates, though sometimes he wondered if it was actually Hector's house and he was just a guest here.

The upper floor of the house was split into two large rooms that led off the landing. One was where Xav slept. The other was his studio. A room with a high-beamed ceiling and flooded with natural light.

The studio had been his priority when house hunting. Money was no longer an issue, thanks to a fortunate encounter fresh out of university with a well-connected gallery owner. Xav had worked hard while he learnt his craft, holding down various jobs to pay his student fees, knowing that his mother couldn't afford to help. As far as he was concerned, he had been due a little bit of luck.

He never took it for granted, though, putting in the graft and leading a nomadic lifestyle as he moved from city to city, throwing everything into his work and the commitments that came with it.

Bristol, London, Rotterdam, Paris: his home had changed more frequently than his girlfriends. Eventually, though, he had burnt out and, hankering to put down roots, he had returned to Norfolk. He was single, a little bit cynical, but had a firmer idea of what he wanted from life.

Now he painted mostly for himself. He still had dealings with a couple of big galleries, but with his bank balance healthier than it had ever been, he could afford to be choosy, and he wanted to work with some of the smaller shops and businesses.

This studio was his sanctuary and where he spent most of his time, and it was the one room he had taken care in furnishing. The space was dominated by his easel, the rest of the room casually dressed with sofas and a couple of coffee tables. Some of his favourite work hung on the walls. He didn't entertain up here; in fact, this studio was his sacred place and he resented anyone setting foot inside it, but the room was big and had looked bare without any furniture.

He stared at the blank canvas. A fresh start, a new piece of work. The possibilities were endless and he loved this moment, the first lick of paint as he told a story with his brushes.

Of course, he already knew what he was going to create. There was no point in fighting it. The urge was too strong. By giving in to it, he could put it in a box and finally be done. This one wasn't intended for public eye. It would be his own personal indulgence.

He never painted faces, but today was different, and although he had only seen her briefly, she was already imprinted in his mind. The almond-shaped eyes, almost black in colour, her wide, expressive mouth with the fuller top lip, her dark hair falling like a curtain of raw silk around her shoulders.

His heart had hitched when he had seen her and for a moment he had been lost for words, could only think about reaching out to touch her to check if she was real. Thank God he hadn't. Was he losing his mind?

For a long time, he had blamed Lana Hamilton for what had happened to Sebastian, but he was older now, probably not wiser, but time had at least taught him that it wasn't Lana's fault. The only one responsible for the whole sorry mess was Sebastian himself.

Xav didn't hate his brother, but his emotions were now divided, unable to reconcile the man he had grown up with as being a coldblooded killer. Of course he loved Seb, but his brother couldn't seem to accept what he had done, still clinging to denial.

For a while, Xav had believed the protestations of innocence. Lana had been wrong. But eventually he had come to accept that the evidence was stacked against Sebastian. He had tortured and killed his girlfriend, and the knowledge of that messed with Xav's head. When did his kind and loving big brother become capable of such an act?

Their mother still visited Sebastian regularly. Although Xav was close to her, she refused to be pressed on whether she still believed in her son's innocence. Xav hadn't been to HMP Woodhill in over six months and knowing he was overdue to visit was sitting heavily with him. He just wished Sebastian would admit to the truth so they could all try to move forward.

As for the anger, he still experienced when he thought about Lana, it was borne out of frustration at the situation rather than directly at her, along with a good dose of guilt. It hadn't been his hands around Camille's neck, but he still shouldered a sense of responsibility, sharing the same blood as her killer.

Lana didn't know any of this and probably thought he still hated her, and it was easier to let her believe that. Because he couldn't be around her. Knew that the insanity of the situation would be his undoing.

How had it got to this with Ollie and Lana? His best friend and the first girl he had given his heart to. The three of them had been so close growing up, yet now they were strangers.

Xav set his brush down, frowning at the canvas as he reached for his water bottle.

Lana hadn't changed. Well, not much. Her hair was longer and she seemed to have overcome her aversion to dresses. Their encounter had been brief, but in those stunned few seconds, he had noticed everything: the familiar scent of her twisting in his gut, her little gasp of shock, and the blush-pink outfit she wore with its ditzy print pattern.

His Lana in a pink dress. It had made him double blink.

Not *his* Lana any more, he reminded himself, taking a drink, the cold water quenching his parched throat as he stared at the face he had painted. It was far from finished, but already he had captured the fire in her dark eyes and knew that she hadn't lost her spark.

The vibrating of his phone cut through the silence and Xav glanced at the screen, seeing his friend Bree's name flash up. For a moment, he toyed with ignoring it, wanting to be left alone to brood and work on the painting. Bree was persistent, though, and Xav knew from experience it was easier just to take the call.

'What's up?'

'Kings Head. I'll see you there in half an hour.'

'I'm working.'

There was a pause. 'Look, mate. I saw Trudy. She told me the Hamilton bitch is back. Figured you could use a drink.'

Xav's shoulders tightened, but he ignored the gibe at Lana, instead glossing over the encounter. 'It was no big deal. Our paths were always going to cross eventually.'

Bree McCarthy had been a close friend of his brother's and both her and Seb had trained together as mechanics. She had been outraged when Lana had pointed the finger at Sebastian, always staunchly believing in his innocence, and she had been one of a few locals to shout about it loudly.

She had also seen it as her job to step into the role of big sister to Xav, and at the time it had been appreciated. Xav and his mother had been treated like lepers by some of the community after Camille's murder. Guilt by association and all that. And Bree, along with a couple of his mother's close friends, had been there to fight their corner.

Now Xav was back and no longer needed a big sister. He was thirty-four and perfectly capable of fighting his own battles, but he didn't forget how Bree had been there for him or his mother when he had moved away, often travelling with her to visit Sebastian. She was probably the closest thing to a best friend Xav had, and he knew she was good for him. Although she was annoyingly persistent at times, at least she stopped him from completely closing in on himself.

'It might not have been a big deal, but it's lovely weather and I've closed the garage early. You should get out. Come on. One lunchtime pint.'

'I've already been out.'

'I'll see you in half an hour.'

Bree ended the call before Xav could protest again, and he scrubbed his hands through his hair, not appreciating being bossed about, and really not liking that she was perhaps right.

He stared at the canvas of Lana, annoyed she was still under his skin. There had been countless women over the years. Why did this one stick?

* * *

Fifty minutes later – he was purposely late out of sheer stubbornness – he met Bree in the beer garden of the pub.

She had picked a table that was positioned directly in the sun, sheltering her eyes as she glanced up at Xav. 'Here he is. Finally venturing out of the house. It'll do you good to get some sun on that skin of yours. You look like a bloody vampire.'

Harsh. Xav wasn't that pale, but he guessed the black T-shirt didn't help.

He put his pint down and took a seat opposite her, stretching out his long legs. 'So you just happened to bump into Trudy then?'

It had been annoying him on the drive over, knowing that the pair of them had been gossiping about his encounter with Lana.

'She's worried about you. Said you looked like you'd seen a ghost.'

'She was overreacting.'

'Cut her some slack. She cares, I care. We're looking out for you. It's what friends do.'

It was, and Xav was the one making too big a deal about this. Bree had a point and Trudy was simply trying to do the right thing. Seeing Lana had shaken him more than he cared to admit and it wasn't healthy. Not after all this time.

Rather than admit he was in the wrong, he changed the subject, telling himself to chill.

Thankfully, Bree seemed to get the hint to keep off topic, though one drink for her soon turned into four, her tongue loosening, and the subject of the Hamiltons raising its ugly head again.

'It's not right what she did to Seb,' she mused, words a little slurred now. 'He didn't have it in him to hurt anyone.'

Sebastian Landry was a favourite topic of Bree's when she was drunk and Xav didn't bother to point out that the evidence proved his brother guilty. They had argued over this too many times in the past.

Instead, he finished the Coke he had switched to after his beer and grabbed his phone and car keys from the table. 'You going to be okay walking home?' Bree's pretty, honey-coloured eyes were glassy and her cheeks flushed. They had been sitting in the sun, which probably didn't help the effect of the alcohol.

'Yeah, yeah, I'm fine.'

'I can drop you off.'

That earned him a grin. 'You're a good kid, you know that?'

Xav smiled to humour her. At thirty-eight, Bree was only four years older than him. Neither of them had been kids in a long while.

'I love you and Seb like brothers. Never forget that. And I'd do anything for either of you.' Tears glistened in Bree's eyes. Too much alcohol always made her emotional. 'Maybe I should drive out to Mead House. Tell that stuck-up bitch that she's not welcome here.'

Xav's stomach dropped. Somehow he managed to keep his tone even. 'You don't need to do that.'

'But I should. For you, for Seb. For your mum.' He could hear the passion and the anger as she spoke. 'This is your home and she needs to stay away. Leave you alone.'

'No. You really shouldn't.' This time, Xav was firmer. 'Today was a chance encounter. She...' He couldn't bring himself to say her name out loud. 'She was more shocked than I was. The house is going on the market and soon she'll be gone. Out of our lives for good.'

Was he getting through? From Bree's glazed eyes, it was hard to tell.

'Come on, mate. Let's get you home.'

He put an arm around her and helped her stagger from the pub, insisting she get into his car, despite her protestations. Sober, she was one of the kindest people he knew, but drunk she could go either way. She could be the happiest person in the room or the most tormented and that sometimes exposed a darker, uglier side.

Pulling up outside the building where she lived, Xav helped Bree up the stairs and into her flat, settling her on the sofa and removing her boots. He glanced at the key fob for her pick-up, wondering if he should hide it somewhere or take it with him.

She already had her eyes closed, though, and was out for the count, lightly snoring.

Xav filled a pint glass with water and left it on the coffee table beside her, then he let himself out of the flat, certain that a bad situation had just been swerved.

10

'I saw Lana Hamilton today.'

Trudy paused arranging the flowers on her father's dresser and glanced at the chair where he sat. He was deep in concentration, frowning at the sports pages of his newspaper. She had bought him a Kindle, but he still preferred to read his news the old-fashioned way, so she indulged him, picking up his favourite broadsheet each morning before heading into work.

'I said I saw Lana—'

'I heard you the first time!' Angus Palmer snapped, finally glancing up, paper crumpling beneath tense fingers and his dark eyebrows knotted.

Trudy barely flinched. There had been a time when this bear of a man had been able to make her cower, but those days were long gone and the only power he yielded over her now was with his voice. They both knew that she was the one in charge, even if he did like to bluster.

If she left, he would have no one.

Of course she would never do that. He may have failed as a

father, but he was the only one she had. Family was important to Trudy and always had been. The news they had received at the start of the year had come as a shock. She was determined to be there by his side.

'Just checking those ears are working,' she teased, smiling when the frown deepened. He was so easy to wind up these days. 'I thought you'd be interested. I know how much you cared for Kitty Hamilton and her family.'

That earned a grunt, but they both knew it was true.

Her father had been upset when he had learnt about Kitty's death, and Trudy was convinced the news had played a part in the stroke he had suffered the following day. She hadn't thought he was going to make a recovery and perhaps it might have been kinder, especially with the other diagnosis he was dealing with, if he had peacefully slipped away. When he had started to regain his speech a couple of weeks ago, it had surprised everyone. The only tell-tale sign now was in the slight slurring of the odd word.

The Palmers and the Hamiltons went back a long way, ever since both families moved to town. Not so much with Trudy's generation. She had never really been close with them. But her grandfather had been Kitty Hamilton's doctor for years, her father taking over when he retired.

Of course, that was before the accident.

The Hamiltons weren't the only ones to suffer tragedy. The car accident that had taken the use of Angus's legs had also stolen Juliet Palmer's life. Trudy had still been in her teens at the time and she had never fully recovered from losing her mother.

'Lana is looking well. I believe Ollie is back too.' She kept her tone even. 'I'm heading out to Mead House tomorrow afternoon when I've closed the shop. They are selling Kitty's paintings. I thought you might like to come with me.'

Angus finally gave up on his paper. 'I'm fine here.'

Was Trudy mistaken or had his face paled a little?

'Oh come on, Dad. It will do you good to get out of the house. Have a little fresh air. And it will be nice for you to see the place before they sell it. I know you have many fond memories there.'

'I said no!' he snapped.

He really was in a disagreeable mood, so she decided not to push it for now.

Personally, she was looking forward to going, remembering how, as a child, she had been wowed by the huge rooms with the high ceilings and the glitter of the fancy chandeliers.

The Palmers had always had money, but they weren't in the same league as the Hamiltons. Plus, of course, Angus had always been particularly tight. It hadn't been until Trudy had inherited her maternal grandfather's estate that she had been able to afford her little shop or any items of real luxury.

She wondered what kind of mood Lana would be in tomorrow. She had looked shocked when she bumped into Xav. Had she not realised he had moved back to Norfolk? How was she going to react when she realised he and Trudy were more than just friends?

Trudy wasn't sure if she should say something to her or not. She didn't want Xav to be angry with her. She had known he was upset this morning, the encounter with Lana catching him off guard. He refused to talk about it, though, and she hated how he kept shutting her out.

After they had slept together, things were supposed to progress, but instead it felt like he was trying to put distance between them.

It wasn't her. Deep down, she understood that. Xav must find it difficult to trust women after Lana's betrayal. But Trudy would keep working to pull his walls down. She had never been in love before, at least not as deeply as this. Of course, there had been boyfriends, but none of them had made her feel the way she did when she was around Xav. They were meant to be together and eventually he would realise it too.

While she was going to Mead House tomorrow, it was simply business. If it came down to taking sides between them, then she was firmly Team Xav.

11

Ollie wasn't about when Lana returned to the house and Elise was out by the pool, lying on one of the sun loungers, wearing only a skimpy, yellow bikini. The irritating woman was treating the house like a holiday home.

The encounter with Xav had dampened Lana's spirits and she wasn't in the mood for conversation, so she headed straight upstairs, figuring she might as well tackle the difficult task of going through Camille's things, the same way she had done with Kitty's.

There were enough memories here to distract her and even though Camille had been gone for half of her life, Lana kept expecting her to walk through the door, to tell her off for snooping through her things, and the pain of her loss hit her suddenly and sharply in the gut.

Time had mostly soothed the edges of grief and the pain was largely a dull constant ache, but one she had become used to. She could think about Camille these days without that overwhelming sense of loss that threatened to pull her under, focusing on happier times. Every so often, though, something would catch her off guard, and the stark and bitter realisation that she would never get to hug her sister again or hear her bubble of laughter crushed down on her as hard as it had the first time.

Lana didn't realise she was crying until she tasted the damp salty tears on her lips and she angrily palmed them away, embarrassed that after so long, a memory could upset her. Did Ollie ever get emotional like this? Again, it wasn't something they had ever really talked about.

When they were younger, she had been able to pick up on her brother's emotions. She knew when he was sad or in pain, and always when he was lying. After Camille's death, it was as if he had learnt to block her out. That sometimes left her feeling so alone.

Sure, she had plenty of friends, and there had been lovers and more serious relationships over the years, but Ollie was her only family now Kitty was gone.

As children, they had been identical and with Lana's tomboyish ways and her fondness for short hair and jeans, it had been difficult to tell them apart.

Ollie had been born eight minutes earlier, but Lana was the more responsible one. Certainly she knew how to have fun, but unlike Ollie, she also thought of others and of the consequences of her actions.

They had been so close once, but Camille's murder had seen them unravel. The gulf with her brother widening as the years passed.

She had hoped Kitty's death would bring them together again, but with Elise here it was looking unlikely.

Swiping away her tears, Lana continued to fill boxes with her sister's things. It was in the bottom drawer of the bedside table that she found the real treasure. A navy, leather-bound book that had Lana's throat thickening. She managed to swallow, knowing before she opened it, exactly what it was: Camille's journal.

Her sister's neat and looping scroll was immediately familiar, and Lana wasn't ready for the kick of memories it stirred. The pages were yellowing slightly, but the journal itself was still in good condition and she leafed through a few pages, knowing this was definitely one for the keep pile.

She started to close the book when she spotted something sticking out among the pages. Another piece of paper? Carefully, she opened the book, found herself at the entry dated a week before Camille's death. It had been marked by a pharmacy receipt for the tablets Lana knew her grandmother took, and the receipt was recent, date stamped, she realised, for the day of Kitty's death. A sharp pain stabbed at her, reminding her again of her recent loss. When her grandmother had bought the tablets, she would have had no idea she wouldn't get to take them. That her life had been about to end. And she had spent that last day looking through Camille's journal.

Was there any relevance to that?

The thought had been instant, but Lana quickly realised it was also foolish.

She was trying to link dots that weren't there. Her grandmother's death had been an accident. That she had been reading Camille's journal the day she died was simply a coincidence. Besides, there were no secrets in this book. The police had gone through it thoroughly before returning it to the family and Camille's killer was in jail. Kitty had clearly just wanted the memories, as Lana did now.

Not wanting to be interrupted, she closed the bedroom door, then sat down on the bed and went to the first entry.

Her sister had started the journal in July 2004, around the time she became involved with Sebastian Landry, their, at first, secret romance documented by a teenage girl who was smitten and head over heels in love.

Went to the coast with S tonight and we talked non-stop. We have so much in common. We like the same music. I swear to God I nearly died when I found he had Jeff Buckley in his CD player. And we both love Muse too. He's so bloody lucky, getting to see them headline Glastonbury last month. He said maybe next year we can go together. Oh my God. He is already thinking long term about us. My heart wants to burst.

The entry went on, explaining more about their evening together, some of it in quite graphic detail, and Lana blushed, flipping the page.

It was more the same, Camille's adoration for her new boyfriend clear in every word.

She had dated before, but Sebastian appeared to be her first real love.

A longing burned inside Lana, recalling her own teenage summers. The warm days and sometimes even hotter nights all rolling into one and seeming like they would never end. They were mostly filled with innocent fun, but she remembered the flicker of excitement when Xav had started to view her with different eyes when she had returned home from boarding school the summer before Camille died.

She had noticed how his gaze lingered, recalled how it made her feel, a fizz heating everything up inside her. Then there was the first time he had kissed her, a little tentative, so unlike the teasing, confident boy she had grown up with, his lips brushing gently against hers and making her tingle. Their teenage romance had been perfect. Until it had abruptly and devastatingly ended.

Trying to push him from her thoughts, she continued to read.

Camille and Seb became official. Inseparable too. If they weren't out and about, they were snuggled up on the sofa or hanging around the pool. If Nana Kitty wasn't around, they would sneak upstairs to Camille's bedroom, though as the months passed, they started spending more and more time at the summer house.

Lana would often hear her sister sneak out when she thought they were all asleep, and she remembered that last awful night. How she had been woken by whispering outside, then peered out of the window just in time to catch a glimpse of Sebastian as he disappeared into the orchard.

At the time, Lana had thought they were happy. It wasn't until after Sebastian's arrest that she learnt of his fight with her sister that last day. Several witnesses had seen them yelling at each other, before Camille tore off the heart pendant on the black ribbon she always wore. A gift he had made her. Throwing it at him before she stormed off.

He had gone there that night with the necklace, knowing that he planned to kill her.

Although they had been able to piece some of it together, no one would ever truly know what Camille's last moments had been like, because Sebastian clung to denial, saying he wasn't there. It hurt that he refused to give their family closure.

Lana opened the journal to the point her grandmother had marked. The week Camille had died. Things had been okay with Sebastian before the argument, hadn't they? Reading through the entries, though, they were far shorter, lacking the emotion and passion of the earlier ones. In fact, Sebastian was barely mentioned at all.

Camille had always been obsessed with her journal, carrying it everywhere and guarding it as though it contained a thousand secrets, but this was just mundane stuff. Documenting the weather, catching up with friends, even mentioning what she ate. It seemed like she was going through the motions rather than revealing her innermost thoughts like in the earlier entries. Why had her journal entries changed so dramatically? She must have still been in love with Sebastian, because Lana heard her sneaking out of the house to meet him late at night. Why then wasn't there any talk about what they got up to or their plans for the future?

Getting up, she wandered over to the window, looking out over the sprawling lawn. Elise was still down by the pool, lying on her belly now, engrossed in a magazine, and there was still no sign of Ollie.

Towards the end of the garden, across the orchard, was the top of the summer house. The place where Camille had spent her final moments.

Until now Lana had stayed away, unable to face going down there.

Maybe it was time to conquer her demons.

12

The garden room doors were already open and the warmth of the late-afternoon sun hit Lana as she stepped outside. If Elise was awake, she didn't stir, her face buried in her towel and the magazine she had been reading now lying on the floor. Next to it was a half-empty tumbler. Margarita, judging by the colour of the liquid and the wedge of lime in the glass.

A small, portable radio was tuned into a station that was playing cheesy eighties pop. The volume was low, but Lana caught the chorus of Bananarama's 'Robert DeNiro's Waiting', as she passed.

As she crossed the patio, the woman let out an inelegant snore and Lana jumped, smiling to herself. She suspected Elise would be mortified if she realised she had made such a vulgar noise.

A fragrant, sweet scent clung to the air as she entered the rose garden and a fresh pang of grief stabbed at her. This had been her grandmother's favourite place. It was still well tended, the plants and bushes a myriad of colour.

Heading into the orchard, the memories turned darker and a tiny ball of apprehension knotted in her gut. She was getting closer to the summer house and wasn't sure if she was brave enough to go inside alone.

Camille was long gone, her killer behind bars. What was it that scared her?

She could understand why Ollie didn't like it. It was worse for him as he had been the one to find their sister's body. Kitty sending him to look for Camille when she didn't show up for breakfast. To this day, he had never spoken about it with Lana or disclosed anything he talked about in the counselling sessions he attended. She was aware of his pain, though. At least she had been before he shut her out.

There had been talk initially of pulling the summer house down, but it had never happened, Kitty simply choosing to pretend it didn't exist. She had been torn, not wanting the reminder, but also knowing it was her last tie to her granddaughter.

The hedgerow had been allowed to grow, mostly blocking it from view, and even from a distance, Lana could see the weeds had run rampant. The gardener didn't touch this area at all and as she picked her way along the broken path, trying to avoid clumps of stinging nettles, the shadow of overhead trees only added to the ominous atmosphere.

The building was still intact, though the once white wood was now a dull grey and splintered in places, while the windows were covered in cobwebs. Despite the warmth of the afternoon, Lana's skin prickled and she rubbed at her arms.

So far away from the house, with the door and windows of the summer house shut, Camille would have known it was unlikely anyone would hear her screams.

Lana's heart squeezed a little tighter as she imagined the terror she must have felt and began to wish she had stayed up at the house. Down here, it was harder to escape her sister's torment.

She should go. Find the gardener and ask if he would be

prepared to clear the summer house. Although she had only spoken to him on the phone, he seemed affable enough.

But did Lana owe it to Camille to at least peer inside? To see the spot where her sister had taken her last breath?

She already knew the answer, her feet reluctantly carrying her forward.

Her fingers closed around the cool door handle and she pushed down, part of her hoping it wouldn't open. The door had once needed a key, but it hadn't been locked in years, and there was a low groan as it moved forward, the stale odour of neglect spilling out. When was the last time anyone had been down here?

Lana brushed at the spiderwebs across the entrance, hating that tension was tightening the muscles in her shoulders. There was nothing for her to fear here. Still, the step she took inside was tentative.

The table and chairs were covered in a thick layer of dust. Three, she noted. The one that Camille had been sat on had long ago been taken away. There was a deep rip in the sofa, the old clock was still on the wall, though the batteries had long stopped working, and the mirror above her grandmother's bureau had a huge crack in it.

Lana looked at the floor, the place where her sister had died instantly recognisable, even in the shadowy light. It had been heavily scrubbed, the wood lighter in that particular spot.

The knots in her shoulders wound a little tighter.

She shouldn't have come down here.

A sound came from outside, the distinctive crunch of footsteps, and she froze.

Was it Elise? Lana struggled to see her brother's girlfriend coming down here.

She crept to the door and peered outside, licked her dry lips as she glanced around the shaded area. No one was there, though with the trees and the overgrown weeds and bushes, there were plenty of places to hide.

Beyond the high hedgerow, she could see the top of Mead House and she realised just how far away it was. As a child, it had never really bothered her how spacious the grounds of the house were, but then she had regarded this as a fun and safe place back then.

No one heard Camille scream.

The unwelcome thought popped into her head.

The location of her sister's murder was unsettling her. But she had definitely heard footsteps.

Deciding it was time to go, she stepped out of the summer house, pulling the door shut.

Before Lana had even reached the orchard, a man stepped into her path, a pitchfork in his hand.

13

'Lana?'

He spoke as she was mid yelp, and she took a step back, her heart hammering in her chest.

'It's George. I'm George. George Maddox, the gardener?'

He phrased it as a question, as if he wasn't quite sure himself. But Lana had spoken to him on the phone and recognised his voice.

'Jesus, you scared the crap out of me.'

'You scared me too.' George lowered his weapon, ran an anxious-looking hand over his hair, seeming more spooked than Lana. 'I didn't know you'd come down here. I was finishing up for the day and I heard noises. I thought someone was trespassing, breaking in.'

'Sorry.' She paused, a thought occurring. 'Actually, how *do* you know I am Lana? That I'm not a trespasser?'

'Well, I, um... I might have looked you up on Facebook after we spoke on the phone.' She fought her smile as his worried eyes went wide. 'I'm sorry.'

She didn't want to tell him she was okay with that, but also she would be a liar if she said she hadn't done the same thing herself before.

'Do people trespass?' she asked instead, changing the subject. When he looked confused, she elaborated. 'I mean, has it been a problem here before, with people coming into the garden uninvited?'

'Not in the years that I've been working here. I can't vouch for when Barney was doing the job.' His expression changed to one of sympathy. 'Kitty always insisted she didn't want this part of the garden touched, and she never came down here. I guess that's why you caught me by surprise. I didn't think...' He trailed off, seeming uncomfortable.

'So you never come down here?'

'No.' His face flushed guiltily. 'Well, I might have once, and I'm sorry, I know I shouldn't have. Your grandmother asked me not to.'

'You've been inside the summer house?'

There was a pause before he answered. 'I peeked inside really quickly. But just the once back when I started.' George pulled a face. 'I wasn't being ghoulish. Well, maybe just a little. Shit... think before you speak, George.' He facepalmed his forehead. 'I'm sorry. I was thoughtless and nosey. She was your sister.'

'It's okay. Really, it's okay.' Lana meant it. She appreciated his honesty and respected his openness. Why wouldn't he be curious? 'You didn't know her, did you?'

He shook his head. 'Not really. Barney's my uncle and I helped him out with the gardens a couple of times when I was kid, but I don't really remember you or your sister. I knew Ollie a little. We used to play football together.'

'I didn't realise that.'

'I'm sorry about what happened to your sister. Your grandmother too. I'm sorry I was unable to make it to her funeral.'

Lana nodded her thanks.

'For what it's worth, I liked your grandmother a lot. I thought she was very... cool.'

His lips curved into a wide smile and Lana found herself warming to him. Maybe it was the way he wore a bandana or his eager, lopsided grin that made him look like he was about to go off on a quest with teenage friends to find treasure rather than mow the lawn. Despite the fact the work kept him muscular and in shape, there was a laidback 'Bill and Ted' innocence about him, and she half expected him to come out with 'radical' or 'bodacious'.

From the smell of weed that was clinging to him, she understood why he was so chilled and thanked his slow reactions that he had been hesitant with the pitchfork.

'How are you getting on with clearing the house?'

'It's a slow process,' Lana admitted. 'It's a big place.'

George nodded. 'Well, if you need help with anything, I'm your man. I have a van too if you need to move stuff.'

'That's kind of you.'

'I can stop by in the morning if you like. Friday is my day off.'

Lana considered his offer. 'Well, if you're sure you don't mind.'

She thanked George, taking him up on the offer. As he left to finish packing up his gardening tools, she took a final glance at the summer house.

It was just a building.

Still, as she turned to walk away, her skin crawled, as if somehow it was watching her.

14

It was Ollie's fiancée, Elise, who answered the door to George the following morning, her expression initially bored, though she soon took notice when she realised who it was.

'What do you want?' she demanded, her tone haughty.

It was an act; they both knew that. He had seen her gaze following him around the garden as he worked, and had even taken his T-shirt off on occasion, just to tease her.

As a kid, George had been short and skinny and was the one everyone liked to pick on, but years of outdoor work had given him a tan and honed his physique. How things had changed.

He slowly looked her up and down, his eyes lingering on her cleavage for a moment. Even if he wasn't being obvious, it would have been difficult to miss, as there was an awful lot of it on view.

The move would have earned him a slap from some women, but not Elise. She was doing her best to look annoyed, but he could see the hunger in her eyes.

'Is Lana about?'

Elise's expression hardened. 'Why?'

'Because I'm here to see her.' George smirked.

That burst her bubble. A scowl now on her face, Elise stepped back, yelling up the stairs. 'Lana? You have company.' When there wasn't a response, she rolled her eyes in irritation. 'Wait here!' she snapped at George, huffing as she disappeared upstairs.

He did as asked, always polite and well-mannered, knowing exactly what people expected from him. A smile on his face when Lana appeared.

'Thank you so much for offering to help.' She beckoned him inside. 'Sorry Elise didn't invite you in. Come on upstairs.'

George picked up his toolbox, following after her.

Now, Lana was the kind of girl he would call pretty. She wasn't beautiful like stuck-up Elise. She was less obvious, but there was something warm and welcoming about her. Under different circumstances, he might have liked her.

He hadn't lied when he had told her he had Facebook stalked her. He had, but not just after they spoke on the phone. He had looked her up many times over the years, remembering her from her sister's funeral, her lost expression conveying grief and disbelief. She was so different to Camille and he would never have put the two of them as sisters. Lana, dark and understated, while Camille had been tall and striking with her flame-red hair.

He remembered how the town had been united in grief, horrified at what had happened on their doorstep. Ghastly things like murder didn't happen here in this neck of the woods.

The irony of that had made him smile. They had no idea there was a monster walking among them.

Ollie made an appearance when they stopped for a coffee break. Lana and George were sat at the large table in the kitchen, a slightly dated room that, despite its size, still felt homely. The June sun filtered through the windowpanes of the patio doors and he could see Elise on one of the sun loungers. Rain was forecast for later that afternoon he remembered, amused. That would soon spoil the hoity bitch's fun.

Ollie double blinked when he saw George. George noted he was bare-chested, wearing just a pair of joggers and his dark hair was rumpled. Just out of bed. Lazy fucker.

'I didn't realise we had company.'

'You were asleep,' Lana pointed out dryly. 'This is George. Remember him?'

Of course he didn't. George already knew that. Although they had hung out a bit as kids, when Ollie and Elise had first arrived and found him in the house, there had been no recognition on Ollie's part whatsoever. Luckily, he had only been inside that day to use the loo and fill up his water bottle, unlike previous visits when he had spent time going through Kitty's things, helping himself to the odd bit of loose change he found lying about. It had been easy to pass his visit off as him simply keeping an eye on things.

'Yeah, of course. He's the gardener?'

'Didn't you guys used to know each other as kids too?'

'Did we?' Ollie looked blankly at George.

'Yeah, but it was a long time ago.'

Ollie Hamilton had been one of the more popular kids. Entitled, George remembered. Not surprising he had a short memory.

'George offered to help me clear some of the furniture.'

Ollie looked at his sister. 'I was going to do that.'

'Really? I hadn't got that impression.'

'Why do you think I came up from London? You *insisted* you needed my help.'

George sipped at his coffee and kept quiet as he assessed the relationship between the pair of them. He had thought Camille's death might have pulled them closer together, but it appeared to be otherwise.

They were twins and he could see the strong resemblance. The similar bone structure and dark eyes. Lana's were flashing now with anger.

'It's half your house, Ollie. Half your responsibility.'

'I'm aware of that. You've reminded me enough times.' He looked over at George again, a frown on his face and eyes narrowing. 'Actually, you do look familiar. You used to play football with us, right?'

So the fucker did remember him.

'Yeah, sometimes.'

Ollie was nodding now as the memories all seemed to rush back. 'You've got rid of the glasses. That's why I didn't recognise you. George Maddox. Yeah, I remember.' He pumped George's hand, suddenly full of smiles, his anger with Lana gone. 'This guy used to be a real nerd, glasses always falling off his nose,' he told her. 'We'd stick him in goal just for laughs. Never caught a single ball. Now look at him, all muscled up.'

George laughed along, forced his inane grin up a notch. He would give this prick the gormless stooge he wanted. Play the part. He could see Lana was embarrassed at Ollie's description of him. It must suck having such an insensitive arsehole for a brother.

'I'm having a few of the lads over for poker tomorrow night. You should come,' Ollie suggested.

'I should?' That genuinely caught him off guard.

'You are?' Lana sounded just as surprised.

Ollie ignored her, addressing George. 'Yeah, of course you should. It would be good to catch up.'

Well, this was a turn-up for the books. Invited to play poker with Ollie Hamilton.

Getting close to him wouldn't be a bad thing. It would make it easier to keep tabs on him.

'That should be okay, but can I let you know?'

'Sure thing. Here, I'll give you my number.'

Lana watched the proceedings, seeming irritated, and George knew he needed to be careful to keep her onside too. He apologised as he followed her back up the stairs, leaving Ollie in the kitchen.

'I'm sorry about that. I hope you don't mind that he invited me.'

'It's fine,' she said once they were back in Kitty's bedroom. 'He just caught me by surprise about the poker game. Sorry you got caught up in our family drama down there.'

George made a point of shrugging it off. He had an older brother, albeit not related by blood. One who had made his life hell as a teenager, until he had taken care of it. They still didn't get along, though at least now he had the upper hand. Yes, he understood family drama all too well. 'No bother. I was surprised your brother remembered me, to be honest. Like he said, I was a bit of a nerd back then. I didn't play football with them often. Mostly I used to watch. He was really pally with Xav Landry. It was always the Ollie and Xav show, I remember.'

He dropped Xavier Landry's name into conversation casually, careful to watch Lana's reaction. Foot in mouth syndrome, that was what his wife, Chloe, said he had. What she didn't know was, more often than not, it was intentional.

He could tell from the tightening of Lana's mouth that he had touched a nerve. Her face paling.

Nicely played, George. Now reel her back in.

'Shit. I'm sorry, Lana. I didn't mean to mention him.'

'You've done nothing wrong. Honestly. Xav was Ollie's best friend. Mine too. It's not his fault... what happened.'

They were silent for a moment and George finished his coffee, still putting on an act to look flustered and uncomfortable by his supposed faux pas.

'He's back in town. Do you still know him? Xav?'

Lana's question caught him off guard. He had assumed she wouldn't want to talk about Xav at all.

'Um, yeah, a little I guess. He pays my Chloe to clean for his mum.'

There was a pause. 'How is Joanna?'

Although he was a little surprised by the line of questions, George tried not to show it. Was she fishing? He decided to answer truthfully and see where it led. 'She has arthritis. Chloe says it's why Xav moved back to the area, to be close to her if she needs him. He wanted her to move to Salthouse with him, but Joanna insisted on staying in Holt. She's very independent like that. It's why he got Chloe in.' Plenty of information there for her to sink her teeth into.

'Xav lives in Salthouse?'

'Yeah, he bought a converted barn on the outskirts of the village. Huge bloody place for one man to be knocking about in if you ask me, but I guess part of it is for his studio. He told Chloe he wanted to be close to the coast. I think he spends a lot of time on the beach.'

Lana fell silent, looking lost in her own thoughts, and perhaps George should have left the conversation there. He couldn't help himself but take it a little bit further, wanting to bring up the name of the man she thought had killed her sister.

'He's a good guy. He knows Sebastian did a bad thing. It's been difficult for him to deal with everything.'

Lana looked like she was about to comment when Ollie appeared again. Poor timing and George felt a flicker of irritation. He had wanted to see if Lana was still strong in her belief that Sebastian Landry was guilty.

Ollie was dressed now in jeans and an old T-shirt, though his hair was still sticking on end and a frown was etched on his face.

'So, here I am. Ready and willing to help. What do you need me to do?'

'It's fine, Ollie. We're nearly done in here.'

Ollie nodded, seeming a little put out. 'Okay, so I guess I'll go find a job for myself.' He helped himself to a hammer and screwdriver from George's toolbox. 'You okay if I borrow these, mate?'

So they were mates now? George's skin prickled, though he kept his tone even. 'Sure, go for it.'

'What are you planning on doing?' Lana asked warily.

'Help clear the house. It's what we're here for, right?'

He grinned at her, when she shook her head, disappearing back into the hallway.

'Please try not to make too much mess,' Lana yelled after him.

From the amount of noise that followed minutes later, George suspected the idiot didn't have a clue what he was doing.

Although she looked annoyed, Lana resisted the urge to check on him, instead staying in Kitty's room with George and helping him sort through what pieces of furniture would be going to charity.

Eventually, they were finished and he followed her across the landing to what had been Camille's bedroom.

The colourful bunch of swear words Lana yelled at her brother as she stepped inside had George grinning to himself. He understood why moments later as he followed her into the room. It looked like a bomb site, with wood everywhere from where Ollie had pulled apart the fitted wardrobes.

George held back a little, leaning against the door arch, as he watched another argument ensue.

'What the hell are you doing?'

'Trying to help.' Ollie paused to wipe sweat from his brow. 'That's what you wanted? Right? To clear the house?'

'These wardrobes were fitted. They were supposed to stay.'

'Well, I didn't know that. You haven't exactly given me a list of what we're supposed to be doing here. Just taken over as always.'

'I don't take over. You haven't been interested until now.'

Lana was picking her way across the room now and even though he was enjoying this latest episode of the Hamilton entertainment show, George felt a little sorry for her. Every surface was cluttered with Ollie's chaos.

'What's this?' she asked, bending to pick up a black, leather-bound journal and George's eyes widened in surprise, his stomach tightening as she opened the front cover and leafed through the first couple of pages. Camille's journal was navy. He knew, because had read through it on previous visits.

'A book,' Ollie told her unhelpfully. 'You know Camille used to keep a diary.'

'And I already have it.'

Lana reached inside the top drawer of the bedside table and pulled out the navy journal. She held both up in her hands.

'The navy one is hers.' She looked at her brother. 'So where did this one come from?'

'The bottom of the wardrobe. The floor panel was loose and it was underneath.' Ollie frowned. 'I don't understand what the big deal is. So what if she had two?'

He wasn't getting it, but George understood the point Lana was trying to make and why she was excited. One of the journals had been hidden away, which suggested that Camille had wanted to make sure no one ever saw it. He wiped at the sweat forming on his forehead, knowing it wasn't a result of physical labour, but instead panic.

As Lana explained this to Ollie, George's shoulders stiffened and tension rippled through his body. Why had Camille hidden this journal?

'It might give us some answers,'

Lana's words had George pulling at the collar of his T-shirt. He was suddenly finding it difficult to breathe.

'What answers? We don't need any. We both know Sebastian Landry killed her. He's in prison and rotting away, exactly as he should be.'

'We still don't know what drove him to do it.'

'I don't need to know. Justice has been served. Just drop it. Please.'

'Well, you might not care, but I do,' Lana snapped, heat in her tone.

Ollie stared at her for a moment. 'You know, she was my sister too.' His voice cracked on the last two words, revealing a vulnerability George hadn't seen before. He waited for Lana to react, but she didn't, and after a beat, he dropped his tools, stepping over the mess he had created and storming past George out of the room.

Okay, this was worrying. George needed to know what was in that journal.

He waited quietly in the doorway as Lana stared at both books and debated his next move. She wasn't just going to hand it over and if the black journal was to disappear today, he would surely top the suspect list. But if this book really did contain info on Camille's last days, he needed to get to it first.

'Are you okay?' he asked eventually, playing for time. 'I can go if you want me to. Come back later.' That was good. Offer to leave so he didn't seem like any threat.

She started, seeming to have forgotten he was there, and found a smile for him, though it looked forced. 'No, don't go. And again, I'm sorry. Ollie and I aren't always at each other's throats, I promise.'

George didn't believe that, but he smiled along with her anyway.

He watched Lana turn the journal over in her hands, as if it was gold dust. A long-lost connection to the dead sister or was she hoping, as she had said to Ollie, that it would reveal some truths about Camille and what happened the night of her death?

The book had been hidden under the floorboards for years, away from prying eyes, and George dreaded to think what secrets might be hidden amongst its pages.

15

Lana was distracted after finding the journal, eager to look inside it, but there was still work to do, including clearing up the mess that Ollie had made.

He and Elise had disappeared off out somewhere. Lana had no idea where. She hadn't seen or spoken to her brother since he had stormed out of Camille's room earlier, only realising they had gone out when she heard his car engine. To be honest, she was glad of the respite.

Finally she helped George load up his van, grateful that he was doing a tip run for her as well as taking some of the bulkier furniture to one of the charity shops in town. She would get him a case of beer or a bottle of whisky to say thank you, she decided, her heart sinking seeing a Range Rover appear on the driveway.

She recognised Trudy Palmer in the driver's seat and realised she had forgotten all about inviting the woman out to view Kitty's paintings. She really wasn't in the mood for this now, wanting to digest what had happened this morning and the discovery of the journal. But it was a job that needed doing and Trudy had driven out to the house.

'Lana, hi.' Trudy had pulled to a halt beside George's van and she was already out of her car. She glanced between the two of them, curious, as if she was waiting for an introduction.

'You know George, right? Our gardener?' Lana offered.

There was a pause as Trudy studied him, narrowing her eyes before she smiled in recognition. 'Yes, I think you went to my school?'

'That's right.'

'Well, it's good to see you again. How are you? Lana's keeping you busy, I see.'

'Something like that.' George didn't seem interested in making small talk, turning his attention back to Lana. He had been at the house helping for much of the day and she guessed he was keen to get on his way. 'Let me know if you need anything else,' he told her, hopping into his van. He saluted her before giving Trudy a quick cursory nod, reversing up and heading on his way.

'He's a man of many words,' Trudy laughed as his van disappeared. 'Is he helping you pack up the house?'

'Yes. He's been a huge help.'

Trudy nodded. 'That's good of him.' She glanced back at her Range Rover. 'I almost forgot. I brought someone with me. I hope it's okay.'

Lana looked over at the car, realising there was someone sat in the passenger seat. Trudy's father.

He had been one of Nana Kitty's oldest friends and she hurried round to the passenger door, a smile on her face for him.

'Doc Palmer, how are you?' she asked, opening the door. 'I was sorry to hear about your stroke.'

'He needs his chair,' Trudy commented, going to the boot.

Trudy and her dad hadn't been at Kitty's funeral, as the Doc was recovering from a stroke, and the last time Lana had seen him, just after Camille had died, he had been fit and healthy. She knew he had been involved in a car accident many years ago. That he had suffered a spinal injury and had lost the use of his legs. But she wasn't prepared for the almost frail-looking man who stared out at her. His once thick, brown hair was an unkempt, straggly grey, and deep-set lines now defined his face. He had to be in his mid-sixties, but he looked much older.

He blinked at Lana, the frown lines deepening. 'I told her I didn't want to come here.'

Lana wasn't quite sure how to react to that, wondering when her grandmother's former doctor had undergone such a personality change. She remembered him as being polite and friendly, but he seemed so bitter. Was it the result of being confined to the chair for nearly seventeen years and forced to give up the career he loved?

She was grateful when Trudy joined them.

It took a few minutes to get him out of the car. Lana watched, unsure if she should offer to help, but also not wanting to get in the way. Trudy's car had been adapted, the passenger seat swivelling to allow her to get her father into his wheelchair. Even though the machine did much of the work, it still required physical strength from Trudy and it made Lana realise just how much the disability affected both of their lives.

It didn't help that the Doc continued to grumble and complain, and Lana wondered why Trudy had insisted on bringing him if he didn't want to be here.

'He just sits in the house, reading his paper or staring out of the window. It's not healthy for him,' Trudy confessed a little later on, when they were upstairs looking at the paintings on the landing. 'I thought today might do him good, but he's being stubborn as usual.' They had left Doc Palmer down in the garden room, Trudy suggesting it might be nice for him to look out over the garden, Lana making him a cup of tea and putting biscuits on a plate that he had looked at scornfully.

'It must have been hard for him, losing your mum and coming to terms with not being able to walk.' Lana remembered the Doc had loved his sport. He was a keen cricketer and enjoyed a round of golf. It had to be frustrating, no longer being able to do the things he loved.

'It is. I try my best to look after him, but he can be a stubborn old fool. And, of course, he needs extra care since the stroke.'

'Is it just the two of you?' Lana asked the question diplomatically, unsure of Trudy's marital status. She didn't wear a ring, and from a couple of comments she had made as they had walked round the house, it sounded like she still lived with the Doc.

She nodded. 'He has no one else to take care of him,' she said simply. 'We've had the house adapted and he can do some things himself, but he relies on me a lot. Xav is good with him. He—' Whether she caught Lana's expression or decided she had broached a taboo subject, Trudy abruptly stopped. 'This one is lovely,' she commented in a quick change of conversation, referring to a coastal watercolour hanging in Kitty's bedroom.

Lana fought to keep her tone even. 'It was one of Nana's favourites.'

Xav is good with him. What exactly did that mean?

That Xav was friends with Doc Palmer?

That he was romantically involved with Trudy?

She hadn't really considered whether Xav was seeing anyone. Not that it was any of her business. She was only back for a brief time and he hated her anyway. Who he was dating or even married to was irrelevant.

But Trudy?

She had seen Xav in her shop, assuming he was there on business. Had she got that wrong?

Although Lana was desperate to ask, she also didn't want to know the answer.

Until a few weeks ago, she had been in a relationship of her own. It was being back here, going through so many memories and now being single; it was making her irrational.

A crash downstairs cut through her thoughts.

The Doc. Was he okay?

She exchanged a look with Trudy, both of them rushing to the stairs.

'Dad?' Trudy sounded panicked as she bolted down them. Lana was close behind her.

They found Doc Palmer in the living room, having wheeled himself through from the garden room, and he was sat in front of the mantelpiece staring at the picture of the siblings when they were much younger. The other frame, with the photo of them that had been taken that last summer, just before Camille died, lay smashed on the hearth.

He hadn't broken it intentionally, had he?

'Dad? What the hell have you done?' Trudy sounded mortified as she bent down to retrieve the broken pieces.

'I couldn't quite reach. I was trying to look.'

'It's fine. Just an accident.' Lana's throat thickened. As long as the photograph was okay. That's all she cared about.

'I'll get you a new frame,' Trudy promised, as her father looked on.

'Honestly, don't worry. It's fine.'

Doc Palmer turned to look up at Lana and for a moment she thought he was going to apologise, but then he repeated her own words back to her. 'Just an accident.'

The smile he gave her while Trudy's attention was diverted was sly and knowing, and in that moment, Lana wondered if it had been an accident at all.

16

The beach had always been her thinking place. Whenever Lana was stressed, she would head to the coast to walk by the sea. The sound of the waves rolling in to lap the shore calmed her, while the expanse of ocean always served as a good reminder that none of her problems were insurmountable.

Right now, she needed both the thinking space and the reminder, and the fact she had chosen Salthouse was no coincidence. The North Norfolk coastline stretched for over forty miles and there were perhaps prettier beaches. The golden sands and pine forests of Holkham or the clifftops of Sheringham and Cromer. Salthouse was flatter, more open and perhaps bleaker, but equally it was dramatic, and it was also close to where Xav lived.

Lana tried not to overanalyse her decision as she pulled onto the beach road late on Saturday evening. The old car park was buried deep under a million pebbles following a storm surge a few years back, so she parked on the road, leaving plenty of distance between her car and the other half-dozen vehicles, as the lane was narrow and turning would be tight.

As she crossed the ridge where the car park had once been,

stepping down onto the stony beach, her load lightened a little. It was nearing dusk and the summer showers that had swept in throughout the afternoon had finally ceased, dark clouds clearing. In the next half an hour, if she was lucky, she would witness a spectacular sunset. Something she hoped might help to lift her mood.

The beach itself was desolate, and aside from a couple of people in the distance, she had this stretch to herself. That suited her fine. She wasn't looking for distractions, though she did take a moment to appreciate the view back to the village across the fields and marshes. The trudging terrain as her feet crunched against pebbles was hard work, but that was good too. It made her feel. As did the North Sea breeze as it whipped her hair across her face. Right now, she really needed to feel, and to clear her head as she tried to process what she had read.

The journal.

She hadn't had a chance to look at it until late on Friday evening. Trudy and her father hadn't left until gone five, and Ollie and Elise arrived home a short while later. Ollie bringing Lana a slice of coffee cake from a posh patisserie, which she understood was a peace offering, though he mentioned nothing about their earlier fight. Deciding to put it behind them, she had accepted the cake graciously.

The incident with the Doc and the photograph had unsettled her somewhat, but she tried to also push that from her mind, concluding that his accident had turned him into a cantankerous old man. Whether he had broken the frame on purpose or not, she wasn't sure, but she refused to buy into whatever game he was playing.

She had agreed a price with Trudy, who was keen to take all of the paintings in the house, and they had arranged that she would come back and collect them in a few days.

Finally, after dinner, she had headed upstairs and sat on her sister's bed with the journal, her fingers brushing over the neatly written words as Camille explained her reasons on the first page for starting a new one.

I can no longer keep my feelings to myself, but I can't risk writing them in my regular journal, just in case it falls into the wrong hands. The last few weeks have been eye-opening and for the first time in forever, I feel alive. This journal is for us, and it will stay hidden, along with the rest of our secrets.

Hours had passed, but Lana had been unaware, absorbed in the entries that documented her sister's secret love affair with a man she only referred to by the initial G. There was the occasional mention of Sebastian, always noted by an S, but it was clear from Camille's words that she was no longer in love with him. In a couple of entries, she talked about breaking the relationship off, but for whatever reason she had held back on going through with it. Was this the reason Seb had killed her? Because he had found out she was cheating on him?

And who was the man known as G? Why did their love affair have to remain secret?

Lana honestly had no idea any of this had gone on and the further into the journal she got, the more she had understood, and the more shocked she was at this secret side of her sister's life.

This was not a romance. It was an addiction, an obsession. Her sister had been following a dark path and her entries became more detailed and explicit, making it uncomfortable to read.

G was in charge of this affair, the one calling the shots and setting the boundaries, and it was clear that while he craved control, Camille was more than willing to do whatever he asked.

Lana had been forced to skim over some of the lines, sick to her stomach as she read about the animalistic way the pair of them had sex, how G liked to mark her with bruises and bites in private places, referring to Camille as his property and calling her his 'perfect little whore'.

Her sister had been intelligent and worldly wise as well as beautiful. Why had she let herself be treated this way?

Sebastian had adored her. He was both chivalrous and proud.

He had also killed her.

It had to be jealousy. A moment of rage.

The summer house is our special place. It's where we play our games, Camille had written in this journal.

The summer house had been Camille and Seb's special place too.

As she walked, Lana recalled the humiliating way her sister had been treated before death, how her killer had degraded her, writing vile words all over her body, and she thought of the things G liked to do. The names he called her, how he liked to mark her, and how he thought he owned her. If she didn't know better...

No. Sebastian had been with Camille on the night of her murder. Lana had seen him.

This was messing with her head.

She paused walking, picked up a pebble, and skimmed it out across the water.

After reading the journal, she had struggled to fall asleep and as a result she had been tired all day. Luckily, Elise had disappeared off out mid-afternoon, so she was one less annoyance to deal with. To stay with an old friend in Norwich, Ollie had told Lana when pushed.

Knowing it was just the two of them, she had tried to talk to him about the journal and tell him what she had read. His reaction had shocked her. He had shut her down, refusing to discuss it and accusing her of dredging up the past. Camille's love life had been her own business, he had raged, and Lana needed to stop poking into the past, let their sister's memory rest.

It seemed that despite all the counselling sessions, Ollie still couldn't face up to or deal with what had happened and she was beginning to worry if making him come back to Mead House had been a bad idea. He had always been the more fragile one.

When Greg Corbett, the first of his poker mates, had shown up with his leery grin and boorish jokes, Lana knew she had to get out of the house and find somewhere to blow off steam. That was why she had come to the beach, hoping a late-evening walk next to the roar of the sea would help to clear her head and make sense of things.

She hadn't finished the journal yet, resisting the temptation to skip ahead to the last page, to find out if G had still been in her sister's life the night she was murdered. There were still several entries to go and while she knew it wouldn't be easy reading, she was also compelled. Unlike her brother, she needed to know the full truth.

The sky was darkening now; inky blues and stormy purples were all that she was going to get tonight. She guessed they suited her mood.

The cry of a marsh harrier sounded overhead and she looked up to see its long tail and the distinctive V of its wings as it swooped towards the marsh, no doubt having spotted dinner. Controlled and predatory. Just like G.

In the distance, she could see a couple of fishermen, their lines cast. Both staring out to sea and far enough apart to suggest they weren't together.

It was growing darker by the minute and Lana should really turn back now. Still, her feet carried her forward. She wasn't ready to leave yet. Just a few more minutes.

The breeze was picking up now, a respite from the recent warm days, and the waves growing in intensity. Further out to sea, the water was dark with shadows, but as the swell rose, the last embers of light shimmered across its surface.

One of the fishermen was calling it a day and he had his back to her, packing away his equipment as she neared. The friendly hello Lana was about to greet him with as she passed froze on her lips as he straightened, turning in her direction.

'Xav?'

She had caught him off guard again, saw his eyes widen in shock and readied herself for the same look of revulsion he had given her a couple of days ago. This time, however, he seemed more prepared, arranging his features into a neutral expression.

At first, she didn't think he was going to speak and as they both stood there eyeing each other warily, Lana tried to organise the jumble of words in her head, aware this might be the last chance she got to try to smooth things over between them. She couldn't mess this up.

'What are you doing here, Lana?' He spoke quietly, his tone almost resigned that he had to have this conversation.

Did he mean he wanted to know what she was doing back in town? Surely he must know about Kitty. She decided to answer his question literally.

'I needed to clear my head. I miss the beach.'

'This beach?'

Was he making an accusation?

She simply shrugged. 'It's as good as any.' When his eyes narrowed in suspicion, she quickly added, 'I had no idea you would be here.'

George's voice popped into her head. *He wanted to be close to the beach. He spends a lot of time down there.*

But she hadn't followed him. Hadn't expected to bump into him. *Liar.*

Okay, hoped maybe, but hadn't expected.

'Can we talk? Please.'

He went back to packing up his things, refusing to look at her. 'I don't think that's a good idea.'

'I know you hate me. I get it. And in a couple of weeks I'll be gone. You won't ever have to see me again. But please, I can't leave without at least trying to put things right between us.'

Xav gathered his fishing gear, huffed out a frustrated sigh, looking at her again. In the dying light, the shadows played on his face, making him look dangerously handsome.

'I don't hate you, Lana. I just can't be around any of you Hamiltons. And I don't want you to try to fix things. There is no "us". Not any more. This whole situation is too fucked up for that. My head wants to explode just thinking about it.'

His words made her heart hitch, then fall.

As she scrambled for something to say in response, he cast the final blow.

'I'm asking you politely. Leave me alone. Please.'

As her mouth flapped open and shut, he stepped past her, heading back along the shoreline towards the beach road entrance. She watched him go, could see his broad shoulders were tight with tension. He had been so civil. Heat and anger she could have dealt with, but the cool and stiffly polite way he had dismissed her left her reeling.

As the shadows swallowed him up, Lana realised she needed to get back to her car too. There was just a lone fisherman on the beach now and she could see his silhouette lit by a lamp in the distance. She only had her phone torch and it wasn't a smart idea staying down here in the darkness. Besides, the wind had picked up and she could feel a few spits of rain in the air.

She hurried after Xav, eager not to be left behind. Her feet crunching against the gravelly beach was a sure sign that she was behind him, but he appeared to ignore that as he strode ahead, only casting a quick annoyed look back at her as he approached the stony ridge that led to the road.

He was parked closer to the beach than she was and had dumped his stuff in the boot, already inside his car before she reached him. Part of her wanted to make one last attempt to talk to him. It was killing her that things were going to be left like this. She tried to make eye contact, but he had started the ignition and then his headlights were on, ensuring she couldn't see him. Frustrating as it was, she got the hint.

By the time Lana reached her own car, it was raining steadily. Behind her, Xav was already turning around on the narrow road.

She started her engine, tried to pull forward, realising immediately that something was wrong, when the vehicle struggled to move. Leaving the engine running, she got out of the car.

As she did, Xav sped past, too late for her to wave him down. Not that he was likely to help her anyway.

It was fine. If there was an issue, she would sort it herself. She had too much pride to ask for his help after he had just told her to stay away from him.

With the car lights on, she could see the problem straight away. She had a flat tyre.

Crap.

No, double crap. They were both down.

She had a spare, but only the one. And she was stuck at the bottom of the beach road in the pouring rain. It looked like she was going to have a damp and boring wait for roadside assistance.

As she pulled out her phone and searched for the number, another engine started from closer to the beach.

Was it the other fisherman she had seen? She hadn't heard him behind her and he had looked like he was settling in for the night.

She turned to face the car as the headlights came on, dazzling her, and waved, trying to get the driver's attention.

Whoever it was didn't appear to see her though, as they weren't slowing.

In fact, they were speeding up.

Realising the car wasn't going to stop, Lana tried to jump out of the way, but she wasn't quick enough to completely avoid the impact as it caught her leg, her scream cutting through the air at the blinding pain as metal cut into flesh.

It was a brief glance in the rear-view mirror that had Xav slowing.

Perhaps wise that he had looked, as he saw Lana was out of her car and from the way she was staring at the front tyres, he knew something was wrong.

Not his problem. She would have to call a tow truck.

That was his head talking. That part of him that made sensible and sometimes ruthless decisions. And, of course, he wasn't going to listen to it. He didn't want a conversation with Lana, but equally he wasn't going to leave her stranded. If he drove off and left her, and something happened, he would never forgive himself.

He would leave it a minute before going back, he decided, just to be sure he was right about the car. He didn't want to give her the wrong idea.

What happened next was over in seconds, leaving him no time to react.

First, he saw the second pair of headlights, then he watched the impact as Lana disappeared off the edge of the road.

For a moment, he was stunned, almost disbelieving what he had just seen, but then the adrenaline kicked in and he shoved the gear-stick into reverse.

As he backed up at speed along the narrow road, he could hear the engine of the car that had hit her. It was revving. Why the fuck hadn't the driver got out to check on her? Had he hit her on purpose?

Then the car was hurtling towards him and Xav slammed on his brake. He was convinced they were going to collide, but somehow the car skidded around him, the squeal of tyres as it took the turn onto the main road too fast cutting through the night. It all happened so quickly, the road dark and the headlights bright, and he was too stunned to pick up on any details.

His heart thumping, he reversed at speed the rest of the way back. Fumbling with his seatbelt, he almost fell out of the door, rushing over to Lana's car.

'Lana?' Where the fuck was she?

He found her in the drainage ditch that ran along the side of the road, the headlights picking her up as he stepped round the front of her car. Jumping into the water, he crouched down and scooped her up in his arms. At first, he thought she was unconscious, dead even, but then he heard her groan.

'Lana?' He used the crook of his arm to cushion her head, his free hand cupping her face and tilting her chin up. As he tapped gently on her cold cheek, her eyes fluttered open, her damp face pale, but with no visible sign of damage.

'I jumped,' she managed. 'I saw it coming, but I wasn't quick enough.'

'Are you hurt?' Xav demanded.

'My leg. It caught my leg.' She grimaced.

He tried to look for sign of injury, but it was difficult to see from her position. 'Do you think you can stand?'

'I don't know. Just give me a couple of minutes.'

Her teeth were chattering now, her body trembling against him. Either from shock or the couple of feet of cold water they were in. The rain wasn't helping either. He needed to get her out.

'Can you hold on to me?'

She nodded, fastening her arms around his neck as he slipped his hand beneath her legs to support her. He caught her hiss of breath as she tensed against him, knew she was attempting to mask her pain, and he tried to be gentle as he lifted her out of the ditch.

He set her down on the grass verge, annoyed that she was already trying to sit up as he clambered out beside her.

'Take it steady, okay.'

This was the Lana he remembered only too well. Always trying to run before she could walk.

She was holding onto her right leg and he could see the gash in her knee as fresh blood poured through her fingers.

He needed to get something to help stop the flow.

'Wait here a moment,' he ordered, turning off her car engine and pocketing the keys. 'And don't move.'

It sounded like a stupid instruction, but this was Lana Hamilton. And he was right. She had blatantly ignored him in the time it took him to return from his car, somehow up on her feet with one hand on the bonnet of her car to steady herself as she tried to put pressure on her bad leg.

'I told you not to move.'

'I don't think it's broken.'

'That's not the point,' Xav said, exasperated.

He wrapped a blanket around her shoulder, then crouched down so he could look at her leg. The cut wasn't too deep, though there was a fair bit of blood, and he folded and pressed a towel against it.

'Are you okay to put pressure on this while I call for an ambulance?'

'I don't need to go to hospital. I'm fine.'

Fine was an understatement, though she did appear to be lucky. From what he could see, there was no other damage apart from to her leg. Probably a few scrapes and bruises, but nothing life-threatening. Still. 'You were just hit by a car. I think you need to be checked out.'

Lana shook her head, insistent. 'No ambulance.'

'Lana...'

'Please! I don't want to go to hospital.'

He remembered she had a fear of them, refusing to go to A&E with them when Xav had broken his nose, or visit Ollie when he had to go in to have his appendix out, and she had created merry hell when she had fallen out of a tree, dislocating her shoulder. Kitty had been forced to take her kicking and screaming.

'I'm fine,' she repeated. 'Besides, it's the police we need to call.'

She was right, though he still disagreed with her assessment of fine.

He stared at her for a moment. Her teeth were still chattering, the blanket he had wrapped around her already dampened by the rain, and her hair was hanging in wet strings around her shoulders.

Concern that she was hurt had pushed the fact someone had purposely done this to her to the back of his mind. They did need to address that, but they were both soaking wet, and badly injured or not, she had still been hit by a car.

He made a decision.

Moments later, he had her buckled into the passenger seat of his car and was trying not to overthink the fact that he was driving her back to his house. He would call the police from there, where at least he could get Lana into some dry clothes and dress her leg properly. He could have taken her straight home to Mead House, but his place was closer to the scene of the hit-and-run. They had locked up Lana's car and would deal with it later.

As he drove, he couldn't help but consider the split second that would have changed everything. If he had left a moment sooner, if he hadn't glanced in the mirror, Lana would have been alone. And what then? Would she have drowned in the ditch? Would the driver of the other car have stayed to finish the job? Because both of Lana's tyres were flat, which was too coincidental for his liking, and the driver hadn't left the scene immediately. It wasn't until he had seen Xav reversing that he had sped off.

It had all happened so quickly and he was cursing himself that he hadn't managed to catch any real visuals. It had been a dark SUV, but he hadn't clocked the number plate or the driver. Had Lana? She was deathly pale and still trembling, the magnitude of what had just happened no doubt sinking in, so the question could wait.

He had told her he couldn't have her in his life but knowing that she could be dead right now was like a stab in the gut, and it was raising a lot of questions he wasn't ready to answer.

If she wondered where he was taking her, she didn't ask. He had promised her no hospital, so did she assume he was driving her home? Neither of them had spoken since getting in the car, the low hum of the radio and the sweep of the windscreen wipers against the battering rain the only noise as they both processed what had just happened.

When he pulled off the road into the wooded driveway, he flicked a glance in her direction. She was still absorbed with her thoughts and he suspected shock was perhaps catching up with her.

He helped her inside his home, trying not to think about everything that lay between them. This was just temporary. It had to be.

Someone tried to kill her.

Not his problem. It was a matter for the police and the sooner they arrived, the quicker he could remove himself from this situation. It would be better that way.

An unwelcome voice nagged in his head.

Liar.

18

'You've had no trouble since you've been back?'

That was from the male detective. Galbraith, Lana was certain he had said his name was when he'd introduced himself. It was hard to keep focus, so much having happened in such a short space of time.

Her mind wandered briefly to the figure she thought she had seen in the garden the first night she had arrived. Returning to a house that held so many memories, it could have been her mind playing tricks on her.

'No,' she told him, warming her hands on the second mug of tea Xav had made her. 'Nothing.'

The first one had been too sweet and she had struggled to drink it. It was for the adrenaline, he had told her, insisting she finish the cup. It had been disgusting and she had protested with every sip, but he was right, it had helped, and the shaking had mostly subsided. He had agreed to hold back on the sugar in the second cup. Much better.

'And there's no one in your life back in Cambridge who has been giving you extra attention or who you are concerned about?'

Lana blushed, thinking of Matt. He had been upset, understandably, when she had called time on their relationship and he seemed to have trouble accepting that it was over, but his behaviour wasn't irrational. Was it?

'I had a boyfriend,' she began, aware Xav was paying attention. 'Things ended... I ended it.'

'And when was this?'

'Maybe a month ago.'

Galbraith nodded at his partner, the easier to remember Jones, before jotting in his notebook. 'And how did he take that?'

'He was upset. Wanted me to give things another chance.'

This sounded bad. She was throwing Matt under a bus when he had reacted perfectly reasonably given that Lana had ended things after six years together. He had thought they were going to get married and it had taken him proposing for her to realise she didn't want that.

'It's not him. He's a good person and wouldn't do this.'

Another exchanged look between the detectives suggested they didn't believe her.

She snuck another look at Xav, whose expression was carefully neutral. This had to be hard for him. He had been good to her, finding her a hoodie and joggers, making her the revolting tea, and generally looking after her.

She thought back to his words down on the beach. He had said he couldn't be around her, asked her to leave him alone. Yet here she was in his home. It felt surreal to her and she was a little surprised he had chosen to bring her here, instead of taking her to Mead House.

After he had taken care of her, then called the police, he had disappeared to change out of his own wet clothes and was now perched on the arm of the sofa where she sat, dark hair still damp and starting to curl, and his clean, long-sleeved T-shirt clinging to his lean, toned physique. Close enough to keep an eye on her, though he couldn't quite bring himself to take the empty seat beside her.

She was grateful for everything but knew this was uncomfortable for him and promised herself she would be out of his hair as soon as she was able.

Of course she had to hand over Matt's details, purely, as the detectives told her, so they could eliminate him from their enquiries. She cursed herself, wishing she had never said anything. Matt wasn't behind this. He was a good, kind man, and she was only sorry that she had let things drag on between them for so long. He deserved better and she would message him when she got home and apologise.

She glanced at her phone and saw Ollie still hadn't read the message she had left for him. She had tried to call him a couple of times, but he hadn't picked up. She knew he had his poker night, though, and was probably drunk, but he was unaware of what had happened.

Someone had tried to kill her.

The thought surfaced uncomfortably in her mind, making her shudder.

If Xav hadn't seen. If he hadn't stopped—

No, she couldn't go there.

'Now remember, A&E if you start experiencing any of the symptoms we talked about,' Jones reminded, getting to her feet, as the detectives finished with their questions.

They had pushed for her to go to hospital, but she had steadfastly refused.

'Okay,' she nodded, just to appease them. She had no intention of going.

Her fear of hospitals stemmed back to her earliest memories: her mother hooked up to tubes and drips as the life slowly ebbed out of her. It was irrational, she understood that. Doctors and nurses helped people and they saved a lot of lives. Still, she couldn't quite conquer her phobia.

Xav understood. He knew how it was for her. He had always known.

The door closed on the two detectives and then it was just the two of them again. This time, though, there was nothing to preoccupy them. No calls to make or wounds to dress. Nothing to divert the attention away from the elephant in the room.

In the aftermath of the hit-and-run, conversation with Xav had felt almost normal, like they were settling back into a familiar rhythm. It had probably been caused by the shock, both their guards dropping, because now she could sense Xav's was right back up as he stiffly told her to make herself comfortable while he cleared away the cups.

She tried to relax, rolling her shoulders to shake the tension out of them as she focused on her breathing. Tonight's events had scared the hell out of her and she was terrified that at any minute, she might completely lose her shit. She needed to hold herself together, at least until she was home.

Trying to distract herself, she concentrated on her surroundings. The house was a blend of modern with traditional, all light walls with wide windows and dark wood beams. The converted shell of the barn comprised of two levels: the lower floor divided only by a central and rather beautiful staircase with a black, wrought-iron balustrade. She could see a large tabby sat halfway up, watching her curiously with wide, yellow eyes. The cat was the only truly homely thing in the house. It was too tidy, nothing out of place, and aside from an old photograph of his parents on a shelf, there was nothing personal of Xav here. It seemed more like a show house than a home.

Lana could see him through the rails, busying himself in a

sleek, expensive-looking kitchen that looked like it was seldom used. All glossy black and shiny chrome, with granite worktops and exposed brick on the walls. Anything to avoid dealing with her.

It was a far cry from the small cosy kitchen in his mother's house. There, the units had been cheap and battered and the appliances temperamental, but Joanna had taken pride in her home and it was lived in. There were always fresh cut flowers on the windowsill, the mouth-watering aroma of home-cooked food, and laughter bubbling in the air.

Lana had loved it when she was invited to stay for lunch or dinner. They had all crowded around the table with its blue checked cloth, while Joanna served up pancakes for Shrove Tuesday, homemade hot cross buns at Easter, and hot dogs and baked potatoes on Bonfire Night.

They had been in that kitchen when she had first realised she had a crush on Xav Landry, catching him looking over at her as butterflies fluttered up a storm in her belly, and over a year later, it had been in that room that he had burnt the lasagne he had made in an effort to try to impress her. She wondered if his cookery skills had improved. Joanna had often laughed that given they were half French, neither of her sons were any good in the kitchen.

Lana glanced at her phone, noting Ollie still hadn't read her message, as Xav wandered back through to join her. He kept his distance though, as if coming to close to her might physically hurt him.

There was a horrible silence that dragged on for far too long.

'I should go. I'll call a taxi, get out of your way.'

'I'll drive you home.'

They both spoke at the same time, then laughed uneasily.

'I don't want to put you out. I've already done that tonight.'

Xav studied her for a moment, though didn't correct her. 'I'll drive you,' he repeated simply.

19

Ten minutes later, they were back in the car, the rain fortunately having stopped again, and enduring another silent ride, this time to Mead House.

Lana hunkered down in her seat, the hoodie rising up to cover the lower part of her face. It smelt of fabric conditioner and of another more familiar scent that had been long lost to her. Xav.

She breathed it in, trying to distract herself from the discomfort of her throbbing leg, and for a split second, all felt right in the world.

Which was stupid, because things really weren't right.

Had the attack been random? Had she simply been in the wrong place, at the wrong time?

Tears pricked at the back of her eyes.

Don't go there. Not yet.

She snuck a glance at Xav, glad he was focused on the road and not on her. He had his own demons he was battling, and she was aware of the tension rolling off him as they neared her grandmother's house, could see it in the tightening of his jaw and the whitening of his knuckles as his fingers curled around the steering wheel.

She wanted to reach out and put her hand over his, tell him it was going to be okay, even if it was a lie, but she feared he would recoil.

By the time he turned into the driveway, that tension was shifting into her and she was eager to get inside the house, desperately tired and needing her own space. However, another part of her yearned to keep this tenuous connection, knowing that once it was broken, Xav would be gone.

There were three vehicles on the driveway, suggesting that poker night was still going strong.

Lana recognised George's van. He hadn't been there when she had left the house and Ollie had been convinced he was going to be a no-show. He must have just been running late.

Xav pulled to a halt in front of the house, cutting the engine and opening his door.

'It's okay. You don't need to get out.'

Either he hadn't heard her or had chosen to ignore her as he was already coming round to the passenger side, his touch burning into her arm as he insisted on helping her out of the car.

'What the hell's going on?'

Ollie's angry voice carried across the driveway and Lana glanced over Xav's shoulder, as her brother stormed out of the now open front door.

'Why are you with *him*? Are you wearing his clothes? What the fuck is going on, Lana?'

She was aware of Xav stiffening, but other than that he didn't react.

'I was in an accident.'

'What?' Ollie sounded shocked now. 'What accident?'

'Not an accident. A car drove into her.' Xav was staring straight at Ollie, his hand still on Lana's arm. She wasn't sure if it was there for her protection or his. 'I watched it happen.'

'What?' Ollie repeated, his mouth flapping now as he processed Xav's words. 'Are you okay?' he managed eventually, refusing to look at or address Xav.

'Shaken up, but all things considered, yes. I did message you. I tried to call too.'

'We were playing poker.' He sounded sheepish. 'I didn't know.'

'It's fine, Ollie. Xav looked after me.' She turned to Xav. 'Thank you, for everything.'

'No problem.'

Reluctantly, she broke contact, stepped towards her brother and the open front door.

Ollie was no longer looking at her, though, his attention now fully on Xav. 'You. Stay the fuck away from my sister and this house.'

'Ollie!'

'He's not welcome here.'

'He pretty much just saved my life,' she snapped.

'And his brother killed our sister!'

'Leave it, Lana.' Xav's tone was weary, like he didn't have the time or the energy for this shit.

He was already getting back into his car, didn't even give her a final glance before starting the engine, and the pang of loss ripped through her as he disappeared back down the driveway.

'You are such an arsehole.' She thumped Ollie on the arm, limping into the house. 'After everything he has done for me tonight.'

She could see his friends through the open door of the living room, knew they must have heard the commotion outside, as conversation stopped, all of them looking in her direction.

George raised a hand and Lana nodded back, but she didn't stop as she went upstairs, not in the right frame of mind to make small talk or to discuss what had happened.

'Lana. Wait up!' Ollie was charging after her. He sounded worried. 'We need to talk about what happened.'

'Go back down to your friends. I don't want to talk to you right now.'

'But should you be alone?'

'I'll be fine.'

'Why are you shutting me out like this?' His tone turned sarcastic. 'You went to Xav Landry instead of me?'

'Excuse me?' Lana thought she had misheard for a moment. She had reached the landing now and spun round to face Ollie, who was almost at the top of the stairs. 'I'm shutting you out? Are you serious? You've been shutting me out for years. And you are *never* there for me.'

'What?'

He genuinely looked stunned. Well, too bad. Maybe it was time to tell him some home truths.

'You accuse me of nagging you, but I don't ever really ask anything unreasonable. I just let you carry on, doing your own thing, figuring maybe you'll eventually appreciate me picking up your slack. Honestly, though? I don't think you even notice. And what the hell right did you have to speak to Xav as you just did? He was there for me tonight and thank God he was. Yet you're more concerned with telling him to piss off than you are about what happened to me. That car hit me and it wasn't an accident. The driver aimed for me.' Her voice dropped to a whisper, 'They tried to kill me.' Saying those words aloud had the tears threatening again. 'Camille's gone, and now Nana Kitty is too. You're all I have, Ollie. I know you have your own life in London and I'm not trying to be a part of that or take it away from you, but we used to be so close.'

She prodded at her chest. 'I used to feel you in here. I don't recognise who you are any more.'

The tears were spilling now and when Ollie reached for her hand, she tugged it away, angrily swiping at them.

'Lana, dammit. Come back.'

Ignoring him, she crossed the landing, shutting the door on him when he tried to follow her into Camille's room. She needed to be alone and, afraid he wouldn't respect that, she locked the door, refusing to respond to his pleas to let him in so they could talk.

Ollie was too much hard work these days. Maybe she was the one who needed to change and to accept he was no longer really a part of her life.

Sitting down on the edge of the bed, she ran her fingers over the wound that Xav had dressed. It hurt like hell, every throb a frightening reminder of what had happened tonight.

She reached for the painkillers she had in the bedside drawer, glancing at the journal beside them. She was too shaken to read any more entries tonight.

The trembling was starting again, the tears flowing freely now, and after taking the pills, Lana lay back on the bed, rolling over to bury her face in the pillow as she gave in to them.

She wasn't usually a crier and generally faced her problems head on, but for tonight she needed this moment of weakness. Someone had tried to kill her. Each time she let that thought sink in, it scared her a little bit more.

She had done the sensible thing. The police were investigating and she knew they were taking the attack seriously. Lana didn't know if she had been a victim of chance or if she had been targeted intentionally, but right now she had to trust they would find out whoever was behind it and why.

Truthfully, she hoped it was a random encounter, even if it

would make the driver harder to trace. If she had been attacked on purpose, then the chances were that whoever had done it might try to kill her again. And that scared her more than anything.

20

Camille Hamilton was my first kill, though it wasn't meant to be that way.

She was supposed to be a simple lesson. Nothing more, nothing less. I would punish her and she would leave alive. That was the plan. But she was thrashing in the chair, pleading with me not to hurt her, and I could smell her fear.

That sounds stupid, right? You can't smell an emotion.

Wrong.

The heavy air was thick with her sweet perfume, her body odour and later, the stench of bodily release. And it was ripe with another musky, almost pungent scent. Fear.

A switch in my head flipped as I fed on the power I had over her and I remember thinking, I can end this now.

I had her necklace in my pocket and had been planning on keeping it. A memento of my revenge for the wrongs done to me. I barely even remember reaching for it or pulling the ribbon taut, wrapping it around her neck, the heart pendant tight against her throat.

At first, I don't think I even realised what I was doing, but then I came to my senses and I understood it was wrong, knew that if I kept strangling her she would die, but I simply couldn't stop myself. I wanted to kill her.

There are consequences to spontaneous actions and I learnt the hard way how dangerous that is. Camille has nearly been my undoing on several occasions.

I don't look in the mirror and see a killer. I am a respectable, functioning adult. I work hard, I care about others, and I think I am empathetic.

Okay, so, yes, I am methodical and sometimes obsessive and I can be calculating when I need to, but I simply see myself as a problem solver. When there is a problem, I try to fix it. It's as easy as that, and if fixing it means ending someone's life, I will.

Lana Hamilton is an unlucky lady. She has managed to place herself in my sights. How unfortunate for her.

She may have narrowly escaped with her life tonight, but there will be other chances.

What she doesn't realise is that she is now an obstacle in my way. And the problem with obstacles is that they need to be removed.

21

Wake, rest, sleep, repeat.

It was the pattern Lana followed for the next few days, as the trauma of the hit-and-run took its toll, both physical and mentally. Her body was a patchwork of bruises, and tender from where she had landed in the ditch, the cut on her leg needing painkillers to dull the throbbing ache, her mood contemplative and despondent as she tried to come to terms with what had happened.

She had messaged her ex-boyfriend, warning him that the police might be in touch and apologising. Matt hadn't been happy and she guessed she couldn't blame him. It stung that he hadn't asked if she was okay, though.

She had ignored DC Jones's advice to go to a doctor, so had been surprised when one came to her, Ollie having called in a favour from an old friend. Initially, she had been angry with her brother, though when told there was no serious damage and that rest would be sufficient to heal the wound, she was both relieved and grateful.

Whether their last argument had made him think or not, Ollie was being a little more thoughtful, bringing her cups of tea and considering her when it came to meals. Even Elise had checked in with her a couple of times to see if she needed anything, though Lana suspected she had been put up to it, as she still wasn't overly friendly or keen to stick around. Not that she particularly wanted her company.

There had been no word from Xav. That didn't surprise her, though it didn't ease her pang of emptiness, and aside from one follow-up call from the police, she had been left to chase them for updates.

Unfortunately, it wasn't looking positive. Xav had been the only witness and he had been more focused on Lana than whoever had hit her. And the police had spoken to Matt, who had an alibi placing him in Cambridge.

Knowing that someone was out there who meant her harm, who might try to hurt her again, at first frightened her, but as boredom and frustration set in, her fear turned to a more productive anger. She had done nothing wrong, nothing to warrant being attacked. She had not deserved this.

The first day she had mostly slept, but restlessness had her needing stimulation. Initially, she had been wary about picking up Camille's journal again, not sure if she was in the right frame of mind to read it. There were only so many sites she could browse though, and she had already ploughed through the two paperbacks she had brought with her.

She kept glancing at the journal and curiosity eventually won.

The entries were more of the same, offering nothing new in terms of content, but what was apparent was Camille's growing obsession with G.

Lana barely recognised her sister from this journal, but every word was written in Camille's familiar handwriting. How could she have missed this huge change in her?

She knew the answer. It was because she had been a teenager herself and wrapped up in her own first love.

The romance she had shared with Xav that last summer had been nothing like this. It had been innocent and tentative. Sweet, even. Camille's words made Lana feel like a voyeur and sick to her stomach. Her sister had been so in love with Sebastian. How had she changed so suddenly?

Lana thought back to the year before her sister had died, the summer of 2004. After years of being the tomboy sister, she had finally felt the pair of them were connecting. It had been the day she had learnt that Camille was dating Sebastian Landry, early into the summer holiday, Lana and Ollie having just returned from boarding school after sitting their GCSEs, that the sisters had taken that first tentative step towards really bonding.

Lana remembered how she had overheard Camille arguing with their grandmother in the kitchen.

* * *

'You have a bright future ahead of you,' Kitty was saying, her voice raised in anger. 'You're off to university in September and you need to focus on your studies, not boys.'

'I can still work hard and see Seb.'

'You should keep your options open. Meet new people, make new friends. University is supposed to be the best time of your life.'

'Seb and I love each other.'

'You're eighteen, Camille. You have no idea what that means.'

Suggesting Camille wasn't in love was perhaps the wrong thing to say to her spirited sister. Camille's temper could be as fiery as her hair and the argument stepped up a notch.

Lana lost interest in the TV show she was watching and used the pretence of getting a drink of juice from the fridge, before taking it to sit at the kitchen table. From here, she could see and hear everything.

'I know he makes me happy and I want to be with him. Why do you want to ruin that for me?' Camille demanded.

'I'm not trying to ruin anything, sweetheart. I just want you to make the right decisions. I know he makes you happy now, but what about further down the line? He's never going to be able to give you the life you are used to.'

'So there it is. You're finally getting to the crux of the problem.'

'I have no idea what you mean.'

'The life I am *used to*.' Camille had her hands on her hips. 'You don't think he's good enough for me.'

'I never said that.'

'You implied it. Seb's family don't have much money. They're not rich enough for you.'

'I didn't imply anything, but yes, if we are going to be entirely honest, the Landrys are good people, but there's no getting away from it: they are poor. I know Joanna works hard to keep a roof over her family's head, but Sebastian and Xavier have fewer prospects than you. They can't afford to go on to higher education. Look at Sebastian. He's had no choice but to take a job working in a garage.'

'And what the hell is wrong with that?'

'How is he going to provide for you, pay to give you nice things in life?'

Camille scoffed. 'Seriously? Will you listen to yourself, Nana? It's 2004. I thought you were more forward thinking than this.' She raised her chin defiantly. 'Maybe I will be the breadwinner. I can pay to give Seb nice things.'

Lana listened and sipped at her juice as the fight continued, both women too stubborn to compromise. She hadn't realised her grandmother felt this way about the Landrys. Xav practically lived at Nana Kitty's house when her and Ollie were back from boarding school and Lana had believed her grandmother to be fond of him. Did she feel the same way about him too? That he wasn't good enough?

That caused a dilemma for her young heart and the secret little crush she had developed on her brother's best friend. Nothing had happened, of course. Xav had no idea of her changing feelings towards him, and Lana would sooner die than tell him. But knowing that Nana Kitty might frown upon any relationship had just added a whole new problem.

The fight eventually ended with her sister storming from the room, after angrily pointing out that it was up to her who she dated and her grandmother needed to butt out.

Lana left it for a short while before following her sister upstairs.

It had always been Camille versus the twins. Lana connected better with her brother, preferring the rough and tumble play, and held little interest in her sister's life. But more recently, she was curious. Boys liked her sister, but they never looked at Lana, and she worried it was because they saw her as one of them. She didn't really dress or act much like a girl. Camille knew about fashion and dating, and Lana, who, along with Ollie, would be turning sixteen in August, had been trying to connect more with her sister.

She knocked tentatively on Camille's bedroom door, before easing it open.

Camille was sat on her bed, cross-legged, and writing in her journal, and she glanced up scowling, a flash of temper in her black eyes. 'Get out!'

She hurled a cushion at the door and Lana hastily retreated. Sulking, she went to her bedroom and threw herself on the bed.

How was she supposed to figure out the mysteries of attracting boys by herself? She didn't really have any female friends and her grandmother would be no help.

Eventually, Camille came to find her. Lana heard the door open, but refused to look up, and the mattress dipped as her sister sat down beside her. She recognised her from the scent of her perfume.

'I'm sorry I shouted at you.'

Lana was never one to hold on to her anger and she rolled over at Camille's apology, saw her sister's pale cheeks had lost their flush and her eyes were no longer scowling.

'What's it like, kissing a boy?' she asked curiously.

Camille studied her for a moment before bursting into delighted laughter. 'Why do you want to know? Is there someone you want to kiss?'

Lana blushed furiously. 'No! I just wondered.'

Did Camille know? Had she realised about Lana's secret crush? She would die of embarrassment if anyone found out. Especially Ollie or Xav himself. How would she ever look at him again?

Her heart thumped under her sister's intrigued gaze.

Eventually, Camille got up. 'Come on.'

Come on where?

Lana climbed off the bed, curious as she followed Camille down the hallway and back into her room.

'Sit down.'

Lana looked at the dressing-table stool, hesitating before doing as told. As she looked in the mirror, Camille stood behind her and Lana assessed both their reflections. She didn't hold a candle to her vibrant sister. 'You're so pretty. No wonder Sebastian likes you.'

Camille's lips curved in appreciation. 'You're pretty too, Lana.'

'Not like you.'

'No, you're not like me, but you're still pretty.'

When Lana shook her head and started to look away, Camille caught hold of her chin and tilted it back up. She ran her fingers through Lana's short, dark hair. 'You're rocking the Demi Moore look and you have great bone structure. We just need to emphasise it. Your eyes too.' As she spoke, she twisted Lana on the stool to face her, then picked up pots of make-up and brushes, delicately stroking brushes over her face. 'I think we go subtle, let your natural beauty shine through.'

Lana didn't really have a clue what Camille was doing, even though she was explaining as she worked, but she was enjoying this time alone with her big sister, just the two of them talking. They had never done anything like this before.

'So what do you think?' Camille asked eventually, turning Lana back to face the mirror.

It was her reflection, but somehow she looked different. Her eyes bigger, her skin subtly glowing, her lips a little more defined. She touched at her face.

'This is really cool.'

'All of the boys will be looking at you now.'

'Really?' Lana wasn't so certain, but Camille seemed confident.

'Are you sure there isn't one you like?'

Xav Landry's face immediately popped into Lana's head, his olive-green eyes sparking and his cheeky grin wide as he teased her, and her face heated under the make-up.

'Nope. There's no one.'

Camille smiled as if she knew better, but she didn't push. 'That's a shame then. All made up with no one to impress.' She caught hold of Lana's hand, pulling her up from the stool and over to the row of wardrobes. She took out one of her dresses and Lana screwed her nose up.

'That's too girly.'

'Okay, we'll start gently. Take off your T-shirt.'

Lana did as instructed, though protested when the dress was replaced by a floaty, cropped boho blouse in delicate floral colours.

'Just trust me.'

Five minutes later, she was wearing the blouse, not liking how her belly was exposed, along with a pair of hoop earrings and a baker boy cap that she really wasn't sure about, but then Camille showed her the mirror again and her mouth dropped open.

She looked so grown-up and, dare she say it, kind of cool and edgy.

'I guess it's okay,' she mumbled, not wanting to let on that she really liked it.

She was still wearing the outfit later when Ollie and Xav returned from football and although her brother teased her mercilessly, Xav did a double take when he spotted her, his eyes widening.

'Wow, what happened to you?'

'She's been playing dress-up,' Ollie snorted.

Although Xav laughed and Lana blushed, she took it in her stride, grinning madly to herself when she snuck a glance at Xav a few minutes later and caught him watching her.

She thought her secret crush was safe, but when she glanced in her sister's direction, to where she was sat on the sofa reading a book, Camille looked up with a sly smile on her face and gave Lana a wink.

* * *

There were so many fond memories of that summer and Lana had put them down to her growing crush on Xav and the tentative signs that maybe he liked her back. But the closeness with Camille had been a big part too. Things had changed, though, the following year and it had taken reading her sister's journal and looking back at those last months for her to realise things hadn't been quite right.

Lana had thought they were still close, but truthfully she had been preoccupied by Xav. They had taken to sometimes hanging out together without Ollie after a trip to the cinema where it had just been the two of them, Ollie having pulled out at the last minute due to a sickness bug. Their friendship gradually becoming something more.

Camille and Seb had been dating for a while and Lana had assumed her sister was happy, but maybe she was wrong. Camille's door had always been closed that last summer and she spent a lot of time alone in her room. At meals, she was quiet and contemplative, and often had a far-off, dreamy look. And where she had once been so touchy-feely with Sebastian, it had reached a point where Lana seldom saw them holding hands or hugging each other.

She hadn't thought much of it at the time, figuring they were just settled in their relationship, but if G had been on the scene, it put everything into a new perspective.

The summer house had always been Camille and Sebastian's special place, but if she went to the summer house with Sebastian, when, and where, did she meet up with G? Had she ever taken him there or did they have somewhere else?

The thought crossed her mind that maybe the whispering she had heard late at night hadn't been Sebastian. Lana had naturally assumed it was, but perhaps Camille had been meeting up with this mystery G.

Except for that last night, of course. Lana had been woken by voices. Her sister and Sebastian. It had definitely been Seb because she had climbed out of bed and looked out of the window, had seen him crossing the lawn.

That was what she had told the police at the time and her eyewitness statement had played a big part in Sebastian being convicted.

Because it had been Sebastian with Camille that night. She knew that, right?

Suddenly, she wasn't so sure.

22

Word had spread quickly about the hit-and-run incident, and Trudy had been wondering if Lana would want to delay the sale of the paintings until she was back on her feet.

Although she apparently had only minor injuries, the incident was likely to have taken its toll on her emotionally. Trudy recalled how her father had been following his car accident. Despondent, upset and unable to focus.

Of course, that particular crash had stolen her mother from her, so it was only natural he had struggled in the aftermath. Things had been different for Lana, but still it had to be scary for her, knowing the driver had hit her intentionally.

Bree McCarthy was the one with all the details, having been told them first-hand by Xav, and it upset Trudy, knowing that Xav had reached out to Bree and not to her.

It was difficult at times dealing with the closeness Xav and Bree shared and, okay, yes, some of Trudy's problem was that Bree was striking to look at and extremely capable. Although her most recent relationship had been with a woman, Bree was bisexual, and it often plagued Trudy, wondering if anything had ever happened between her and Xav. Bree insisted they were just friends, but was she telling the truth?

The hit-and-run must have been traumatic for Xav to witness too, especially as it had forced him to spend time with Lana. A woman he didn't like or want in his life.

It surprised her then that he wanted to fix Lana's car.

She learnt he had persuaded Bree to do the work, and had agreed to cover the cost, though Bree was still grumbling about it every step of the way, keen to remind Trudy, when she stopped by to see her, that she despised the Hamiltons and thought Xav was off his head wanting to help Lana. This was for him, not for Lana.

'He's too soft and should cut that bloody woman out of his life,' Bree moaned.

'He couldn't just leave her lying in the road.' Trudy tried to play peacemaker, a role she had to adopt far too often.

'Ditch.'

'Pardon?'

'She was in the ditch. He should have left her to drown.'

The harshness of Bree's words shocked her. Trudy knew she disliked the Hamiltons, and that she had been one of Sebastian Landry's closest friends. Correction: was still his friend, and one of his staunchest defenders. But she'd had no idea she felt this strongly about them.

'Lana has done nothing wrong,' she pointed out, trying to be diplomatic.

'Nothing wrong?' Bree gave her a hard look. 'She was the one who put Seb in prison.'

Not personally, Trudy thought, but didn't point it out. She didn't want an argument. Lana had only told the police what she had seen.

'Why was he with her anyway?' she asked instead, keeping her tone casual. As far as Trudy was aware, Bree had no idea how she felt about Xav. They had never spoken about it and Trudy hoped Xav had kept his mouth shut that they had slept together.

'He bumped into her on the beach, apparently. Sounds to me like she was following him. I mean, why else would they be down there together?'

Trudy didn't even want to consider the question. It already stung a little, knowing that the two of them had been together, talking.

Did Xav still had feelings for Lana? She knew they had been together when they were teenagers, but that was years ago, and their romance had abruptly ended when Sebastian was arrested for Camille's murder.

She tried to think logically and not let herself be swayed by Bree's words. There was nothing going on between Xav and Lana, and even if they had cleared the air, Lana would be going back to Cambridge again soon. Whatever this brief connection was, it would soon be broken.

As Lana hadn't contacted her to cancel, Trudy decided to assume their appointment still stood for her to collect the paintings.

After leaving Bree's workshop, she stopped to pick up a colourful bouquet of gerberas, roses and peonies for Lana, before driving out to Mead House. She had a replacement photo frame to give her too, still mortified that her father had broken it during their last visit.

Ollie Hamilton answered the door, a blank expression on his face as he looked her up and down.

He didn't remember her then.

'Hi, I'm Trudy Palmer. Doctor Palmer's daughter. Is Lana about?'

His eyes narrowed. 'You're here about the paintings?'

No 'Hi, how are you?' or 'How's your dad doing?' Ollie was

clearly still the same dismissive and self-entitled arsehole she remembered.

Refusing to let it get to her, Trudy painted a bright smile on her face. 'I am. Is this still a good time for her? I heard about what happened.'

He shrugged and held the door wide. 'I guess. Come on in. I'll go find her.'

Ollie disappeared, leaving Trudy alone, and she glanced around, a little self-conscious. She wasn't an unconfident woman, but there was something about the size and stature of this house that always reminded her of being a child.

Back then, her father had been quick to tell her she should be seen but never heard. If she ever spoke out of line, the punishment was swift. Trudy had learnt from a young age it was safer to do as she was told. It wasn't until later that she began to question that authority and think for herself.

'Who are you?'

She turned at the sharp tone, saw it belonged to a scowling blonde, her bikini covered by a see-through cover-up that left little to the imagination.

'Trudy Palmer. I'm here to see Lana.'

'Oh.'

This was Ollie's fiancée, she guessed. She had heard he was getting married.

The woman was beautiful, but cold, looking at Trudy as if she was a piece of dirt, and Trudy hated that old feeling of insecurity bubbling inside her. It annoyed her that she was now a grown adult, yet felt the need to explain herself.

'Ollie's gone to find her. He knows I'm here.'

The last few words were spoken to the woman's back as she chose to dismiss her, disappearing down the hallway. Anger and humiliation heated Trudy's face. Elise was obviously as self-absorbed as Ollie.

She shuffled from one foot to the other as the seconds ticked by, a bad habit she had when she was anxious, and one her father had tried to force out of her.

Eventually, she heard her named spoken. 'Trudy?'

She glanced up to see Lana making her way down the stairs and could tell from the way she was gingerly walking that she was still in pain. She was wearing a T-shirt and a pair of what looked like pyjama bottoms, her hair scraped back in an untidy knot, and she didn't look ready for visitors.

'I'm so sorry, I'd forgotten you were coming today.'

'My fault. I should have checked it was still okay. Do you want me to come back when you're feeling better?'

'No, please. You're here now, and I don't have any plans, so as long as you don't mind me dressed like this.' Lana pulled at her T-shirt and grimaced.

'Of course not.' Up close, Trudy could see the evidence of bruises. On her forehead, collarbone and arms, and there were no doubt more under her clothes. 'How are you feeling?'

'Like I was hit by a bus,' Lana quipped, the hint of a smile touching her face.

Remembering the flowers and the picture frame, Trudy handed them over. 'I brought these for you, and a replacement frame too.'

'That's kind of you. Thank you. How is your dad?'

'He's okay. I really am sorry about the other day.'

'Honestly, forget about it. Would you like a coffee?'

When Trudy accepted, Lana led her through to the kitchen, the pair of them making small talk while she put the flowers in water and made the drinks.

'So how did you hear about what had happened?' Lana asked as she filled the mugs, passing one to Trudy. She pulled a face. 'I suppose everyone in town knows.'

'Well, it made the local paper.' Trudy followed Lana outside to the patio. Here gave a full view of Kitty's pretty top garden and she could see George hard at work, cutting back shrubs.

When he glanced up in their direction as she took a seat at the table, she offered him a smile. He gave her a hard stare before turning back to his work, and she shifted uncomfortably on her chair.

'Was it really in the paper?' Lana drew her attention back. She looked as if she was cringing.

'Only a brief article. I doubt everyone saw it. But that's not how I found out, anyway. Bree was the one who told me,' she admitted.

'Bree?'

'She's Xav's best friend. The one who sorted your car.'

'She did?'

She hadn't known? Immediately, Trudy regretted telling her.

'It was no big deal. He knew the car needed moving and Bree's a mechanic. It made sense.'

'I'll need to get in touch with this Bree, thank her and settle up.'

No, because then she would know that Xav had covered the cost and she might read too much into it. She needed to understand that it wasn't healthy for Xav to have her in his life.

Not sure how to respond to Lana's comment, Trudy changed the subject. 'Do the police have any leads?'

Lana shrugged unhappily. 'Nothing. It's such a remote area and Xav was the only witness.' She trailed off, looking wistful for a moment. 'I don't know what would have happened if he hadn't been there.' She looked at Trudy now, curious. 'You're friends with him, right?'

More than friends. Where is this going? 'We're close.'

'How is he?'

That was a loaded question. Did she mean how was he following the hit-and-run or how was he in general? Perhaps this was an opportunity. To put Lana straight and make her back off.

'He's struggling, to be honest,' she said, testing the water. 'It's difficult for him having you and your brother back, and it's stirring up a lot of bad memories.'

When Lana's face fell, Trudy rearranged her expression to one she hoped conveyed sympathy. It was time to give Lana a dose of the truth.

'He knows Sebastian did a bad thing and it's a burden he carries, even though it was not his fault. I know there is history between you, but I think the kindest thing you could do for him, Lana, is to leave him alone.'

'But I—'

Trudy raised her hand, quick to cut off Lana's protest. 'If you truly care about him like I do, then you'll listen to what I'm saying. This is taking a toll on his mental health and it's hard for me to watch him suffer.' Was she getting through?

To her relief, Lana nodded. 'Okay. We'll be gone in a few weeks anyway,' she said, looking thoughtful for a moment, before brusquely changing the subject to the paintings.

* * *

Later, as Trudy drove away from Mead House, she mused over their conversation.

Lana had stayed off the topic of Xav after the warning, but she had seemed distracted. Was she thinking about him? Was she annoyed that Trudy had said something?

It was killing her not knowing the full details of what had happened between Xav and Lana the night of the hit-and-run. Had they planned to meet at the beach or had Lana gone there purposely to find him, as Bree suspected?

She doubted Xav would tell her and she had too much pride to ask him. As she indicated, taking the turn off to Salthouse, she wondered how he would react if he knew she had just warned Lana to stay away from him. He valued his privacy and she suspected he might be angry with her for sticking her nose in. Whatever happened, he must not find out.

The most important thing was, Lana had agreed to leave him alone. Hopefully she would stick to her word. The sooner she was gone, though, the better it would be for all of them.

23

'Why didn't you tell me that Xav sorted my car?'

Ollie glanced up from the skirting board he was painting, shoulders sagging slightly when he saw his sister standing in the doorway of his old bedroom, her hands on her hips suggesting she was spoiling for another fight.

Her words the night of the hit-and-run had been a bit of a wake-up call for him, making him realise just how badly he had been behaving.

It was coming back to this house. Deep down, he knew that. Camille's death had affected him more than he liked to let on and he tried to mask it by pretending to the world he was over it. And now he had almost lost Lana.

The thought of her dying too scared the hell out of him. And she was his twin, which somehow made it worse. It didn't matter that they had grown apart. He had always known that she was there and would be, no matter what. Realising he had that wrong had him reassessing everything.

Of course, he hadn't shared those thoughts with her. Was too embarrassed to admit the truth. But he was now trying to make up for the way he had treated her. He had been more considerate and had tried to make Elise do her bit too. He had thought about Lana when ordering food in, as well as on the couple of occasions he had cooked, and he had been helping around the house. He was also doing his best to protect her from Xavier Landry.

Ollie didn't know what had happened that night on the beach between them, or why they had even been together, but he didn't like how Xav had conveniently been there when Lana had nearly lost her life. Something was off about that whole situation and he didn't trust Xav or his intentions one bit. The car thing was a ploy to get closer to her, he understood that, but he wasn't sure what Xav's endgame was. All he knew was he had already lost one sister to a Landry. He wasn't prepared to lose Lana too.

And, of course, she was blinkered where Xav was concerned. Always had been. She wouldn't see that Ollie was just trying to protect her. He could tell that from her hostile stance right now.

'I'm planning on paying him back,' he told her, resting the paintbrush on the side of the tin and getting to his feet. He wouldn't be in Xav's debt. They had once been the best of friends and Ollie had loved him like a brother. How things had changed. Now all he felt was anger and bitterness.

'He paid for it too?'

Okay, so apparently she didn't know that bit. Ollie mentally kicked himself.

When the car had been unexpectedly delivered back to Mead House the day after the hit-and-run, he had pulled out his wallet, expecting to have to settle the bill, surprised when he was told it had already been taken care of. By Xav Landry of all people.

He had recognised Bree McCarthy, recalling she had been a friend of Seb's, and still was, judging by the scowl on her face. She didn't want to be there and it was clear it was under duress. Although she hadn't outright admitted it was Xav who had pressured her into fixing the car, replacing the slashed tyres, Ollie had easily been able to join the dots.

As he had watched Bree climb into the passenger seat of the car that had followed her to the house, Ollie understood that Xav was up to something, and he didn't like it one bit.

There was no way he planned to tell Lana.

Or at least that had been his intention.

Trudy Palmer must have opened her big mouth. It was the only way Lana could have found out.

Ollie cursed the woman, wishing he had sent her away instead of letting her in the house.

Unfortunately, he was now left with no choice but to come clean.

'He's up to something, Lana, and I don't like it.'

'What? Don't be ridiculous.'

'So he just happened to be in the right place at the right time when someone slashed your tyres and he was still in the area when that car hit you? It's all a bit convenient, don't you think?'

'No, it's really not.' Lana's eyes were flashing with temper now, her cheeks flushed. She had been a shadow of herself the past few days. Although her anger was directed at him, Ollie was relieved to see she had her spark back.

'And now he's paying to have your car fixed? Why would he do that?'

'I don't know why, but he was on that beach first. I was the one who bumped into him, not the other way around.'

'Did you know he was going to be there?' Ollie asked, his tone tight. Had she purposely sought Xav out? Why would she do that, knowing the terrible link between their families?

Lana took a little too long for his liking before she answered. 'No, I didn't.'

Was she telling the truth? Once, a long time ago, he would have known. Now he wasn't sure.

'I want you to stay away from him. He's bad news.'

'You want me to or you're ordering me to? You're not my keeper, Ollie. In fact, last time I checked, you weren't really interested in being part of my life.'

Ouch. That stung. 'Is that what you really believe?'

'Well, it's true, isn't it.' Lana looked a little flustered, as though realising maybe she had gone too far, but being as stubborn as Ollie, she pushed on. 'I never hear from you these days unless you want something and you kicked off about coming back here to help me.'

'I still came though! And you're wrong. I care about you. I love you. You're my twin sister.'

She had no idea just how hard it had been for him to come back. That he had vowed to stay away from here forever. Going down to the summer house and finding his sister's body had traumatised him, the scene he had walked in on playing on a constant loop in his head. Lana didn't understand; she had never had to deal with that and didn't have to carry the burden he did.

'You're treating it like a holiday, though. We're here to sort the house!'

'What do you think this is?' He indicated to the paint tin. 'Is this what people do on bloody holiday?'

'Okay, fair enough. You've been helping a bit the last few days,' she conceded. 'It might be nice if your fiancée stopped treating the place like a hotel, though. And would it hurt for her to be a little more civil towards me? She's going to be my sister-in-law. You never even told me you were engaged.'

She had a point there. He should have told her. Truth was, it had been such a whirlwind affair, he had barely had time to adjust to everything himself, let alone spread the word. And if he was entirely honest, he didn't really know a whole lot about Elise Gladstone himself.

They had met on a night out and, refreshingly, she had made the first move. He had shallowly been sucked in by her revealing cleavage and learning that she was a model. After that, it had seemed only a matter of days before she was moving herself into his flat and pressuring him to put a ring on her finger. Ollie had been so smitten with his new hot, sex-mad girlfriend, he hadn't really taken the time to get to know her and he had yet to meet any of her family. And Lana was right. Elise had been off with her, and he had no idea what her problem was.

He had brought it up with her a couple of times, but on both occasions, Elise had turned it into a big fight, and deep down, it had him wondering if he was making a mistake. He always had been a bit impulsive.

In his typical Ollie way, though, he was pushing the problem to the back of his mind. Right now, this was about him and Lana, and whatever the hell was going on with Xav.

'You're deflecting,' he told her, going on the defensive. 'This isn't about Elise. It's about you staying away from Xav Landry. Whatever you think of me is irrelevant. I'm just trying to look out for you. I don't trust him.'

'Because he's a Landry?'

'Because his brother killed our sister.' Ollie's temper was close to snapping. What part of this wasn't she getting?

'What if he didn't?'

Lana's words had him pausing, thinking for a moment he had misheard her.

'Say what?'

This time, she spoke slowly. 'I said, what if he didn't?'

Ollie wasn't quite sure how to respond, so he gave an awkward-sounding laugh. 'Of course he did,' he said eventually. The haunted look on Lana's face was unnerving him.

'I've been reading Camille's journal. The one that was hidden. Did you have any idea that she was seeing someone else behind Seb's back?'

'What? Who?' Ollie's mouth was dry and he was suddenly finding it hard to swallow.

'She only calls him G. She was obsessed with him. I think she had a lot of secrets she kept from us. And from Sebastian.'

Was this true? Camille and Sebastian had always been together.

'So, what are you suggesting? That this G person killed her?'

'I don't know.' Lana shoved a frustrated hand back through her hair. 'Maybe.'

'But how?' Ollie narrowed his eyes. 'You saw Sebastian. He was there.'

Lana didn't answer him immediately and he could see the conflict on her face, that she was struggling with the words. When she spoke, her voice was a whisper.

'What if I was wrong?'

Seriously, was she really now doubting herself?

She had always been so certain it was Sebastian Landry she had seen. And of course Seb denied it, but he was lying. Ollie was sure of it.

It was Xav. He had been putting ideas in Lana's head, manipulating her into believing his brother was innocent. She was getting confused reading the journal.

She had tried to make Ollie look at it, but he couldn't bring himself to read Camille's words, to have the reminder of that last summer. The idea made him feel sick and he refused to talk about it, shutting Lana down whenever she brought it up.

'Sebastian Landry killed Camille. You're doubting yourself over a stupid book and a conversation with your ex-boyfriend. This is why you shouldn't see him. He's trying to twist things in your head.' He raised a warning finger. 'I mean it, Lana. Stay away. I won't lose another sister.'

He didn't give her time to respond, leaving her open-mouthed as he stormed from the room.

The sooner they could put this damn house on the market and get away from here, the better it would be for both of them.

24

The beauty of summertime meant windows were generally open, and people never seemed to realise how far their voices carried when they were raised in anger.

It was George's good fortune that he had been working in the top garden, close to the house, when Lana and Ollie had started fighting. Elise was sunbathing nearby, scowling whenever he threw a smirk in her direction. She looked like she wanted to kill him rather than fuck him. Funny how things had changed.

He focused on pulling weeds as he listened to the pair of them arguing about Xavier Landry, resisting the urge to laugh when the conversation turned to Elise.

It was obvious she had heard too, because she shifted on her sun lounger, a frown on her face as Lana gibed about how she was treating Mead House as a hotel. Elise's gaze slid over to George again, their eyes meeting for a brief moment, and he couldn't resist the tiniest goading smile.

Unimpressed, she sneered her nose at him and flipped onto her belly, burying her face in her arms so she didn't have to look at him.

She could be as testy as she wanted. She only had herself to blame.

What was spoken about next had him stilling.

With Lana in Camille's bedroom, it had been difficult to get to the journal and it seemed she had read enough of it to cast doubt in her mind over what she had seen the night of her sister's murder.

Fuck.

Suddenly, George's T-shirt was too tight, his body heating beneath it, and he was struggling to breathe steadily. If Lana went to the police, if they took her seriously, this had the potential to be very bad indeed.

Even though he now had a fool-proof plan in place, he needed to act quick.

He glanced again at Elise, realised she was still paying attention to the raised voices, her chin now propped up on her folded arms as she listened intently. And she didn't look happy at all.

25

Lana had never been particularly good at taking orders, and when people tried to push her in one direction, she tended to rebel and go the other way.

Trudy Palmer had asked her to stay away from Xav, which to Lana had felt a little bit like a ticking-off and had her itching to do the opposite, but it was Ollie's attempt at laying down the law that had really pissed her off.

Xav had asked her to leave him alone, but that had been prior to the hit-and-run incident, and before he had taken it upon himself to get her car fixed. No one had forced him to do that and it would be rude of her to not say thank you or at least to try to repay him. Besides, she still had the clothes he had lent her. She had to return those.

These were the various excuses she had come up with as she drove out to Salthouse on Wednesday afternoon, the idea of seeing him again heating everything up inside her as she thrummed with both anticipation and nerves, scared to address the real reason why she was going.

What if she had been wrong about Sebastian?

Until the argument with Ollie, she had kept those words to herself, but now she had spoken them aloud, it had given her confidence in them, even if Ollie had tried to shoot her down.

How was Xav going to react, though?

If it turned out she was wrong about Camille's journal and that someone else could have been involved, she was going to have given him false hope, but if there was a chance she could be right, she would have been responsible for sending his brother to prison for all of these years.

The idea that she might have done that to an innocent man made her want to throw up.

After the fight with Ollie, she had finished Camille's journal, the last words taking her up to the day before her sister's murder. And the later entries had made it clear that Camille and G had been meeting in the summer house too.

She had been so certain it had been Sebastian she had seen that night, but had she been mistaken? The voices she had heard had just been whispers and her eyes had been sleep-heavy, the garden lit only by the moon. It had looked like Sebastian from behind, but it had been at a distance and he hadn't turned. She had never seen his face, only the briefest flash of his profile. Had she somehow convinced herself it was him simply because it was who she had expected to see?

Her testimony had been persuasive enough to convince the jury. Sebastian didn't have an alibi for that night and his DNA was all over the summer house. Other witnesses told of his fight with Camille, the day of her death, how they had seen her hurl the necklace at him. Sebastian insisted he had thrown it away, but there was no way of proving if he really did.

When everything was added together, he hadn't stood a chance, but what if he was telling the truth? What if the necklace had somehow fallen into the wrong hands?

Maybe Lana should have taken the journal straight to the police, but if it turned out that she was on to something and she hadn't had the courtesy of telling Xav first...

No, she owed him at least this much.

It was early evening by the time she pulled into his driveway, her gut tightening as she spotted his car. He was definitely home.

She pulled up beside where he was parked, taking a moment to steady herself before grabbing the bag of clothes she had washed and ironed, and getting out of the car.

How was he going to react when he saw her? Would he ask her to leave him alone again or would the door that had been firmly wedged shut before the hit-and-run still be open a crack?

The aches from the accident were exacerbated by the tension that was tightening all of her muscles, and her body was a patchwork of bruises. Hopefully, he would take sympathy on her and let her in. She just needed ten minutes of his time.

She knocked on the door.

Waiting on the porch for him to answer, her stomach somersaulted nervously and she glanced around at her surroundings to try to distract herself. When she had been here before, it had been dark, plus she had been too shocked to take in any scenery, but now she could see that the barn was flanked by trees and open fields that rolled in the direction of the coastline.

He still hadn't come to the door and, wondering if maybe he hadn't heard her, she knocked again.

This time, she heard his voice coming from above her, his tone vaguely annoyed.

'Door's open. Come on in.'

Well, at least he was talking to her.

Pushing open the door, she stepped into the house, glancing at the immaculate kitchen and towards the central staircase.

She had only been on the ground level previously and was a

little surprised Xav was suddenly comfortable enough to invite her upstairs, which was where she guessed his studio was.

The elegant iron banister was cool under her palm as she climbed the steps, finding herself on a landing with a high-beamed ceiling and a feature window that looked out towards the marshes.

'Give me five minutes. I'm just cleaning up.'

Lana had been so distracted by the view, she hadn't taken in the rest of the upstairs. One door she could see led to what she suspected was a bedroom, given the bank of wardrobes on the far wall; in the other she could see Xav, his back to her as he tidied away brushes. An easel stood between them, the canvas on it tilted slightly away so Lana couldn't see what he was working on, and as she stepped further into the room, a pretty tabby cat with wide yellow eyes brushed past her legs, the sound of paws hitting wood as it disappeared downstairs.

'Hi.'

Her voice had Xav dropping the brush he was holding and spinning round to face her, his expression startled and his green eyes wide. 'Lana? What are you doing here?'

'You told me to come in.'

As she said the words, it clicked. He had been expecting someone else.

Okay. This was awkward.

The silence stretched, Xav looking uncharacteristically flustered, while Lana's cheeks flamed.

'I, um, I brought your clothes back.'

She went to take another step into the studio, but he reacted quickly, moving forward to take hold of her elbow and guide her out of the room, pulling the door shut behind them.

Well, that firmly told her that she wasn't welcome up here.

For a moment, she thought he was going to escort her down the stairs and out of the barn, but then he seemed to check himself, letting go of her arm and rubbing a paint-spattered hand over his unshaven jaw.

'How are you feeling?'

'Like I was hit by a car,' she quipped, the corner of her mouth curving as she studied him, looking for a sign, anything to tell her that the old Xav was still in there.

He was frowning so hard, she was beginning to wonder if he had completely lost his sense of humour, but then she saw the quick flash of a grin and a little of the tension ebbed out of her shoulders.

'Here.' She handed him the bag of clothes. 'I washed them. They're clean.'

'Thanks. How did you get here? Did you drive?'

'Yeah.'

'Is that a good idea after what happened?' He was frowning again. Two little lines creasing between the dark slash of his eyebrows.

'I'm fine. Just a bit sore.'

'What about the car that hit you? Do the police have any news?'

Lana shrugged. 'I've spoken to them a couple of times, but I don't think they're going to find the driver.'

'It wasn't an accident.' He sounded annoyed. 'It was deliberate.'

'They know that. But they haven't said I was specifically targeted.'

'Your tyres were slashed. I disagree. Just be careful, Lana.'

The idea it wasn't a random attack sat uncomfortably in the pit of her stomach and she was keen to change the subject. 'Actually, that's another reason I'm here,' she told him, trying to keep her tone breezy. 'My car.'

'What about it?'

'You had it fixed and brought home for me. Thank you. You didn't have to do that.'

Xav shrugged. 'It was no big deal.'

'You paid.'

'Only for materials. A friend did the labour. She owed me a favour.'

'I'd still like to pay you back.'

'I don't need your money, Lana.'

Was it her imagination or was he sounding a little defensive? Her offer must have annoyed him, because he was suddenly guiding her back down the stairs and she suspected towards the front door.

'I was hoping we could talk,' she protested.

'I'm sorry, but I'm expecting company.'

Lana knew it wasn't a lie. After all, he had mistaken her for someone else. If she left now though, she would have no reason to come back.

'I really do need to talk to you, Xav.'

When he seemed to waver, looking as if he was about to remind her they had nothing to discuss, she quickly added, 'It's important.'

'Okay.' He sounded more resigned than intrigued. 'What's up?'

Lana had practised this moment on the drive over, but her rehearsed words had all vanished. 'I found something,' she started, unsure where to go from there.

Xav raised his eyebrows in question, his expression impatient as he waited for her to continue.

'Camille had a journal.'

Now he was looking irritated. 'We know that. It was used during the trial.'

'Not that one. There's a second book.'

'What?' His tone was sharp.

'There's a second journal, Xav. One she had hidden.'

'Why are you telling me this now? She died seventeen years

ago.' He sounded resigned and Lana knew she was losing his attention.

'Because we only found it while we were clearing out her room. It was hidden under a loose panel in the bottom of the wardrobe.'

Xav took a moment to absorb what she was telling him. 'Okay,' he asked slowly, his tone a little wary. 'So what's your point? Seb is in prison.'

'Did he have any idea that she was seeing someone else?'

If she didn't fully have his attention before, she did now.

'Who?'

'I don't know.'

'You don't know?' He sounded sceptical.

'She just refers to him by the letter G.' She let him consider that, before adding, 'They used to meet in the summer house.'

Lana watched the flicker of several emotions pass over his face. 'I still don't understand why you're dragging this up,' he said eventually, his frustration clear. 'It's irrelevant whether she was seeing someone else. You saw Seb that night, remember? That's what you told everyone.'

'I did.' She tried to unstick her tongue from the roof of her mouth, swallowed heavily and forced the words out before she lost her nerve. 'But what if I was wrong?'

Her cheeks heated as Xav stared at her, the silence dragging on as she waited for him to react, broken only by the ticking of the clock.

Say something.

Eventually, he broke eye contact, turning to skulk over to the window, his back to her as he planted his palms on the edge of the worktop, broad shoulders stiff as he stared out at the view.

Lana waited, aware her heart was thumping miserably. She knew her words had upset him but wasn't sure how to make things right. Whether she even could.

'Xav?'

'Just go.'

There was no anger behind his words, just resignation, and somehow that was tougher to deal with.

'Xav, please.'

'Go, Lana. Now.'

Knowing she didn't have a choice, that by staying she would only upset him, she backed towards the door, trying to think of something she could say in parting. Anything that might make this easier. Xav wouldn't even turn to look at her, though. What hope did she have?

Opening the front door, she let herself out, closing it behind her, nausea tightening her throat. She hadn't wanted to hurt him and had simply done what she believed was the right thing.

The sound of an engine drew her attention towards the road and Lana turned to see another car pull onto the driveway, parking behind Xav.

She vaguely recognised the woman who got out, though couldn't quite place her, but she saw the open hostility in her light-brown eyes as she glanced her way.

She knew who Lana was, then.

'Hi.' Lana made an effort to smile at her, determined to be civil, but her greeting was ignored as the woman stepped past her and went straight into Xav's house without knocking.

Was she Xav's girlfriend? Lana tried to ignore the stab of jealousy that was burning in her gut. They were obviously close if she just let herself in. Or was she the best friend Trudy had mentioned – Bree?

Lana preferred that possibility.

Although, whoever she was, it was clear the woman already disliked her and her estimation was going to sink further when Xav told her about Lana's latest revelation.

There was nothing she could do about that, though. She had done what she had come here to do and she had given Xav the heads-up. Why then did her burden feel heavier?

Climbing into her car, she decided it was time to involve the police. She would go back to Mead House and get the journal, then, in the morning, she would drive to the local police station and hand it in.

26

The journal was missing.

Lana opened the top drawer of the bedside table where she knew she had left it, then, seeing it wasn't there, immediately doubted herself, checking both of the lower drawers and under the bed.

She remembered seeing it this morning.

So where was it?

Ollie.

She had spoken to him about it earlier and he had refused to believe it possible that anyone other than Sebastian Landry had killed Camille. He must have taken the journal to look at it.

While it was annoying that he had been going through her things without asking, the weight of worry lifted as she went in search of him, and she was hopeful that if he was reading it, he might now be prepared to listen to her.

She found him in the kitchen, seasoning a simmering pan of ingredients, a sight that still had her double blinking, even though it was the third meal he had made in the last few days. Ollie was the king of ordering in. Since when had he become so domesticated?

'If you wanted to look at Camille's journal, you could have asked first.'

He hadn't heard her approach over the loud music that was playing – some kind of gangsta rap that Lana didn't recognise – and he jumped at her voice, dropping his spatula on the floor.

'Jesus, Lana. Don't do that.'

He barked at Alexa to turn down the volume, scooping up the spatula and going to the sink to rinse it.

'What are you cooking?'

'A jalfrezi. You hungry?' he asked, as he returned to his now sizzling pan. 'This is the Ollie Hamilton signature dish. Made with my own twist.'

She hadn't been, the conversation with Xav having pretty much killed her appetite, but now she was here and she could smell the cooked onions and tomatoes, and whatever spices he had used, her belly was rumbling.

'Yeah, a little. Since when did you get so good in the kitchen?'

'I've always been able to cook.'

'But you order in takeout most of the time.'

Ollie shrugged. 'Sometimes it's easier.' He glanced back at Lana. 'Anyway, what were you saying when you came in?'

'Camille's journal. Where is it?'

He gave her a blank look. 'Why would I know?'

'Because it's not where I left it.'

'Okay. Well, I haven't touched it.'

'You're sure?'

'Of course I'm sure. I think I would remember if I had taken it.'

Was he telling the truth?

She studied his dark eyes, which were a mirror of her own, saw them narrow slightly as he frowned in irritation.

'Lana, stop looking at me like I'm lying. I don't have it. I thought I made it clear earlier; I have no interest in reading it.'

She believed him. But that didn't explain where the journal was.

'I don't understand where it's gone.'

'Maybe you put it somewhere else.'

'I didn't. I remember...' She tailed off, realisation dawning.

Elise.

'Where is she?'

'Where's who?'

'Your fiancée.' She snarled out the word and Ollie's expression went from annoyed to worried. As Lana stormed from the kitchen in search of Elise, she heard the clatter of pans and utensils before her brother's footsteps caught her up.

'Do not go making accusations. You don't know she took it.'

'There are only three of us in this house, Ollie, so who the hell else would it be?'

Elise hadn't been outside and she wasn't in the lounge or the garden room. Remembering that she had heard the sound of a shower running before coming down to the kitchen, Lana headed to the stairs.

'Why would she want Camille's journal?' Ollie tried to reason as he followed her. 'She didn't even bloody know her.'

Lana didn't bother replying. She had tunnel vision, was focused only on finding Elise and getting the journal back. Her old bedroom door was closed and she didn't knock before entering, catching a wide-eyed Elise wearing just a towel wrapped around her head.

'What the fuck? Get out!'

Ignoring her, Lana stormed around the room. 'Where is it?'

'Where's what?' Elise reached for her robe, hastily slipping it on and tying it at the waist. 'Nolly! What the hell is going on?'

Ollie had his hands up, trying his best to play peacemaker as Lana pulled open drawers, pushed piled-up clothes to one side. 'Can you please just stop a minute,' he demanded, his voice raised.

Lana paused her search, locking eyes with Elise. 'You took a journal from my room. I want it back.'

For a moment, Elise looked stunned. 'No I didn't. I haven't been in your room.'

'You're lying. It's gone and you're the only one who could have taken it.'

'I'm not lying.' Elise's tone was cold, her expression hardening. 'And you have no fucking right to burst in here and accuse me like this, you complete psycho.'

'Jesus, that's enough.' Ollie was between them now as Lana clenched her fists. She wasn't a violent person, but Elise was really pushing her buttons. 'Both of you need to back the hell down. Lana, you can't just throw accusations around without any evidence.'

'Yes, you fucking nutjob,' Elise goaded over his shoulder, before his attention snapped to her.

'And you, quit it with the name calling. She's my sister.'

His intervention had Elise pouting, her eyes wide with shock that he hadn't automatically taken her side, while Lana was wondering when her brother had grown a backbone.

He surprised her further by questioning Elise. 'You swear you didn't take the journal?'

'No! Of course I fucking didn't.' Her pretty face was red with rage. 'I already bloody told you that.'

Ollie turned to Lana and shrugged, looking uncomfortable at being caught in the middle. 'She says she didn't take it.'

Lana scowled at Elise, who was still shooting her daggers. Was it possible she was telling the truth?

But if she hadn't taken the journal, where had it disappeared to? Someone had it.

'She does not get to treat me like this, Nolly. I don't care if she's your sister. Either she goes or I do.' Elise's tone was haughty and Lana's blood heated again.

'Oh, go, please do. Last I checked, it isn't your house anyway, and you've done sod all since you've been here.'

'Lana!' Ollie sounded exasperated, taking her arm and pulling her to the door. 'Look,' he pleaded. 'She says she doesn't have the journal and we have no proof that she's lying. Will you please just leave the room so I can try to calm her down?'

He didn't allow her time to respond, giving her a gentle shove out of the door, then quickly shutting it. The turning of the key in the lock told her she wasn't getting back inside, which perhaps was for the best. She needed to shake off this anger. It was unproductive and the tension was only exacerbating her aching bones.

For her own peace of mind, she went back to Camille's bedroom and did another thorough search for the journal.

Was she overreacting? Had she simply misplaced it? Being back here in the house, spending all this time in her dead sister's room, it wasn't easy. There were so many memories, both good and bad. Perhaps she was losing her grip on reality. Questioning what she had seen the night of the murder, making accusations about the journal being stolen. It wasn't healthy.

But, no, the journal wasn't here, she concluded, and she hadn't misplaced it.

As for what she had read and what she had seen, she knew she was right to be questioning everything.

But how was she supposed to go to the police now?

Of course, she could make them aware of the journal's existence. Ollie would back her up on that, and George too, as both of them had seen it. Lana was the only one who had read her sister's words, though. She could tell the police about her sister's mystery lover, referred to only by the initial G, explain the sordid nature of their relationship, and how they used to meet in the summer house late at night, but would they actually believe her or be able to do anything without physical evidence? She had wracked her brains trying to think who G could be, even considering George at one point. It was only remembering what Ollie had said, about how he had been a runt of a kid and badly bullied that made her knock him off the list. Camille had spoken about a commanding and experienced lover. That hadn't been George.

And if she was to tell the police she might be mistaken, that perhaps she hadn't seen Sebastian Landry that night after all, how were they going to react? Would she be in trouble?

The journal was key. Without it, she had nothing.

She stewed over it for the rest of the evening and later that night as she settled into bed, the window open and a light breeze swaying the curtains; she thought back over the day and how she had managed to completely mess everything up. If she had the chance to do everything again, the journal would have stayed with her at all times. As for Xav, she still wasn't sure if she had done the right thing telling him about G or not. He deserved to know, but at what cost? All Lana had done was open old wounds. And now he wasn't speaking to her again. She had badly misjudged that one.

As her eyes drifted shut, her memories pulled her back to that summer seventeen years ago and the voices she had heard outside the window. Just who had Camille been with the night of her murder?

* * *

The beeping from her phone woke her a short while later and frowning, she reached for it, seeing that she had a text from an unknown number.

It was gone eleven-thirty. Who the hell was messaging her this late at night?

She opened the text.

Lana. It's Xav.

How had he got hold of her number? Curious, she read on.

Can we meet? Tomorrow if you're free. I want to see the journal.

She reread the message, debated whether to reply, but decided
it was best to wait until the morning. At least that would give her
time to figure out what the hell to say to him.

How was he going to react when he realised she no longer
had it?

Putting her phone down again, she closed her eyes and tried to
drift back into sleep.

Instead, she was restless, tossing and turning, damning Xav for
messaging her so late. It was going to be a long night.

27

It had been Bree who persuaded Xav to get in touch with Lana.

She had shown up just after Lana had left, getting the brunt of Xav's temper. He wasn't sure what kind of game Lana was trying to play or exactly what it was she was trying to achieve, but he wanted no part of it.

Going through the trial, listening to the awful things that were said about Sebastian and having to come to terms with the fact they were true had been hard enough. Having her now show up and say that maybe she had made a mistake had been like a red rag to a bull.

Of course, with hindsight, he realised he should have asked questions, but his initial reaction had been anger, simply wanting her out of his house. He didn't question whether there was any truth in what she was saying, immediately assuming that it was some kind of misguided olive branch.

Because surely she had to understand it was a terrible idea to give him false hope.

Xav hadn't planned to tell Bree what had happened, but he was snappy and irritable, and completely distracted, and it was obvious that Lana was responsible, so he had vented.

Given that she hated the Hamiltons, her suggestion, that he should talk to Lana, had come as a shock. But she'd reminded him that this wasn't about Lana. It was Sebastian's life they were talking about and, if he was innocent, they owed it to him to clear his name. They needed to get their hands on that journal.

One problem. Xav didn't have Lana's number and, after his encounter with Ollie the other night, going to Mead House would be a really bad idea.

Determined not to let him off the hook, Bree had made a call to Trudy, reasoning that she probably had Lana's number.

She was right and although Trudy had been more wary about whether it was a good idea, worried in case it was some fanciful notion on Lana's part, and scared Xav might get hurt, she did agree Xav needed to see the journal.

He had messaged Lana late last night, deciding to get it over with. Figuring that once the text was sent, he couldn't change his mind.

It was now 9 a.m. and she hadn't responded.

Probably because you kicked her out of the house.

Well, technically there had been no kicking and he hadn't shouted at her or been heavy-handed. He had simply told her to leave.

But then she had to appreciate that she had just given him the mother of all shocks.

Surely, she would understand that he needed a little time to process everything.

Her call came almost an hour later.

Xav was in the studio when his phone started ringing. Setting his paintbrush down, he took a moment to wipe his hands clean on an old rag before answering, putting the phone on loudspeaker.

'Xav?' Her voice echoed around the large room, sounding a little unsure, as if this might be some kind of trick.

'You got my message?' he said, dispensing with any greetings.

'Yes. Late last night.'

'So is today okay?'

'Yes, but—'

'Can you come here? Say in an hour?'

'Okay, but, Xav, there's something you need—'

'We can talk when you get here.'

'Xavier!'

He didn't let her finish whatever it was she was going to say, unwilling to prolong the conversation. This was already hard enough.

* * *

He was in the kitchen feeding Hector when he heard the sound of her engine and he had the front door open waiting for her as she stepped out of the car.

Her movements were a little slow and jerky, reminding him that she would still be hurting from the hit-and-run, and he winced at the stab of guilt telling him to lighten up and stop being such an arsehole.

Not an arsehole, he rationalised. He was just keen to know if this really was something or if he was wasting his time. He refused to get his hopes up.

Not yet.

'Did you bring the journal?' he asked, eyes narrowing as she straightened up, clicking her fob at the car. Her hands were otherwise empty and she had only the tiniest shoulder bag with her. As for what she was wearing – a pretty little sage-green dress dotted with tiny white flowers, the hem skimming an inch above her knees, the wound from the hit and run still visible, and the cleavage subtle, but revealing just enough to intrigue – there were no pockets he could see that would hold any kind of book. If she was trying to remind him of what he could no longer have, it was working, but annoyance pushed his frustration to one side when she shook her head.

'Lana! I asked you to bring it.'

'I tried to tell you on the phone, but you hung up on me. I can't find it.'

'You can't find it?'

Was she actually being serious? This was a joke, right? Xav studied her for a moment, waiting for her to say that it was, that, yes, she had left it in the car. Even though it would be a stupid and insensitive joke, he really didn't care. But he could tell from her expression that she was being deadly serious.

'I'm really sorry.'

'Damn it, Lana. I don't have time for these games.'

He shook his head as he turned and stormed back into the house, not bothering to shut the door because he knew she would follow.

'This isn't a game. Xav! Don't walk away from me.'

The sound of her footsteps had him rolling his eyes, but when she caught hold of his arm to try to stop him, his temper snapped and he turned on her.

'Then what is it? Last night you had found this magic book that you were convinced was going to clear Seb's name, and now you want me to believe that you can't find it. I would have thought that given how important it was, you might have taken better care of it.' He paused to catch a breath and she went to speak, but he held his hand up. He wasn't done yet. So many years of frustration and anger had built up at this shitty situation. He needed to vent.

'Actions have consequences. My mother lost her son, I lost my brother. People treated us like we were lepers, as if what Seb had done was some family trait, that we were all murderers. All of these years, I have struggled to comprehend what he did. He's my brother and I love him, but I have hated him too. And now you just casually show up and tell me you might have made a *mistake*? A mistake is forgetting to pay a bill or putting petrol in your car instead of diesel. For fuck's sake, Lana. This is a man's life.'

The outburst shocked Xav as much as it appeared to shock Lana. He hadn't realised how much pent-up rage he had been holding on to.

All worded out, he huffed out a breath, readying himself for her reaction.

He was expecting temper, just wasn't sure on what scale, so she caught him completely off guard when she burst into tears.

Fuck!

Lana wasn't much of a crier. At least, she never had been. He could only recall two times he had reduced her to tears. The first when he and Ollie had ganged up on her when they were kids, the second time was following a stupid fight that last summer when she had thought he was going to break up with her.

Then, of course, there were the tears for Camille. But he hadn't caused those ones. His brother had.

The fight went out of him. He had never been able to deal with Lana's tears.

'I didn't mislay the journal. I think someone's taken it,' she managed between sobs. 'And I know how shit it's been for you. It's been shitty for me too. You lost your brother. I lost my sister. And she's never coming back.'

'Lana—' He tried to intervene, but she was on a roll.

'It's been hard coming back here, remembering what happened, and even though I had to tell the police what I saw that night, I didn't want to. I desperately didn't want it to be Seb, because I knew it meant I didn't just lose Camille, I was going to lose you too. I never wanted to hurt you, Xav. Not then, not now. And finding that journal, realising I could have been wrong, that I might have played a part in an innocent man going to prison, that Camille's killer could still be out there...'

The tears were falling harder now and she was struggling to get her words out.

Xav cursed himself for being such a self-absorbed, insensitive bastard and making it all about himself. Of course she had suffered too. He had been so caught up in his own pity, how had he failed to see that?

He wasn't sure he had any words left, so he acted instead, closing the gap between them and folding her in his arms.

She didn't resist, sinking into him, her sobs muffled against his shoulder and his heart hitched as he breathed her in. He had forgotten how it was to hold her, how perfectly she fitted against him. All these years had passed and in a way he guessed he had grieved for his brother, but he hadn't realised he had mourned losing Lana too.

They stood that way for a few minutes. Lana eventually breaking the silence long after her tears had stopped.

'I'm sorry I don't have the journal.'

She had turned her head slightly, her breath warm against Xav's neck as she spoke, her arms still tight around him, as though she was reluctant to let go.

'It's not your fault. I'm sorry I got mad at you.'

'I've looked for it everywhere. Someone has to have taken it.' There was a hint of panic in her voice and he gave in to the urge to stroke his hand over her hair, telling himself he was simply doing it to offer comfort as he let his fingers comb through the silky strands.

'We'll figure it out.'

We? Not *I* or *you.* He had just made them into a team. Was that a good idea?

He decided not to question it too much for now. If Lana was right and someone had taken the journal, it suggested they didn't want Camille's words being made public, and that added weight to the theory that Sebastian hadn't killed her.

Xav hadn't allowed himself to even believe it was a possibility, unwilling to be disappointed, but now he had a tiny sliver of hope.

They would need to tread carefully, though. If Seb was innocent, then Camille's killer was still out there.

He thought back to the hit and run. Was it connected?

Either way, if whoever had killed Camille knew that Lana had read the journal, that she was questioning what she had seen that night, there was a very good chance she could now be in danger too.

28

'So, apart from me, who else knows about the journal?' Xav asked, bringing two cups of coffee over to where Lana was sitting on the sofa. He placed them on the coffee table, then took a seat beside her, pulling one leg up under him as he turned to face her, seeming relaxed around her for the first time since she had been back.

Lana had barely slept, dreading telling him the journal was gone and blaming herself for not taking more care with it. She had known he would be angry with her, but she hadn't expected it would present the opportunity to clear the air.

She wasn't stupid and didn't expect things to go back to how they had once been, but at least Xav was no longer looking at her like it physically pained him to be in her presence.

'Ollie was the one who found it, when he was taking the wardrobe apart in Camille's room,' she told him. 'George and I were with him.'

'George?'

'George Maddox. The gardener.'

Xav nodded. 'I know him. His wife cleans for Mum.'

Lana wanted to ask how Joanna was. Xav's mum had always

been so kind to her and had been thrilled when she realised the pair of them had started dating. Opinions changed, though, and no doubt Joanna would be of a different view now. It didn't feel appropriate to ask after her and Lana told herself to stay on topic.

'He's been helping us with the house.'

'And his name begins with G.'

'He wasn't having an affair with Camille. I've already considered him. The man my sister wrote about sounded experienced and dominant in their relationship. George was younger than Camille and Ollie says he was a bit of a nerd.'

'True,' Xav agreed. 'But he knows about the journal and he has the correct initial, so we keep him on the list.'

'The list?' Lana asked, faintly amused. 'We have a list?'

'Yeah,' Xav decided. 'We should.'

His mouth curved into a grin, his cheeks dimpling and creases fanning from the corners of his eyes. It was beautiful and achingly familiar, and Lana realised it was the first time she had seen him properly smile since she had been back.

'Okay,' she nodded, her voice a little thick. 'Do you have a pen and paper?'

While he went to get them, she swallowed and took a steadying deep breath. She needed to pull herself together. This was about Camille and Sebastian, not about her and Xav. There was no point yearning for what she could no longer have.

'So, you, Ollie, George,' Xav said, returning to the sofa and writing the three names down on the jotter pad he had fetched. 'Who else?'

'Ollie's fiancée, Elise, is staying in the house.'

'Ollie's getting married?' He sounded surprised.

'Apparently so.'

'What's she like?'

Entitled, rude, lazy. Lana didn't say any of those things, but she took her time thinking how to answer, which provoked a laugh from Xav.

'You don't like her, do you?'

'I never said that.'

'You don't have to. I can see it written all over your face.'

Really? Was she that transparent?

'I guess we haven't got off to the best start,' she admitted.

'But Ollie loves her?'

'Apparently so. It's been a bit of a whirlwind thing. She's quite high maintenance.'

'And she knows about the journal?'

'Yeah,' Lana said, hesitating before adding, 'Well, she does after I accused her of stealing it.'

'Lana!' Xav was laughing again.

'It's just the three of us living there and Ollie swears he didn't take it. I was working on process of elimination.'

'Okay. Adding high-maintenance fiancée to the list,' Xav said, still sounding amused as he wrote down Elise's name. 'Anyone else?'

'Not that I can think of.'

Xav was silent for a moment. 'So you found the journal before that night on the beach? Before the car hit you?'

'Yeah, why?'

Even as she asked the question, Lana understood where his train of thought was going. 'You think it's connected?'

'It's a bit of a coincidence, don't you think?'

Was it? She had only just started reading the journal the day before the hit-and-run, and although she had learnt about G, she hadn't truly believed that he could have been her sister's killer, not until later. Was Xav right? Had the driver of the car been the person involved with Camille?

She had fallen silent and must have looked worried because

Xav caught hold of her hand, his thumb tracing a pattern over her palm, the action both comforting and intimate, stirring a thousand butterflies in her belly.

'I think it's maybe best not to let anyone else know about any of this. Just to be on the safe side, okay?'

Lana nodded. He was right. She really hadn't thought any of this through.

'So you're absolutely sure no one else knew about the journal the day you found it?'

She had already gone over the day in her head. 'No one. It was just the four of us in the house at the time.'

Xav tapped at the notepad with his pen. 'This is a pretty short list, Lana.'

It was, and she understood the implications of that.

'Ollie wouldn't hurt me.'

Xav agreed. He and Ollie may no longer be on speaking terms, but they had once been the best of friends. Ollie would never hurt his own sister.

'Okay, so that leaves two. George and Elise.'

'You think one of them took the journal?'

Xav nodded. 'Logically, yes.'

'And they might have been driving the car.'

It wasn't a question, but he answered anyway. 'Possibly. If it's connected.' He gave her hand a squeeze. 'When do you know for definite that you last saw the journal?'

'Yesterday, just before I came to see you. It was gone when I got home.'

'So Elise was in the house. Where was George?'

'He would have finished work for the day. It was just Elise and Ollie in the house.'

'What about the night on the beach? Do you know where George and Elise were then?'

Lana thought back, remembering. 'Ollie had invited George to a poker night. He was at the house, though he did arrive late.'

'What about Elise?'

'She was in Norwich, staying with a friend.'

'She's from Norfolk?'

'Apparently so.'

'So they both possibly have alibis.' Xav was thoughtful for a moment. 'George drives a van. Does Elise have a car?'

'Not at the house. She caught a cab.'

'But she can drive, right?'

Lana shrugged. 'I have no idea. I don't know a huge amount about her.'

Which was a worry. Ollie had gone rushing in head-first and brought Elise into their lives. She was living in Kitty's house, had access to all of their things. Lana already didn't trust her, but was it possible she was dangerous too? And if the answer was yes, if Elise had taken the journal and had driven the car into Lana, then what was her motive?'

She voiced that question aloud now, understood from Xav's pause that he was already wondering the same.

'We need to find out more about her and whether there is any possible link between her and Camille in the past,' he said eventually.

Lana nodded. 'She's out in the garden a lot. If Ollie's not about, I'll see if I can sneak into their room and go through her stuff.'

A hint of a smile touched Xav's lips. 'I was thinking more along the lines of trying to talk to her, see if you can ask some leading questions and find out anything that way.'

'She's not exactly approachable, and I made things a whole lot worse when I accused her of stealing the journal.'

'Well, start with an apology and see where it leads.'

'An apology?'

Lana must have looked aghast, because Xav's smile was widening.

'Smile sweetly and tell her you're sorry for jumping to conclusions.'

'But I'm not sorry.'

'I know that and you know that, but if it helps to get her talking, it will be worth it, right?'

'I guess.'

'Just be careful, Lana, okay? If she was driving that car...' Xav trailed off. They both knew what he had been about to say. He didn't need to voice the words aloud.

'I'll stay safe,' she promised.

Xav didn't seem convinced, and she wasn't sure if she found his concern flattering or unnerving.

Her stomach churned uncomfortably. Until this moment, it hadn't really sunk in. She could be sharing a house with someone who wanted her dead.

'The bedroom doors still lock, right?'

Lana looked at Xav, frowning. 'Yes. Why?'

'Okay, until we know the deal with Elise, I want you to promise me that when you go to bed at night, you'll keep your door locked.'

'You're actually scaring me a little now.' She laughed nervously, but the smile had dropped from Xav's face and he was looking deadly serious.

'Promise me, Lana.'

'Okay, I promise.'

29

George generally called in on his mother at least once a week and he always tried to time it when he knew she would be home alone.

It wasn't that he had anything against his stepfather. The old man was okay, but when it was just his mum, there was less chance Derek would be there. Therefore he had been dismayed to find his stepbrother sitting in the kitchen when he stopped by on his way home from work.

'Do you want a cup of tea, love? I was just making Derek another one.'

The idea of even sitting down at the same table didn't exactly fill George with joy, but what choice did he have? He had only just arrived, so he could hardly walk back out.

'Thanks, Mum.'

He pulled up a chair, gave an unsmiling nod to Derek. 'All right?'

'Can't complain,' Derek told him with the same level of enthusiasm.

This forced pleasantry, it was all a charade for their parents. George had hated his older stepbrother from the moment fourteen-year-old Derek Golden had entered his life. Derek was six years older and he had made George's life a living hell until George had eventually found a way to stop him.

These days, they barely spoke, and their dislike for each other was mutual. But Derek knew better than to even look at George the wrong way, aware of what the repercussions could be and how George held all of the power.

Their relationship was civil for their parents' sake, but coolly so, and that suited George fine.

Derek was a pathetic mess. He drank too much, struggled to hold down a job, and his marriage had crumbled. If George liked him, he might have pitied him, living in his shitty little flat, with few friends and no life to speak of. He wasn't even a hard man any more, his muscles having turned to flab.

George didn't need to resort to blackmail. He was now bigger and stronger. He could easily kick Derek's arse if they ever came to blows. Having a lingering threat though, one which would result in a prison sentence if he ever revealed the truth, was better. It ensured his stepbrother never stepped out of line. They both knew that if Derek's dark secret ever got out, his life would be over.

30

Lana waited for the right moment to approach Elise.

The idea of apologising to the woman made her bristle, but Xav was right. They needed to know more about her and the easiest way to do that was to try to befriend her.

Despite Elise's ultimatum that one of them had to leave, the three of them were still co-habiting, so it was likely Ollie had managed to smooth things over. The atmosphere in the house remained frosty, though, with Elise deciding to pretend Lana didn't exist. She hadn't spoken a word to her since being accused of taking the journal.

The apology, when it came, was going to be difficult.

Lana and Xav had already found out what they could online before Lana returned home, which was very little. Elise Gladstone was thirty-three and, according to her photos on social media, she liked shoes – a lot. Her Instagram feed was filled with pictures of her feet in jewelled sandals, sky-scraper heels and leather boots. She also preferred pouting to smiling, judging by how her mouth was scrunched up on every picture. It looked like a cat bum, Lana had observed, perhaps a little unkindly, but earning a snort of laughter from Xav.

Google didn't tell them much more. Ollie had told Lana that Elise was a model and there were a few shots online, though the pictures looked dated, suggesting she had been young at the time.

Lana ignored Xav's idea to friend request her on Facebook. She would stoop to the apology, but no way was she going that far.

She had been messaging with him a lot since she had returned home, and although it had mostly been about Elise, the odd personal comment or question had crept in, making it almost feel like old times. Of course it wasn't, and when she found herself smiling hearing the ping of her phone receiving another text message, Lana had to remind herself they were allies for now, but that this situation was only temporary.

Have you spoken to her yet?

It was the third time he had asked and her answer was the same.

Not yet. I'm waiting for the right moment.

Xav's reply, when it came, was a little more impatient.

It's been twenty-four hours, Lana. I know it means swallowing your pride, but you just need to get on with it.

He was right, she knew that. But it didn't make it any easier. Leaving her phone on the bedside table, she went in search of Elise.

She found her in the kitchen, a cocktail shaker in her hand and the various open bottles on the counter suggesting she was making margaritas. It was barely lunchtime, but that didn't seem to bother Elise.

She played for time, going to the fridge for a bottle of water, then glancing in Elise's direction, willing her to turn round. The woman knew she was in the room. She was just choosing to ignore her.

Lana cleared her throat, swallowing down her irritation. She hoped Xav understood how difficult this was for her.

'Elise?'

When she got no reaction, she tried again.

'Elise? I was hoping we could talk for a minute.'

Again, she thought she was going to be ignored, but then Elise turned to give her a look that managed to fall somewhere between sullen, wary and bored. When she didn't say anything, only huffing out a little sigh, Lana pressed on.

'I want to talk about the other night when I came into your room... uninvited.' The last word grated, because technically it was her room, not Elise's. She managed a smile, hoped it didn't look as forced as it felt.

'What about it?'

'I was wrong. I shouldn't have accused you of taking the journal and I shouldn't have come in without asking.' Lana's face was heating. The mortification of this moment making this harder than she had imagined it would be. 'I'm sorry.'

There it was. The apology was out. She waited for Elise's reaction, hoping her expression was contrite, or at least neutral. If Elise realised she didn't mean any of the words, then all of this would be a waste of time.

She studied Lana and sniffed disdainfully. 'No, you shouldn't have come in and you had no right to accuse me. It was very upsetting.'

'I'm sorry,' Lana repeated, unsure what else the woman wanted to hear.

'Okay, well, as long as you realise you overstepped a line, I suppose I will forgive you this time.'

Seriously, where did this bitch get off?

Deep breaths, Lana.

She watched as Elise filled her glass. As she picked it up, she gave Lana a dismissive look. 'Was there anything else?'

Anyone overhearing the conversation would think Lana was the hired help.

She thought of Xav, of Sebastian in prison, and of her sister, whose killer may very still be at large, and reminded herself that she was doing this for them.

'Actually, I was hoping we could start over. We haven't got off to the best start and you're going to be my sister-in-law. Can we please try again? I'd like us to be friends.'

The withering look Elise gave her had Lana's hackles going up and she clenched her fists by her side in annoyance.

'Look, no offence, Lana, but I'm marrying your brother, not his family. I'm not really interested in having any kind of relationship with you. We'll be gone when you've finished packing up the house. So let's just make the best of a bad situation and tolerate each other, okay?'

When Lana didn't respond, because, quite simply, how was she supposed to, Elise added patronisingly, 'It's good that you acknowledged you were in the wrong. I'm glad you realise that. Perhaps you can learn from your mistake.'

Lana watched her go outside, the rage building.

Who the fuck did Elise think she was?

Part of her was tempted to follow after her and push her in the pool, but she reined herself in. While it would be momentarily satisfying, she knew it would achieve nothing.

Instead, she skulked off towards the stairs, planning to go and text Xav, tell him how his bright idea had worked out. She had grovelled for no reason and now she had to spend the rest of her time in this house with the vile woman, who would no doubt be lauding it over her. They should have just gone with her original idea of snooping through Elise's things.

As she reached the landing, Lana glanced towards her old bedroom. The door was closed, but she knew neither Ollie nor Elise were in the room. Her brother had gone food shopping and Elise had only just gone outside.

Before she could change her mind, Lana crossed the landing, knowing Xav would disapprove, but also that they were left with little choice. She had tried the civil approach and had it thrown back in her face. Now it was time to do things her way. Of course, if Elise caught her snooping, it would completely undo the apology she had just forced herself to give, but given that the woman wasn't interested in having any kind of relationship with her anyway, did that really matter?

Once inside her old room, she closed the door, crossing to the window. She tried to keep to the shadows as she peered out, spotting that Elise was in the pool.

Knowing that she was safe for the moment, but not wanting to waste any time, Lana went straight for the woman's handbag, which was hanging on a hook on the back of the door. She emptied the contents onto the bed. It was mostly items of make-up and the only thing of interest was the purse. Lana went through it, saw credit cards that confirmed the woman's identity and a licence that told her Elise could drive. It was registered to Ollie's address. That was quick work. There were a couple of appointment cards – one for a hair salon, another for the dentist. Both local to where she lived. And the cash compartments were empty, albeit for a couple of receipts. One was for groceries, the other for a cafe breakfast. Lana glanced at the details, tensing when she realised it was dated for the morning after the hit-and-run for a place in Sheringham.

Just along the coast from Salthouse.

Elise had allegedly been in Norwich then and staying overnight with a friend. So why was she eating breakfast in Sheringham?

Lana needed to get a photo of the receipt.

Replacing all of the items as she had found them, except the receipt, she hung the bag back on the door, then left the bedroom, going to Camille's room to fetch her phone.

She glanced out of the window, saw Elise was now on her sun lounger, drink in hand.

Back in her old room, Lana took a photo of the receipt, before returning it to the purse. She sent it to Xav with a shocked face emoji, then went through the bedside drawers.

There was nothing else of interest that she could see, but she checked everything anyway, just to be certain.

She had just opened her old wardrobe when her phone pinged with Xav's reply.

Are you snooping?

Quickly she typed a response.

Your idea was shit, so I've gone for plan B. I apologised and suggested being friends, and she shot me down. Apparently she is marrying my brother, not his family. I just found this receipt in her purse. She was supposed to be staying with a friend in Norwich, so why was she in Sheringham?

Other than clothes and lots of unsuitable shoes, there wasn't anything much to see. Lana checked the pockets of a jacket but found them empty.

She was about to slide the door shut when she heard a voice outside the door.

Shit!

It was Elise talking, but Ollie was still out, wasn't he?

Panicking, Lana glanced around for a place to hide. There was the en suite, but was there no time to cross the room? It had to be the wardrobe.

Lana quickly stepped inside, trying to make space between the clothes. She was sliding the door shut when Elise came into the room.

'I don't care. You promised you would delete it.'

There was no response. Who was she talking to?

There was the narrowest of gaps where the door met the wall and Lana kept her eyes trained on it. She caught a brief glimpse of Elise as she paced the bedroom, seeming agitated. Her phone was pressed to her ear.

'That's not fair. I did exactly as you asked.'

What was she talking about?

She held her breath as Elise's voice came closer.

'I want it deleted and I want you to do it now!'

Shit. Was she about to open the wardrobe door?

But then she was turning on her heel, swearing insults at whoever was on the other end of the call. Lana saw her fling her phone at the bed, then, moments later, she disappeared from view and there was only silence.

Lana waited a couple of seconds, then eased the door open an inch, relaxing a little when she realised Elise had left the room. The bedroom door was open. Lana decided she would leave it another minute before making her escape.

The sight of the phone on the bed was sorely tempting. Elise generally had it with her at all times and if anything was to reveal her secrets, the phone would. Including the number of who she had been talking too. It was too great a risk, though, and Lana couldn't risk Elise coming back. Not now she knew she was in the house. Besides, her phone would likely be locked anyway.

The sound of running water had her tensing again and she realised it was coming from the bathroom.

She had been wrong. Elise hadn't left.

Fuck.

Lana glanced at the bedroom door. If she was quick, she could make it.

She opened the wardrobe further, peering out. She could hear it was the shower that was running. Was Elise already in it?

Tentatively, she left her hiding place, carefully sliding the door shut behind her.

It was about ten steps to cross the room. She just needed to move quickly.

As she glanced one more time at the bathroom, her phone pinged with another text. The noise was too loud.

Lana froze. Elise would have heard it over the water, she was sure.

Move, dammit.

'Nolly?'

Lana fled for the bedroom door, not looking back to see if Elise had stepped out of the bathroom. She limped across the landing to Camille's room, quickly locking herself inside. Her heart thumping as she waited.

Had she been seen?

It took a few moments for her breathing to return to normal. If Elise realised she had been in the room, she wasn't reacting. Still, Lana's fingers trembled as she pulled her phone out of her pocket and opened Xav's most recent text message.

Just be careful, okay?

She managed a smile at the irony. He had no idea that his message had almost just got her caught.

31

Lana was taking risks and it was scaring Xav more than he cared to admit.

He had told her not to go snooping, but she hadn't listened, and okay, what she had found threw up plenty of questions, ones that suggested Elise might have been the one driving the car. But that also made her dangerous. If she had already tried to kill Lana once, chances were she would attempt to do it again.

He didn't like that one bit and wanted Lana to keep her distance from the woman, at least until they figured out what she was up to.

The receipt was worrying, as it proved Elise had been in the area at the time of the hit-and-run, and not in Norwich as she had claimed, and the conversation Lana had overheard definitely sounded fishy.

He started to message her, intending to suggest she come over, but before he could send the message, another one pinged through. Bree reminding him they had scheduled drinks and checking on the time they were meeting.

Crap. It was Friday. Her birthday.

He couldn't cancel and leave her sitting home alone. He was

also a shitty friend, because he had been so wrapped up with Lana, he had forgotten to wish her a happy birthday.

He did so now and told her he would drive and pick her up at 5 p.m., then quickly got himself in the shower. He would send Lana a message when he got to the pub.

After stopping en route to buy a birthday bottle of Scotch, he collected Bree, taking her to her choice of venue, the Ship Inn at Weybourne. It was only three miles from Xav's house, but he hadn't yet decided if he would drive home or leave his car at the pub. He figured he would see how the evening panned out.

He realised as they walked into the pub that it wasn't just the two of them. Trudy stood up to greet them with a beaming smile on her face, and his heart sank.

Bree hadn't warned him she was coming.

She gave each of them a hug, wishing Bree a happy birthday, then lingering for a moment longer than was comfortable with Xav. Her overpowering perfume filled his senses and he had to ease himself out of her embrace.

'I'll get drinks,' he told them both, going to the bar while Bree and Trudy went outside to find a table. While he waited for the order, he sent a quick message to Lana, checking she was okay.

Her reply pinged back as he was carrying the tray of drinks out into the beer garden.

'Coke?' Bree questioned, raising her eyebrows.

Xav shrugged. 'I'll probably drive home.'

Bree didn't seem too impressed with this idea, muttering something about Xav not being much fun to Trudy. 'And now he's on his phone,' she complained.

'Two seconds and it's going away, I promise. I'm just checking in with Lana.'

He read her message, telling him she was fine, then reminded her to keep her bedroom door locked, just as a precaution, before slipping his phone back in his pocket.

'Has she given you the journal?' Trudy immediately asked.

Xav hesitated, unsure how much of it he was willing to share. Both pairs of eyes were on him though, and he guessed he did have them to thank for encouraging him to talk to Lana.

'No. It's gone missing.'

'Missing?' Bree repeated.

'Lana thinks someone has taken it and, after talking to her, I'm inclined to agree.'

Irritation niggled him as he saw Bree and Trudy exchange a look, one he recognised as scepticism.

'Are you sure it ever really existed?' Trudy asked, eventually. The gentleness of her tone was well meaning, he was sure, but it only served to annoy him further.

'Are you suggesting she made it up?'

'I'm just saying that Lana has been desperate to talk to you since she returned to town. Maybe this was her way of trying to get your attention.'

'Bloody cruel, though,' Bree muttered, looking unhappy. 'She's playing with people's lives here and giving false hope.'

'No, she's not. The journal exists. I know Lana. She's not lying about it.'

'Okay, so where is it? Who would take it and why?'

This was where Xav was reluctant to say too much. At least without concrete evidence. 'Someone who doesn't want my brother's name cleared.'

'And do you have any idea who that person could be?' Trudy asked.

'No.' He had left it a moment too long before answering and although he kept eye contact with Trudy, he suspected that she knew he was lying.

'Well, I can see she has you convinced.' Bree sounded resigned as she sipped at her drink. 'Just do us all a favour, mate. Think with your head where Lana Hamilton's concerned. I don't trust her one bit.'

'You were the one who suggested I contact her,' Xav pointed out.

'Because of the journal. She led you to believe she had proof. Something that could help clear Seb's name.'

'She never said she had proof.'

'Okay, but she gave you hope, let you believe this journal was important.'

'And it still is.'

Bree sighed. 'Look, I know you still have feelings for her. Just don't let them cloud your judgement. Personally, I am reserving mine.'

'Do you have feelings for her?'

Xav glanced at Trudy. Her question had been casual, as if she was just mildly curious, but he understood why she was asking and realised it presented him with the perfect opportunity to get their relationship back to being purely platonic.

'Things with Lana are complicated. But, yes, I care about her and I still have feelings for her.'

It wasn't a lie as such. Just something he hadn't quite accepted yet.

Trudy held his gaze, her expression void of emotion. 'I see.'

For a moment, the three of them fell into an uncomfortable silence and Xav was wondering if maybe he shouldn't have used Lana to get Trudy off his case. Perhaps it would have been kinder to be honest and tell her their long-ago one-night stand had been a mistake, certainly as far as he was concerned.

Luckily, Bree came to the rescue with a subject change and the topic of Lana and the journal were dropped.

Xav was still a little annoyed they were doubting him, but he tried to shake off his irritation and make an effort, for Bree's sake, and he was relieved when Trudy did the same. After a few minutes of awkwardness between them, she seemed to put it behind her, and for that he was grateful. He may not be attracted to her, but she was a good person, and he was happy to be her friend as long as she understood nothing else was on offer.

They were on their third round, Xav having just returned from the bar with another tray of drinks, when things went downhill.

Bree was the first to react to the newcomers in the beer garden, pausing mid-sentence, a scowl on her pretty face. 'You've got to be fucking kidding me.'

Not sure what she was referring to, Xav turned in his seat, locking eyes with Ollie Hamilton.

Tension crept up his spine as the smile slipped off Ollie's face and was quickly replaced with a scowl. He was with Ryan Hayes and Greg Corbett. The pair had gone to school with Xav, but had severed ties with him long ago, making their allegiance to Ollie clear.

Ollie had never been as forgiving as Lana, and it pained Xav that the boy he had been so close to growing up, who had been his best friend, now viewed him with such disgust.

Xav was the first one to break eye contact and to turn away. It wasn't that he was scared of Ollie or afraid to get into a fight. He was perfectly capable of using his fists if he had to and had been involved in plenty of brawls when he was younger, trying to defend his brother's name, but he didn't have the heart for this one.

Unfortunately, Bree did, and she was eyeballing Ollie, taunting him into making a move. 'I would love to flatten that little worm,' she hissed.

Bree might be several pounds lighter than Ollie, but Xav had no doubt she could kick his arse.

'Just leave it, okay. He's not worth it.'

'Look at him, though, so fucking superior. He really thinks he's something special. The great Ollie Hamilton. That family are a curse.'

'Xav's right, Bree,' Trudy urged. 'Look, we're having a nice evening. Please don't let him spoil it.'

She seemed to be the voice of reason, as Bree turned back to her drink. She was still muttering under her breath, but Xav could see she was rolling the tension out of her shoulders, prepared to let it go.

It was too little too late, though, because Ollie was striding over, evidently having caught some of what she had been saying, while Hayes and Corbett watched on in amusement.

'Do you have a problem with me being here?'

He was addressing Bree, but Xav was the one who answered. 'No one has a problem with you, Ollie. Go and enjoy your drink.'

Ignoring Xav, Ollie repeated his question, a scowl on his face. 'I asked if you have a problem with me being here?'

Bree smirked across the table at Xav and Trudy. Before either of them could react, she turned in her seat. 'Look, we're trying to enjoy our evening and you're disturbing us. So how about you take that smug, pretty boy face of yours and run back over to your friends. Leave us the hell alone.'

'Don't talk to me like that.'

'Excuse me?' Ollie's tone had been pompous and Bree's expression darkened as she climbed to her feet. Seeing their friend in potential trouble, Hayes and Corbett closed in on the table. 'Talk to you like what?'

'Bree. Leave it, please.'

'Stay out of this, Xav. It's time someone told this sanctimonious little prick some home truths.'

'Is that so? What the fuck is your problem with me?' Ollie's chin was raised and he was trying his best to be intimidating, but Xav remembered him well enough. He had plenty of bluster and was overconfident at times, but he was never very good at seeing things through. Besides, unless he had changed, there was no way Ollie would stoop to hitting a woman.

Unfortunately, Xav wasn't so sure about his friends. Ryan Hayes wouldn't get involved, but Greg Corbett would be loving this and didn't seem to have a problem with who his punches landed on.

'My problem isn't just with you. It's with your whole damn family. You Hamiltons think you're something special, but you're a disease to this town.'

'Bree, that's enough.' He needed to defuse this situation. Nothing good would come of it.

'Shut up, Xav.'

She was riled now and Ollie's face was darkening, his fist clenching as he took another step closer. Xav watched him closely, ready to step in if necessary, even though he knew Bree was perfectly capable of defending herself.

'This town took my sister.' Ollie threw a withering glance in Xav's direction before locking eyes with Bree again. 'His family took my sister.'

'Maybe your sister deserved it.'

'Bree! Stop it,' Xav tried again. It was a low blow and cruel too.

Ollie's eyes were wide with shock. 'Take that fucking back.'

'Make me!' Bree taunted.

Xav had no appetite for this. They were adults, not hormonal teenagers looking to prove themselves, and besides, this whole pathetic feud was between him and Ollie, no one else. He started to get up, hoping to talk down the situation, but Trudy was already on her feet and placed a hand on his shoulder, beating him to it as she moved round to Bree's side of the table, pushing herself between her and Ollie.

'Look, you're both being ridiculous,' she told them, attempting to smooth things over. 'Let's sit down and talk this through.'

'I can't believe you need women to fight your battles.' The snide comment came from Corbett, who Xav ignored, knowing he was trying to inflame the situation.

'Sit down, Trudy,' Bree ordered. She looked furious; her eyes locked on Ollie's.

'Take back what you said about Camille,' Ollie demanded.

'Why?' Bree shoved at him, provoking. 'Because you don't want to accept that she might have been a slut who got what she deserved?'

'That's enough!' Xav was on his feet now. 'Bree, you've crossed a line.'

She was being unnecessarily spiteful and in that moment he was more annoyed with her than he was with Ollie. Before he could react, though, Bree shoved Ollie hard and his hand shot out, either to steady himself or hit Bree, Xav wasn't quite sure. But Trudy was still trying to separate them and in the jostling, she managed to put herself in the line of fire.

Xav heard the smack, watching in horror as she crumpled on the floor.

Accident or not, he refused to stand by. He wasn't quick enough, though, and the crack of Bree's fist as it slammed into Ollie's nose was so loud, it had him wincing.

Corbett was stepping into the foray now, eager to get involved, as Ollie cupped his face, blood spilling through his fingers, howling in pain.

Xav was aware of a kid screaming, and other pub-goers gasping in shock, then the cavalry arrived in the form of a couple of bar staff and other drinkers, pulling Corbett, Ollie and Bree apart.

Trudy was on her knees and Xav helped her to her feet. 'Are you okay?' he asked her, trying to see where the slap had landed, which was difficult as she leaned straight into him. He put a tentative arm around her, knowing she hadn't asked for this. She had been trying to play peacemaker.

Damn Ollie and Bree. This was a nice countryside pub and as it was still early evening, there were families here. He was ashamed to be in their company.

As he suspected would be the case, the landlord wanted them all to leave. Xav had no issue with that, wishing he had never come out in the first place. He apologised to the staff, leaving his number and telling them to call him if there was any damage that needed paying for, then he helped Trudy outside to where Bree was waiting, still pumped up with aggression and beer, only regretting that she hadn't hit Ollie a second time. Fortunately, there was no sign of Ollie or his friends, who it appeared had already left.

'I told you I would give that little prick what he had coming to him,' Bree said, wandering over.

'I asked you to drop it. You were completely out of order back there.'

'Oh come on, Xav. He deserved it.'

'And did Trudy deserve it too?' Xav stormed, his temper finally snapping.

He seemed to finally get through to Bree, whose expression turned contrite.

'Shit, Trudy. I'm sorry you got caught up in that.'

'I'm okay, honestly,' Trudy insisted. 'It was my fault. I was in the way.'

'See, she's okay,' Bree agreed, her bluster immediately coming back. 'No thanks to Ollie bloody Hamilton, though.' She paused, scowling at Xav. 'Will you please stop throwing me daggers. I never hit her.'

Xav laughed harshly. 'If you and Ollie hadn't started, she wouldn't have been in the firing line in the first place.'

'I was trying to look out for you and your brother!'

'I don't need you to look out for us, Bree. I can take care of myself!'

The pair of them were silent for a moment as they stared at each other, neither willing to back down.

Bree was the first to speak. 'Well, you've made it clear where we stand. As I guess you don't need me, I'll get out of your hair.'

She raised her chin defiantly, turning on her heel.

Oh, for Christ's sake.

'Bree, come back and get in the car.'

'Thanks, but I'll walk. I need to clear my head. I have some things to think about.'

'You know, considering how capable and headstrong you are, you're being a real bloody drama queen right now,' Xav shouted at her back.

His comment had her pausing, her shoulders tensing as she considering his words, spinning round to face him.

'You're a fine one to talk,' she pushed back. 'I don't know what's got into you tonight. That Hamilton bitch is messing with your head.'

Xav's temper spiked. 'Leave Lana out of this.'

'She's trouble, Xav. And she's got you thinking with your dick instead of your brain. Bloody Hamiltons. This town will be better off without them. You wait and see.'

'Last chance for a ride,' Xav offered, ignoring Bree's gibe. He held the passenger door open for Trudy.

'Thanks. But no thanks. See you around, Xav,' Bree shot back.

He didn't push it. It was still early and it was only about four miles back to Holt. Hopefully the walk would sober Bree up.

As he climbed into the driver's seat, he turned to Trudy. 'You okay?'

She nodded, still seeming a little in shock. 'Yeah, I think so. Not quite the night we were expecting, eh?'

'Bree's her own worst enemy,' Xav muttered, starting the engine. 'I know she means well, but she needs to get her temper under control.'

'Will she be okay walking home?'

'Yeah, she'll be fine. Hopefully it will sober her up a bit.'

As he spoke, they drove past her and, glancing in the rear-view mirror, Xav saw her stick her middle finger up at him. There was no reasoning with her right now. He would call her in the morning and hope she had calmed down.

'The Hamiltons are not her problem. I don't know why she has such a bug up her arse about them.'

'And are they yours?' Trudy asked quietly.

Xav flicked his gaze briefly at her. 'They'll be leaving once the house is on the market,' he said, ignoring the actual question.

He wasn't sure quite what she was implying, but suspected it had to do with the earlier conversation about his feelings for Lana. Trudy needed to understand that even after Lana had left town, nothing was going to happen between them.

Now, though, wasn't the time for that conversation. He would take her home and get some ice on her face. Then, once he knew she was okay, he would check in on Lana and make sure she was too.

He only hoped that Ollie's actions hadn't completely destroyed the tenuous connection they had rebuilt.

32

Sleep wouldn't come and Lana found herself rolling from one side of the double bed to the other, trying to find a cool spot and a comfortable position.

It didn't help that the night was muggy, the temperature and humidity levels seeming to climb rather than drop as the evening wore on. But that wasn't the only reason.

Her mind was too awake as she replayed recent events, still trying to accept that her brother's fiancée may have been the one trying to kill her, plus processing the news that Xav had given her when he had called.

In the early, obsessed with each other, stage of their teenage relationship, they had spent most evenings on the phone, usually talking until one of them fell asleep. This call had been different, though, Xav checking in to make sure she was okay, then admitting to the incident that had happened with her brother.

She had been furious. Not with Xav, who was blaming himself, but with her brother, and she wanted to be sick when she found out that he had hit Trudy.

Accident or not, how bloody dare he behave like that?

He hadn't come home, so she had no idea where he had gone after he had been thrown out of the pub, and she assumed Elise was in her room. That was what she had told Xav when he asked, and he reminded her again to lock the bedroom door when she went to bed.

He could have left the call at that, but he seemed as reluctant to get off the phone as Lana, and they ended up talking as he drove home from Trudy's, then went up to his studio. As it was still early, he told her he planned to paint.

'Call me if you need to or if anything happens,' he had urged before they eventually said goodnight, and she believed he really meant it.

While everything else was falling apart around her, her friendship with Xav was the one thing that appeared to be back on track. Another reason why she was now struggling to sleep.

Things would never go back to how they were before, she understood that. But it didn't stop her wanting what she couldn't have.

* * *

The crash when it came startled Lana awake and for the briefest moment, she couldn't recall where she was. She must have eventually drifted off, she realised, remembering everything.

It had to be Ollie who had made the noise. He was probably drunk and had tripped over something.

She glanced at the alarm clock, saw it was almost 11 p.m.

As she settled back down, annoyed he had woken her, she waited for the sound of his footsteps on the stairs. When they didn't come, she found herself stewing. Had Ollie hurt himself?

Annoyed as she was with him, he was still her brother. Throwing back the duvet, she climbed out of bed. She was wide awake now and wouldn't sleep while she was worrying about him, so she might as well go and check he was okay.

She pulled on an oversized T-shirt and went to the door, for a moment wondering why it wouldn't open. Remembering why she had locked it had her hesitating and she glanced at her phone lying on the bedside table. Perhaps she should take it with her. Just to be on the safe side.

Clutching the phone in her hand, she unlocked the door and stepped out onto the dark landing. She was met only with silence and for the first time it actually occurred to her that perhaps she had dreamt the noise.

No. It had woken her, and it had definitely come from within the house.

Flipping on lights, not liking the ominous feeling that came with the dark, she made her way to the top of the stairs and peered over the banister. Straight away she could see the front door was wide open.

'Ollie?'

There was no response and her gut twisted a little tighter. Suddenly she wasn't quite so convinced it was her brother. She glanced towards the other end of the landing and her old bedroom door. It was closed, but that didn't mean Elise was inside. There had been no reaction to Lana calling Ollie's name, but maybe Elise was a deep sleeper.

Aware that her growing apprehension was because she didn't know what she was dealing with, Lana strode over to the door, knocking loudly.

She might annoy Elise by waking her, but was that really any great loss? The woman already hated her.

She waited a few moments, then when there was no response, she rapped her knuckles again.

Still nothing. If Elise was in the room, surely she would be awake by now.

Lana glanced at the door handle, knew it wasn't her wisest idea, but her hand closed over it anyway. She tried to open the door, but found it locked, which suggested Elise was definitely in the room. The only way out was via the window, but that involved climbing down the tree outside and somehow Lana couldn't see Elise doing that.

She returned to the top of the stairs, called for Ollie again, and debated her next move when he didn't answer.

Someone had opened the door. It was possible it was Ollie or Elise, and that made her reluctant to call the police. She had no proof there was an intruder in the house and couldn't see from this distance whether the door had been forced open. If it turned out to be a false alarm, she would have wasted their time. She was panicking over nothing; she was sure of it. The apprehension she was feeling was because of everything else that had happened. She was sure of it.

Still, that didn't stop her fetching a hammer from the toolbox, which was luckily still in her grandmother's room, and flipping on more lights before she descended the stairs. There was no harm in being cautious.

Even if she was right about Elise being the driver, take away the car and she was just a woman. Lana was certain she could take her down if it came down to a physical fight.

She did a quick sweep of the hallway, peering into the kitchen and the living room, lighting each room, before closing and locking the front door.

'Ollie?'

It was the third time she had called him and there was still no answer. Lana knew she wouldn't be able to go back to bed until she had figured out what the hell was going on. She was too unsettled, tension knotting her shoulders and tightening her grip on both the hammer and her phone.

Xav had told her to call him if she needed to. He had said he would be working, but what if he had decided to call it a night? She didn't want to disturb him over something stupid.

Another crash had her rooted to the spot and for a moment almost too frightened to breathe.

It sounded as if it was coming from the garage.

Ollie hadn't taken his car, but it was possible he had gone in the garage for something.

Her fingers were trembling as she tried his number, frustrated when it went straight to voicemail.

Without allowing herself to overthink it, she scrolled down to Xav's name and pressed call.

He didn't keep her waiting, answering within three rings. 'Lana? You okay?'

Straight away she knew she had done the right thing. He sounded wide awake and concerned.

'I think someone is in the house,' she blurted.

'What? Have you called the police?'

'I don't know if it might be Ollie or Elise. Ollie isn't here. Elise has locked the bedroom door. Oh God, what if it is Ollie and he's hurt?'

'Lana, slow down. You're not making sense. Just take a moment and breathe, okay?'

She did as asked, annoyed she was flaking out on him.

'There was a crash downstairs,' she told him, trying again, this time making an effort to concentrate on her words. 'It woke me up. I thought it was Ollie coming home, but now I'm not so sure.'

'And Elise is in bed?'

'I don't know. I think so. Her bedroom door is locked, but I knocked, tried to wake her. She didn't answer.'

'And where are you now?'

'Downstairs. I'm in the kitchen.' Her voice dropped to a whisper. 'Xav, the front door was open. I definitely locked it.'

That had his attention. 'Okay, I'm calling the police. Go wait upstairs and make sure you keep the bedroom door locked until they get there.'

'But what if it is Ollie? What if something's happened to him? I heard another noise. In the garage. I need to check if it's him.'

'No, Lana, listen to me. Go back upstairs and lock the bedroom door.'

'But if I—'

The sudden sound of music thumping against the wall distracted her. It was that awful rap crap that Ollie liked to listen to and it was coming from the garage. Moments later, she heard the sound of an engine starting.

Xav's voice sounded in her ear. 'Lana, talk to me.'

'I think it's him.'

'Who? Ollie? Are you sure? Have you seen him?'

'There's music coming from the garage.'

'He was drinking, so I'm pretty sure he wasn't driving.'

Lana wasn't listening. She was looking at the connecting door, could see now that the key was in the lock.

'Can you please just go upstairs?' Xav pleaded. 'If you haven't seen him, you don't know for sure that it's him.'

Of course it was. Lana had panicked and now she had Xav worried. But it all made sense now. Ollie had been out drinking, but he was back and rather than go to bed, he had gone to prat around in the garage with his car. It wouldn't be the first time he had done something like this. She remembered when he was younger, especially after Camille had died, he used to spend a lot of time sitting in his car, his music on full whack. It was his way of coping, of having alone time. If he was upset about what had happened at the pub, he would be looking to blow off steam. That's why he hadn't come up to bed. She just needed to make sure he wasn't planning to drive anywhere.

Realising she had solved the mystery, the tension ebbed out of her. 'It's okay. I know Ollie. It will be him,' she reassured Xav. 'I'm sorry I disturbed you.'

'Lana! Don't you dare hang up.'

She stepped into the garage, saw headlights on, could barely hear Xav over the purr of the engines.

Two engines, she realised.

Ollie's car was running, the music blasting, but so was her grandmother's old Mercedes, and from what she could see, both vehicles were empty.

What the hell?

Where was Ollie?

Perhaps Xav was right and she should go back upstairs. Barricade herself in the bedroom and phone the police. Something weird was going on and it was starting to freak her out.

She took a step back, reaching for the door handle again.

As she did, a figure stepped in front of her, dressed all in black and arm raised.

Lana didn't have time to react, barely even saw the metal pipe as it cracked against the side of her head, her world turning to black before she hit the floor.

33

Ollie's face was throbbing, his ego bruised and his mood black.

What was supposed to be a fun catch-up with old friends had turned into a nightmare of an evening, much of which had been spent waiting in A&E with a bloody and broken nose, only to be told to take some painkillers and leave it to heal by itself.

Ryan and Greg had taken him there but were quick to make their getaway, not even saying goodbye as he checked himself in, and a terse conversation with Elise a short while later, who told him she was tired and, no, she wasn't coming to pick him up, meant he was now enduring an expensive taxi ride back from Norwich to Mead House with a driver who stuck rigidly to the speed limit and whose cab was too hot to be comfortable. The car stereo was also tuned into some mediocre radio show that was playing old school country music. Ollie hated country music with a passion, and had requested a change of station, but the driver was either deaf or ignoring him.

Fucker wouldn't be getting a tip then.

To add insult to injury, he then informed Ollie when they were a mile away from Mead House that his card reader was broken, so it would have to be a cash payment.

Ollie argued with him over that, but with no money on him or in the house, he was left with little choice but to go back to Holt to a cash machine.

When they eventually reached Mead House, his temper was close to snapping.

'Here will do,' he instructed, as the cabbie indicated to make the turn into the driveway. He would walk up to the house. No way was he paying a penny more than necessary.

He handed over the fare and held his hand out for the change so it was clear he wasn't giving it as a tip, receiving a grunt instead of a goodbye, the driver looking unimpressed.

Ollie got out of the taxi, shoving his wallet back in his pocket, and as he walked up the dark driveway, he muttered away to himself about his shitty mates who had dumped him at the hospital, his shitty girlfriend who he hadn't heard a word from since their earlier exchange, and shitty Xav Landry and his arsehole friend, Bree McCarthy.

And, of course, they would all be trying to paint Ollie as the bad guy, because he had hit Trudy Palmer.

Okay, he felt a little bad about that, but he had been trying to steady himself after Bree pushed him. He hadn't hit Trudy on purpose. She had simply been in the way. Nonetheless, shame and humiliation at how the evening had played out heated his cheeks.

Christ, his nose was hurting. His head thumping too. Probably from the stress of the whole situation.

Deciding he would pour himself a whisky when he got in, maybe wash down some painkillers with it, and try to relax before going to bed, he started to speed up.

Through the trees, he could see the front of the house and it surprised him to see lights on. Not just upstairs, but all of the ground floor too. And was that his music he could hear playing? It was gone midnight and Elise had said she was in bed, so it had to be Lana. What the hell was she up to?

* * *

Lana's head was groggy and she was too hot. Those were her first thoughts when gaining consciousness. The next thing she was aware of was the slow rhythmical thumping behind her skull. As she opened her eyes, realising she was in complete darkness, the thump increased both in speed and intensity, her head spinning so fast she almost threw up.

She lay still for a moment, needing the dizziness to pass so she could focus. Sweat was damp on her forehead, dripping down her face, and the pain in her head now so acute, she wanted to cry out. She tried to pull it under control, drawing in a couple of deep breaths. There was hardly any air, though, and what she did manage to inhale was pungent with fumes that were so strong, the nausea crawled straight back up into her throat.

Where was she?

'Hello?'

Her voice sounded muffled, even to her own ears.

What the hell was going on?

She tried to focus, realising that she was curled up in the foetal position, her bare feet pressed up against something, her back too, and what was that noise? She could hear music and something else in the forefront was rumbling away. An engine?

The memories came rushing back. The noise in the garage, the engine of Nana Kitty's Mercedes running.

She could feel the vibrations coming from beneath her, and realised she was inside the car. The last thing she remembered was the flash of someone in front of her. They had hit her with something.

Had they put her in the car? Were they planning on taking her somewhere? She had to get out.

Why was it so dark?

Gingerly, she tried to sit up, but didn't get far. Something heavy was above her, blocking her escape.

Trying not to panic, she reached out again, taking a few moments to explore her surroundings. A small space, metal just above her and to the sides. She couldn't stretch. In fact, had barely any room to move.

The car. She was definitely in the car. But not on the seat and there was not enough room in the footwell. And there was that awful smell of fumes.

It was like the air was closing in and smothering her.

She needed to move and try to clear her head so she could focus. And the engine needed to be turned off. She was feeling woozier by the second.

She used what little energy she had left to push at her makeshift coffin, meeting with resistance and dread clawing at her spine as she realised she was trapped.

Finally, she understood why she could barely move.

She was in the boot.

Using what little air she had, Lana started screaming.

* * *

It was his second visit to Mead House in the space of a week, the one place he had vowed to never return to, but Xav took no notice of that as he pulled off the country lane and sped up the driveway.

Lana's call had scared him half to death, ending abruptly with a scream before the line went dead. Every problem that had existed between them had suddenly become irrelevant. He knew only that he had to get to her and fast.

He had called the police as he was driving but was aware they wouldn't be able to get to the house as quickly as he could and he floored the accelerator, not caring that he was taking the narrow bends far too fast. Normally, he was a conscientious driver, but tonight he didn't have the luxury of time.

He was so focused on the house ahead, every room lit up and the front door wide open, that he almost hit the man jogging up the driveway.

Ollie.

He jerked the steering wheel at the last moment, the car skidding around him, as he leapt out of the way, pulling to a halt outside the house. He was already out of the car when Ollie came stumbling towards him, his face in a snarl.

'You stupid son of a bitch. Were you trying to kill me?'

'I need to find Lana.'

'What? I told you to stay the fuck away.'

When Xav ignored him, heading straight for the house, Ollie caught his shoulder and pulled him round to face him, getting in close.

'You've got a real nerve showing up here tonight.'

There wasn't time for this. Xav gave him a hard shove, then when Ollie came straight back at him, he grabbed hold of the front of his T-shirt.

'Listen to me. Your sister's in trouble. I think she's in danger.'

'What?' The aggression dropped away, concern taking its place. 'What the hell are you talking about?'

Xav didn't answer. He was looking over Ollie's shoulder, could see the smoke coming from the double garage door.

'Where's your key?'

'What?'

Xav pushed him towards the garage. 'Ollie, where's your fucking key?'

Seeing the smoke, Ollie's eyes widened and he started patting down his pockets.

There wasn't time.

The front door was wide open and, without another word, Xav charged into the house. He might not have been here in years, but he remembered the layout well enough.

'Who the fuck are you?'

He spared the briefest glance at the blonde watching him from the stairs, scowling at him, but didn't stop to answer. Across the hall, into the kitchen, to the connecting door that led into the garage. Thick smoke and exhaust fumes were already filling the room.

He heard footsteps behind him as he opened the door.

'Lana?'

Ollie sounded distressed as he followed Xav into the garage.

Two cars, both of the engines running. Xav lifted his T-shirt to cover the lower part of his face, moving between the cars. Lana wasn't in either of them.

He reached inside the Mercedes and shut off the engine, while Ollie took care of his own car.

'Lana?'

Where the fuck was she?

She had definitely been in the garage when her phone went dead.

'The boot.'

Xav looked at Ollie, saw his face twist in anguish as they rushed to the back of the Mercedes. As it swung open, he caught his breath, seeing Lana curled up on her side.

Beside him, Ollie let out a guttural howl.

She wasn't moving and Xav's initial thought was that she was dead. As he tried to register the horror of that, a numbness crept over him, and his body was almost on autopilot as he lifted her out of the boot. She was still warm to touch, burning up even, her hair and skin damp, and he carried her through into the kitchen, laying her down on the cool tiled floor.

'Shut the door!' he yelled at Ollie, who did as told, locking the worst of the fumes in the garage before dropping to his knees beside Xav.

'What happened?'

The blonde was in the room now. So this was Elise, Xav guessed.

He didn't answer her and neither did Ollie, whose focus was entirely on his sister. But he noticed that she didn't seem quite as concerned as she should. Had she done this?

Xav should never have let Lana go back to Mead House alone. He had known there was a threat but hadn't wanted to address the idea that maybe, until they established where it was coming from, it would be safer for her to stay with him.

He pushed that burst of guilt to one side, knowing there was no time for it now, just as there was no time for Elise. He would focus on her later. Instead, he checked Lana's pulse, barely daring to hope when he realised she had one. He was about to attempt CPR when she started coughing, her eyes blinking open.

'Lana?'

Ollie was leaning over her and Xav had to hold him back.

'Give her some space.' He glanced at Elise for the first time. 'Can you get her some water?'

When the woman simply stared at him, seeming fixed to the spot, he barked, 'Now!'

That startled her into action and although she didn't answer, she went to the sink and filled a glass.

Lana was pale and shaken, and Xav could see, now that her hair was brushed back, that she had a gash on her forehead, but she was breathing and, in typical Lana style, she was also moving too fast, already trying to sit up.

'Take it easy,' he instructed, accepting the water from Elise and helping Lana take a couple of steadying sips.

Ollie wasn't waiting any longer, pulling her into a tight hug before Xav had even set the glass down. Xav could see he was fighting to hold on to his emotion. While his own were still under control, he pulled out his phone and called for an ambulance.

Lana wouldn't like it, but she needed to be checked out.

He saw Elise's eyes widen slightly when she realised he was on the phone to the emergency operator and realised she wouldn't know he had already called the police. He didn't know if she was involved in what had just happened to Lana or not but was sure the police would want to speak to her, as it had just been the two of them in the house alone. One thing was certain: Lana hadn't locked herself in the boot.

34

Elise's nerves were on edge when she heard the sirens.

It had just been her and Lana in the house tonight and she knew it looked suspicious.

She had been shocked when she had seen the man she now knew to be Xavier Landry running into the house, Nolly close behind him, and that shock had turned to horror when she had watched them bring Lana through from the garage. Nolly had taken no notice of her reactions, falling to pieces and focusing only on his sister as he realised she was alive.

He was subdued now as the four of them sat in the living room with the two police detectives.

Lana, who had looked half dead at one point, had soon perked up, protesting bitterly when the ambulance had arrived. The para-medics had checked her over and Elise had watched the relief sag out of her when they told her she didn't need to go to hospital. She now sat on one of the two sofas, Xavier by her side, looking like he was guarding over her.

He had the whole brooding artist thing going on and, under different circumstances, Elise might have been tempted, but it was clear he was only interested in Lana. The poor sap hadn't been able to stop touching her since she had woken up, almost as if he was afraid she might crumble away if he broke contact.

Nolly had told her the history between the three of them and Elise didn't get what was so special about his stupid sister. Lana was way too perky and confrontational. And it wasn't as if she was anything special to look at. What had happened to her tonight was all her fault for digging up the past. Why couldn't she just leave her bloody sister's death alone? But no. She had to poke, poke, poke.

Frankly, she was a pain in the arse, and Elise held her solely responsible for the mess she was now in.

She needed to get hold of George, to let him know she was in trouble, but she didn't dare risk doing that while the police were still here.

'So you slept through the whole thing?' the female DC was asking her now. The woman's name escaped Elise. She hadn't really been paying attention at the time of introductions, as she desperately tried to figure a way out of this whole mess. It was the second time the detective had asked the question.

'I already told you, yes.' Elise tried to adopt a bored tone, one that suggested she was fed up with all this and wanted to go back to bed.

'Miss Hamilton heard a crash from her room, which must have come from the garage, but that is below where you were sleeping. Don't you think it's a little strange it never woke you?'

'I had headphones in. I need music to sleep.'

'And you didn't hear her knock?'

'Nope.' Elise glanced at Lana, who, despite looking pale and shaken, was shooting her daggers.

Instead she looked to Nolly for support, annoyed when he refused to make eye contact. He was sat in one of the two armchairs, quiet and contemplative, and she was struggling to gauge what he was thinking.

The questions kept on coming and she answered them the best she could, aware that she was now on her own, and desperate for a chance to escape.

She suspected that neither detective believed her, as they kept asking the same things over and over, as if they were trying to trip her up.

How come she heard Xavier and Ollie if she didn't hear Lana?

Why had she locked the bedroom door?

Did she have any idea who might want to hurt Lana?

Could she verify her whereabouts the night of the hit-and-run?

Was she certain she didn't know what had happened to the second missing journal?

Because, yes, Lana had thrown that into the mix too, giving the detectives something else to chew over, proving to Elise that her apology earlier had been hollow.

George Maddox had a lot to answer for and she intended to give him hell when she next saw him.

That's if she could get out of this mess, because it seemed Lana had been spying on her and knew more than she had initially let on, overhearing Elise's last conversation with George and finding a breakfast receipt that could be incriminating.

Elise was aware of everyone's eyes on her. Xavier looked as unimpressed with her as Lana did, while the two detectives were watching her closely, she suspected to see her reactions. Even fucking Nolly, the disloyal bastard, was paying attention now, and she could see he was questioning everything.

He was so transparent, the accusation written all over his face, and she almost enjoyed his look of disappointment when she confessed she had cheated on him.

She hadn't wanted to admit to sleeping with someone else, and she had lied, saying the affair was with an old friend, but what choice did she have? She couldn't risk the truth coming out, but she was also very aware she had just given up her meal ticket.

When they had first met, Elise had told Nolly she was a model, and yes, true, she had done a couple of low-profile magazine shoots years ago. Her main job had been a doctor's receptionist, at least it was before she was fired for repeatedly showing up late to work.

Down on her luck and unable to pay her rent, she had counted her blessings when Nolly had allowed her to move in, determined to hang on to her prize catch, and pressing for an engagement ring, when she learnt of his inheritance.

She was relieved when the police finally left. The woman detective had warned her to get in touch if she remembered anything crucial and Elise had a horrible feeling that she was their number one suspect, but to be honest, she didn't plan on hanging around long enough to let them gather evidence.

George was the one who had pulled her into this mess. He would have to figure a way to get her out again. And, right now, Elise needed him to come and pick her up.

Yes, she had family here in Norfolk, but they had disowned her after she had slept with her brother-in-law. Even though that was years ago she knew they would not welcome her back with open arms. That left her stuck in the middle of the countryside and her only other alternative was to call a cab. As she no longer had Nolly's credit cards at her disposal, she was reluctant to do that.

George sounded wary when he answered the phone. 'Why are you calling me?'

'Because the police have been at the house asking me a bunch of questions I don't have answers for.'

That had his attention. 'Are you still there now?'

'Yes, but I'm now packing and you have to come get me.'

'It's gone midnight.'

'I don't care.'

'You have to stay.'

'No fucking way. They're all treating me like I should be locked up. This is your fault, you got me into this whole mess. You'd better fix it.'

There was silence on the line.

'George? Are you listening to me? Come and get me now. I'm not playing this game any more and I don't have anything to lose, so come and pick me the hell up if you want me to keep your secrets.'

When he spoke, he sounded resigned. 'I'm not coming up to the house. I'll pick you up at the end of the driveway in twenty minutes.'

Elise heaved out a sigh of relief, glad he had relented.

She was packing her things when Nolly came upstairs to find her. The detectives having finally left.

'You're leaving?'

He sounded more annoyed and accusatory than concerned, and she was quick to turn the tables on him.

'What the fuck do you think, Nolly?'

'How long has it been going on?' he demanded.

'What?'

'This affair. How long, Elise?'

That was all he cared about?

'The whole time we were together,' she lied, twisting the knife in cruelly and enjoying his gasp of shock.

'You bitch.'

'And you're a pathetic, weak man,' Elise snarled, her temper snapping. 'I'm glad I cheated on you. You didn't have my back tonight. You just sat there and let both of those detectives try to tear me to pieces.'

She had worn the trousers throughout their brief relationship and expected him to back down, so he surprised the hell out of her when his tone turned aggressive.

'Seems to me they were asking some pretty relevant questions.'

Bastard.

Elise zipped her case shut, dragging it off the bed. She was not going to stick around for a moment longer and put up with this.

As she pushed past Ollie, he asked another question.

'Do I know him?'

Elise's shoulders tensed. 'Does it matter?'

'To me, yes.' Ollie sounded broken.

'No, you don't,' she lied.

He didn't try to stop her as she left the room and part of her wanted to pull off her ring and throw it back at him, but she knew how much the diamond had cost. No way was she parting with it. She clunked her case down the stairs, heat flooding her cheeks when she realised Xavier Landry was now blocking her path to the front door.

'Should you be leaving?'

What was he planning, to keep her a prisoner here in this house? He couldn't do that.

She wheeled her case awkwardly down the last few stairs, scowling at him. 'Last I checked, I'm free to go, so get out of my way.'

'Where are you going?'

'To check into a hotel. Not that it's any of your fucking business.'

She went to push past him, but he refused to move, so she met his hostile stare, raising her chin a notch, determined to show him she wouldn't be intimidated. 'I refuse to stay in this house with you people after what you all put me through in there. If you really think I hurt your precious Lana, then why do you want me around anyway? The police haven't arrested me, they haven't cautioned me or told me I have to stay here, so you have zero right. I will not be your fucking prisoner. Now get out of my way. My taxi is waiting.'

'Let her go, Xav.' Lana was standing in the living-room doorway, her arms folded and a tired look on her face. 'I don't want her here.'

'That makes two of us,' Elise hissed, desperate to get out of the house. She tried to get past Xavier again, relieved when this time he relented.

It didn't matter that it had started to rain and that she was early to meet George so would have to wait around. She just wanted out.

At least he was coming to pick her up. Her threat had worked and it was good to know that she now held some of the cards.

George Maddox had been calling the shots for too long.

35

2005

It had been during a detention that they had first connected, and although they shared classes and he knew who she was, he doubted she even knew his name.

George was there because the English homework he had handed in contained a slur about his teacher. He had honestly known nothing about it until the work was given back, with a note to stay after class, and his eyes had popped when he looked at the story he had worked so hard on, seeing the crudely written insult at the bottom of the page.

He recognised Derek's writing, understood his stepbrother had set him up again, and he had attempted to set the record straight, but his teacher had been livid and refused to listen. He was made to stay after school for an hour every night for a week.

The first two nights he had been the only kid there. It was just him and Mrs Benson and the hour passed painfully slow. On the Wednesday, there had been a change of teacher and a second student.

He had watched her walk in, taking the desk across from him.

She briefly made eye contact, but the scowl didn't lift from her face. George doubted she would lower herself to speak to him.

Mr Hughes was now in charge of detention and he wanted to be there even less than the kids did. He was one of the younger teachers at the school and known for being a flirt with the other staff, and he kept disappearing out of the room. From the giggling George heard, he suspected he was trying to charm one of the cleaners.

With just the two of them in the room, there had been an uncomfortable atmosphere and George had become self-conscious as he stared at the workbook in front of him, half afraid to clear his throat and resisting the urge to fidget in his seat.

That third night of detention had dragged longer than the others and when he saw the same girl in the room on the Thursday night, he feared he was going to suffer again.

This time, she had arrived first, but where she had ignored him before, she was now watching him with lazy interest. When Mr Hughes had made his first excuse to go for a wander, the girl had surprised him by leaning across.

'What are you in for?' she'd whispered.

When George had told her, her eyes had widened. 'Did you really do that?'

It crossed his mind that perhaps he should say yes. Maybe if he told her he had written the insult, she would think he was cool, but he had hesitated for too long and could see she wasn't going to believe him.

'My stepbrother did it,' he'd admitted. 'He is such a dick.'

Shame had heated his face as she stared at him and he'd braced himself for either laughter or an insult. He received neither.

'I told Mrs Brookes to fuck off,' she'd told him conspiratorially.

'Really?'

When George's eyes went wide, her lips had curved in a smirk.

'Yup.'

'Did you just do it for laughs?' he'd asked, trying to sound casual, barely daring to believe she was interested in having a conversation with him.

The girl had shrugged. 'I guess. I was in a bad mood that day and I had just had enough.'

Mrs Brookes was one of the scariest teachers. George was in awe.

That afternoon had passed far quicker. Although they had to be silent when Mr Hughes was in the room, he wasn't there very often.

The conversation was mostly light to begin with, but then the girl began probing about Derek, wanting to know the history with George's stepbrother.

He had been wary about saying too much, not wanting her to think he was a wimp and hating the idea that she might pity him, so it had surprised him when she had revealed she was facing her own issues.

'The person I have always believed in, who I have trusted the most, has betrayed me. Last week, I discovered everything I have been led to believe is a lie,' she'd admitted. 'I honestly don't know how to feel about that.'

'I'm sorry about that,' George had told her. He wasn't really sure what else he could say. Her face had darkened and he could see the rage in her eyes.

'I guess I am disappointed, and angry too,' she'd continued. 'I have been let down and I want to get even.' She looked at George. 'Does that make me a bad person, do you think? That I want to punish the people who have hurt me?'

'No, I guess not.'

'Would you want to get your stepbrother back if you could? Take revenge?'

He thought about it for a few moments; the idea of making

Derek pay was something he had dreamt about for a long time. 'Yes, I would.'

She had smiled then. 'I think you and I are more alike than we realise.'

It was the next day after their detention had finally finished that she made the proposal.

George was outside unchaining his bike and didn't hear her approach.

'I think you and I could help each other,' she told him, her voice startling him and making him drop the chain.

He wasn't sure he would be any help to her, but still he was intrigued. 'How so?'

'I could make all of your problems with Derek go away. Make it so he never bothers you again. Would you like that?'

George wasn't too sure he believed she could help him, but, yes, of course he would love it. He nodded. 'How would you do that?'

'With a plan. I have an idea. Of course, I would need you to help me too.'

'By doing what?'

'I want to get revenge on the person who has ruined everything for me.'

'You want me to hurt them?' George wasn't sure he could do that. He must have looked worried, because she smiled and shook her head.

'No, I would just need your help in getting them alone. And perhaps being my lookout. I just want to scare them a little. Teach them a lesson. You could do that for me, right? And in return, I will deal with Derek.'

'I guess I could.'

'So we have a deal then?'

George hesitated, but only for a second. He took the girl's outstretched hand and shook it. 'Okay, yes, we have a deal.'

36

So much had happened over the space of one night and Lana's head was spinning.

Of course, it could be the side effects from the carbon monoxide, but the paramedics had told her she was okay and that she was fortunate she had been found so quickly.

She'd had a cracking headache earlier, but that was most likely from the head wound she had suffered, and luckily it had eased. Again, she hadn't required stitches, so she guessed that in the grand scheme of things, she had been lucky.

It was easier to focus on that than what would have certainly happened if Xav and Ollie hadn't found her when they did, or who had attacked her.

Perhaps they shouldn't have let Elise leave, but the woman had been right. They couldn't hold her prisoner. The police hadn't charged her with any crime and although they had seemed dubious of her story about being asleep, they hadn't ordered her not to leave town.

Lana still believed Elise had taken the journal, but had she been the one to lock her in the boot of the Mercedes? Elise was more petite than Lana. Would she really have had the strength to move her body after knocking her unconscious?

It was something her, Ollie and Xav were discussing, the three of them sat in the living room, oblivious to the fact it was gone 2 a.m.

Things weren't quite right between Xav and Ollie, but for now they had reached something of a truce, and for the first time since Camille's death, Lana believed their problems were fixable.

She would never have thought they would be spending time together in this house again, and she had to keep pinching herself that Xav was here beside her right now, a comforting and steadying presence. As awful as they were, she refused to regret the circumstances that had brought him back to her.

'It's a bit of a leap, but it's possible,' he said now, swirling the whisky Ollie had poured him in one hand, the ice cubes rattling against the glass, while his other remained cupped around the small of Lana's back.

'It's more than a leap,' Ollie pointed out. 'Lana would have been a dead weight and heavier than usual. And she is bigger than Elise.' One side of his mouth curved as he looked at her now. 'No offence.'

He was more subdued tonight than she had seen him in a long time. Exhaustion possibly played a part and she didn't doubt he was smarting from having his nose broken by Bree, but mostly she suspected it was learning that Elise had been cheating on him.

While Lana felt bad about that, she was relieved to have him back.

The pair of them still had a lot of issues to work through, but already she was feeling closer to him than in a long time, and in truth, she was glad Ollie had seen Elise's true colours before marrying her.

'None taken,' she told him. 'And you're both right. She would have struggled. That is, unless she'd had help.'

It was a new possibility and one she could see Ollie and Xav both considering.

'I'm still convinced she stole the journal,' Lana pushed. 'And I don't buy her story that she didn't hear anything earlier. It woke me up and I was the other end of the house. What I don't get, though, is why she would want to hurt me. Do you think it's possible she knew Camille?'

Ollie shrugged. 'I guess she could have. I really don't know, Lana.'

They had already grilled him about his fiancée, learning he hadn't known her well at all. In true Ollie style, he had been easily swayed by a pretty face.

He sounded tired, so she didn't push it. Ollie had told the police everything he knew, and Lana was beginning to wonder if he had been targeted. Elise wanting a way in. Again, it seemed a stretch, so for now she was keeping those thoughts to herself, but it still didn't explain who G was or what Elise's motive had been.

Ollie had been so reluctant to know the contents of Camille's second journal and he had looked both nauseous and shocked as Lana had told the police about her sister's secret lover, recounting some of the sick games they had played. He was being forced to face up to a whole lot of truths in one go and she felt a little sorry for him.

He needed rest. They all did. It would be easier to think straight with clearer heads.

Finishing her whisky, she turned to Xav, keeping her voice low. 'Will you stay here tonight... with me?'

Okay, technically it was already morning, but he knew what she meant, and they were sitting close enough on the sofa that she heard the intake of his breath. But when he turned to look at her, his gaze was steady. He didn't speak, instead answering her with a simple nod.

Taking the glass from him, she put both tumblers down on the coffee table, then got up, reaching for his hand. When Ollie glanced over at them, she made things clear.

'He's staying.'

Part of her was waiting for a protest, but Ollie seemed resigned to the fact things had changed, giving a shrug.

Tightening her grip on Xav's hand, she led him from the room and up the stairs to the bedroom.

They didn't bother to undress, just kicking off shoes and crawling on top of the duvet, and as they lay there facing one another, Lana reached out and tentatively ran her fingers across his cheek. She had missed his face so much.

'Is this okay?' she whispered.

Although he had agreed to stay with her, she knew this couldn't be easy for him.

When he nodded again, those earthy-green eyes, framed by sickeningly long lashes, staying locked on hers, her fingers continued to explore. The slash of dark eyebrows, the frown line above his slightly crooked nose, the curve of his jaw, rough with dark stubble, and the softness of his mouth.

He reached up, catching hold of her hand and turning it so he could kiss her palm, his breath hot and his lips soft.

Lana shuffled herself closer, trailing the fingers of her free hand into his hair.

'And what about this?' Leaning into Xav, she brushed her lips across his. 'Is that okay too?'

This time, he responded with questions of his own.

'Should we really be doing this, after what's happened? I thought your head was hurting?'

'It is, though it's not as bad as earlier. Besides, you're here and I've really missed you.'

The words slipped out and for a moment, as Xav broke eye

contact, she regretted saying them out loud. She didn't want to risk him pulling away. Not again.

But then he was looking at her, his gaze heated and the hint of a smile playing on his lips. 'I've missed you too, Lana.'

Her heart swelled. 'I know things are complicated, I know this isn't an ideal time, but...' She trailed off when Xav pressed a finger against her lips.

'Let's not talk about complications right now, okay? Or any of the other crap that's going on. It's just you and me. Lana and Xav. Like it used to be.'

Now it was Lana's turn to smile. 'Okay.' She pressed her lips to his again, this time lingering, a murmur caught in the back of her throat when he deepened the kiss, his tongue sliding into her mouth. It was a warm, familiar memory that heated her up inside and, as he rolled her on her back, the weight of his body covering hers as his hands gently explored, every one of her nerve endings tingled.

Later would be for trying to find out who had attacked her and why, for renewing their efforts to find out whether Sebastian had been falsely imprisoned, and if Camille's killer was still on the loose.

But for now they needed this, the calm before the storm, a few precious hours where they could lose themselves in each other without having to worry about what came next.

37

Ollie was in the kitchen, hair sticking on end and dressed only in a pair of joggers, when Xav wandered down the stairs, and he lingered in the doorway for a moment, watching his old friend as he hunched over the counter staring intently at his phone.

Last night, they had reached a truce of sorts, both understanding there was a bigger threat at play and that they had a mutual goal – to keep Lana safe. They still hadn't cleared the air, though, and Xav wasn't sure if Ollie would ever forgive him for being Sebastian's brother.

That could be a problem, because for the second time in recent days, Xav had almost lost Lana and it had made him realise he couldn't walk away from her again. He didn't know how the hell they were going to make things work or if it would even be possible, but this time he was going to fight to keep her in his life.

He had left her asleep, suspecting she would be out for the count for at least another hour or so and knowing she needed the rest and time for her body and mind to heal. Even though he hadn't had much sleep himself, he had watched her for a while, reacquainting himself with every curve and line of her face. The cut of her cheekbones, the sweep of dark lashes and the fullness of her top lip, then, when she had rolled over and the duvet slipped away, the arch of her back and the intimate curves of her backside.

She had been so many of his firsts. Not his first kiss. That regrettable experience had been with Karen Pointer when he was fourteen, all mushy lips, too much saliva and poking tongues. But Lana had been his first steady girlfriend, the first to steal his heart, and the first girl he had made love to. Well, okay, making love was a stretch; that first time had involved lots of urgent fumbling and had been a bit of an anti-climax for both of them. They had learnt together, though, and their experiences gradually became better.

Last night had been like a warm and familiar embrace, only better. Time apart, plus the gained skill and confidence of having had other lovers, had heightened the intensity of the moment. They hadn't rushed, instead taking their time to rediscover and savour as they drove each other over the edge.

He had made peace with Lana and overcome his reluctance to set foot again in Mead House. Was it possible he and Ollie could fix things too?

Clearing his throat, Xav stepped into the kitchen and saw Ollie's eyes widen slightly as he turned to face him, the plaster across his nose a reminder of how fractured things had been just a few hours before.

'Hey.'

Ollie eyed him warily. 'Hey.'

'Lana's still asleep. Can I get a coffee?'

There was a hesitation and Xav could see the wheels turning, knew that Ollie was deciding which way he was going to play this. Eventually, he shrugged. 'Sure.'

Xav watched him reach into a cupboard, relieved he wasn't going to make things difficult. At least not for now.

Ollie filled a new mug with fresh coffee from the pot, before topping up his own drink. 'You still take it black?'

'Yeah, I do.'

Xav accepted the mug, making the decision to stay in the room. For things to work, he couldn't avoid Ollie.

'How's your nose?'

There was another hesitation.

'Sore. Your friend packs quite a punch.'

Xav was expecting him to add, 'For a woman', but Ollie seemed to catch himself.

'She does,' he agreed, remembering Ollie well enough to know his masculine pride would be dented. 'I wouldn't want to get on the wrong side of her.'

Which had him wondering, would Bree be speaking to him today? Xav had been so wrapped up with Lana last night, it had distracted him from their earlier argument.

He would call her later, he decided, and he guessed he should check in with Trudy too at some point. Make sure she was okay.

Ollie moved to sit down at the kitchen table and although he took his phone with him, he pushed it to one side. Taking that as a sign he was making an effort, Xav went to join him, pulling out a chair.

'So, you slept with my sister last night.'

It wasn't a question, but it was a very direct statement and one that required an answer, and Xav decided he wasn't going to try to creep around the fact.

'I did.'

He waited for Ollie's reaction, meeting his gaze head on, his hand stilled on his mug.

'Do you still love her?'

'Yes.' Admitting it out loud to Ollie made him realise he had never stopped loving Lana.

'I guess we have a common interest then. I want her to be safe.'

'I do too.'

'Then we need to figure out who is targeting her and why.'

Xav nodded. 'Agreed.'

'I don't think Elise was in the garage last night.'

When Xav opened his mouth to speak, Ollie put his hand up.

'Just hear me out.'

'Okay.'

'She weighs less than eight stone and she's physically smaller than Lana. I know we touched on it briefly last night, but I've been really thinking it over and I just don't see how she could manage to knock Lana unconscious, drag her across the garage and put her in the boot. Then there's the clothing. Lana said the person who attacked her was dressed all in black. Elise didn't have an outfit like that. If she does, then she was keeping it well hidden from me. I'm not trying to let her off the hook. I know some of the stuff she was saying last night doesn't add up, but if she's behind what happened to my sister, then she had help.'

Credit to Ollie, he was making some fair points. It had to sting, knowing the truth about his fiancée, but if he was upset, he wasn't showing it.

'What about the journal? Do you think she took it?'

Ollie shrugged. 'I guess that's possible. Lana accused her and Elise went on the defensive. At the time, I believed her when she said she hadn't taken it, but now, in light of what happened last night, I'm not so sure.'

He fell silent, staring at his coffee and Xav mused over what had just been said.

'We need to find it,' he concluded. 'And we have to figure out who Camille was seeing.'

'You and Lana really believe there's a chance Sebastian is innocent, don't you?' There was no scepticism in Ollie's tone. It was as if he was trying to believe it himself.

'Maybe. I honestly don't know. Lana is the only one who has read the journal and now it's gone. But we know there was someone else other than Sebastian, and the fact that the journal has vanished, plus with everything that's been happening to Lana, it has to be connected.'

'Someone beginning with G, right?'

'Apparently so.'

'George Maddox was there when we found the book.'

'You really think the George we knew back then would have been sleeping with your sister? She was nineteen and what would he have been? Fifteen?'

A smile touched Ollie's lips, the first one Xav had seen in a long while. 'I guess not. If you looked at him now, I would believe it, but back then, no way.'

He fell silent as he considered, and Xav suspected he was thinking about the dark nature of Camille's relationship. It had been about power games, of dominance and submission, which suggested an older, more experienced lover. Xav had seen Ollie's face when Lana had revealed details to the police and knew his old friend had been both shocked and disgusted.

'So, not George, but who else?' Ollie spoke eventually.

Xav thought of the people they had known when they were teenagers, the vicar for some reason popping into his head. 'Graham Hunt?'

Ollie shook his head. 'I'll check with Lana, but I'm pretty sure he was away on holiday when Camille died. I remember him coming to the house to pay his respects when he returned.'

'Godfrey Kirton?' Xav grinned as he mentioned the old greengrocer.

'Is he even still alive?' Ollie asked. 'He was about eighty when we were kids.'

'No idea. I haven't seen him in years.'

'Pretty certain he would have struggled on his Zimmer frame.'

Xav hesitated before mentioning the next name, unsure what Ollie's reaction would be.

'What about Greg?'

Ollie briefly met his eyes, knowing exactly who Xav was talking about even though his surname hadn't been mentioned.

'You think Camille would have slept with Corbett?' He sounded a touch defensive.

'I'm just putting names out there, Ollie.'

'I don't see him being her type.'

Xav didn't either, but they should keep him on the list regardless. 'Maybe not,' he agreed. 'But we need to rule him out. We can't just dismiss him.'

'Okay, fair enough.' Ollie finished his coffee and got up from the table. 'Do you want another cup?'

'I'm good, thanks.'

'What about surnames or nicknames?' Ollie asked, taking both mugs over to the sink. 'G doesn't necessarily mean first name, and, let's face it, the suspect pool we have is not particularly inspiring.'

He was right. It wasn't and they spent a few minutes considering other potential lovers, but nothing stood out to either of them.

'Are you heading home soon?' Ollie asked when they had exhausted the list.

Xav looked at him, surprised he was asking. 'In a bit. I have a hungry cat waiting.'

'Funny. You always struck me as more of a dog person.'

'I still like dogs. I'm going to wait for Lana to wake up before I go. Why do you ask?'

'Because I'm gonna go upstairs and get dressed, then check the garage again and outside. See if there is anything we or the police missed last night.' Ollie kept his tone casual. 'I wondered if you fancied helping me.'

It was another olive branch and Xav wasted no time taking it.

'Yeah,' he nodded. 'I do.'

* * *

It was a fruitless task, but one they had to do. Ollie couldn't just sit around and wait for the police to come up with answers when his sister's life was in danger. At least with Xav helping him, they had two sets of eyes covering the ground and spending time together pulled at memories from the past, reminding him of how things had once been between them. Before things had become messy.

Things were still a little tentative between them and Ollie wasn't sure what the future would hold. He only knew that for now, their alliance was best for Lana. He still wasn't sure how he felt about Xav or about Lana letting him back into her life, but he realised he had to make an effort. And although he wasn't yet quite ready to admit it, he had missed his old friend, and was regretting the wedge that had been driven between them by Camille's murder.

Was it really possible Sebastian was innocent? Had they been wrongly hating and blaming each other for all of this time?

But if it was true, then who had killed Camille?

Was it the person who had been trying to hurt Lana?

They needed to find out who Camille's lover had been. But how? The suspect list was woefully short and, at the moment, Greg Corbett sat top of it. Granted, he made more sense than someone like George Maddox, but seriously, Corbett? Although he was Ollie's friend, even he would admit that the man had the manners of a pig and very few redeeming qualities. He had been single for as long as Ollie had known him. Was he even capable of seducing someone?

Camille hadn't been short of admirers. She could have had anyone. No, there was more chance of her dating a woman than Greg Corbett.

The thought passed briefly, though stuck.

Was it possible that G could be female?

Ollie remembered his sister. Beautiful, fiery and confident. She had never shown any interest in girls, but then he had to admit he had only really known her to be with Sebastian.

Had that been her big secret?

No. He was clutching at straws now.

The garage gave no clues, only proving that whoever had attacked Lana had covered their tracks well. Outside, there was more ground to cover and after half an hour of searching with no success, they were about ready to give up and go back in the house when Xav found the part-smoked cigarette.

It had been in the border along the edge of the driveway and as he scooped it up, studying it, Ollie watched as his expression turn from confused to concerned.

'What have you found?' he asked, jogging across.

'Probably nothing,' Xav muttered, but still he held out the cigarette for Ollie to take.

He studied the roll-up, wrapped in pale-pink paper. 'Not many of these about.'

'I think there are few different brands that make them.'

'But how many people smoke pink cigarettes?' When Xav didn't answer, rubbing his hand across the back of his neck, Ollie narrowed his eyes. 'Do you know anyone who smokes these?'

From the look on Xav's face, it was pretty bloody obvious he did, and as he waited for him to answer, Ollie wondered if it would be with the truth.

'Bree McCarthy does.'

'So she was here then?' Ollie's hackles were rising.

'We don't know that, Ollie. A discarded roll-up on the edge of the drive. It could have come from anywhere.'

'You were with her last night. Was she smoking these?'

'She always smokes them.'

'Did she say she was going to come here?'

'No. Trust me, I would remember if she had. We got into an argument after she hit you and she refused to get into the car. She ended up walking home to Holt.'

So she didn't have an alibi. Ollie's mind was work overtime. 'So it is possible she could have been here then.'

'I guess, but she would never hurt Lana.'

'You sure about that? She seemed to have quite a lot of pent-up aggression against us Hamiltons last night.'

'I still think you're jumping to conclusions over a cigarette.' Even though Xav continued to defend her, it was half-hearted, and Ollie could see from his face that he knew the cigarette was uncommon. 'She was close to Sebastian, and true, she's not a fan of you or Lana, but she wouldn't try to hurt either of you.'

When Ollie tapped at his broken nose, Xav quickly added, 'Intentionally.'

'We need to rule her out, though. That's what you said about Greg, right? We can't just dismiss her.'

Xav's jaw tightened slightly, but he nodded. 'Fair enough. I'll talk to her.'

'I don't see how that cigarette got here by accident, Xav.'

'She was here the other day, remember, when she brought Lana's car back. Maybe she dropped it then. Or maybe George smokes them.'

He could tell from Xav's expression that he realised he was clutching at straws.

'What's Bree short for out of interest? Bridget? Brianna? Sabrina?'

A muscle in Xav's cheek twitched, the name spoken with reluctance. 'Gabriella.'

Ollie stared at him, aware his look said it all.

'It's not Bree. I know her. Besides, we're looking for a male.'

'Are we?' When Xav's eyes widened, he added, 'We were considering Elise last night. Bree makes far more sense. She's gay, isn't she?'

'Bisexual. And your sister wasn't.'

'Maybe she was,' Ollie said, admitting his earlier thoughts. 'We know she had secrets.'

Xav let out a frustrated huff. 'You're really running with this theory, aren't you?'

'I am. Think about it, Xav. The initial works, she hates the Hamiltons, she has lived around here all her life, so knew Camille. And we can't be certain she went straight home last night. She's also a tough girl. Elise would have struggled to get Lana in the boot of that Mercedes, but Bree would have managed it. Plus she understands cars. She would have known to use the Mercedes. That the emission levels were more dangerous. And now we have the cigarette.'

'And how do you explain the journal? We both know she didn't steal that.'

'Honestly? I have no idea. I'm still trying to piece everything together and make sense of it all. Look, you told me earlier that you still love my sister. If that's true, then you want her to be safe. I'm sorry Bree is your friend, but the facts speak for themselves.'

Xav brooded for a moment, but then he nodded, his tone resigned. 'I can talk to her. Ask her outright.'

'That would just tip her off.'

'So what do you want to do?

'We need to try to get into her flat, snoop around.'

'Are you serious?' He could tell Xav wasn't impressed with the idea at all. 'She's my friend. I'm not breaking into her home on a hunch.'

'It's hardly a hunch.'

'It's not concrete evidence, Ollie. Besides, you can't. She's taken today off, so she'll be at home.'

'What about her workshop?'

Xav's tone was suspicious. 'What about it?'

'Could we get in there?'

'Without her permission?'

'This is for Lana. Okay, maybe it's a long shot, but if Bree did attack her, wouldn't you want to know?'

Ollie's question was met with a moment of silence, before Xav admitted reluctantly, 'I have her spare key.'

'To the flat?'

'No, the workshop. She gave me one for safekeeping after she locked herself out once.'

'Okay, that's good.' Ollie's mind was ticking over as he formulated a plan. 'So you go and see her at home, try to have a snoop around if you can, and I'll go to the workshop.'

'We're not the bloody Hardy Boys, Ollie.'

'Well, do you have a better idea? You can't just confront her. If she is guilty and we tip her off that we're on to her, she'll know to cover her tracks. Look, if we find anything we can go to the police.'

'And if we do it, what about Lana?'

'I guess we should tell her our suspicions.'

'I don't want to leave her alone in this house.'

He had a point. Lana had been attacked twice now. They needed to make sure she was safe.

'My place has a decent alarm system and a deadbolt on the door.'

'Okay. So she can wait for us there.'

Xav fell silent for a moment and Ollie could tell he was still brooding over the details.

'Look, mate. It sucks that Bree is your friend, but she was supposed to be your brother's friend too. If I am right about this, then she has left him to rot in jail for seventeen years. You know what they say about keeping your enemies close. Maybe her intentions aren't quite as honourable as you think.'

Xav's jaw was twitching again, his expression darkening. 'Okay. Let's do this.'

The plan for Derek was simple.

The girl said she was going to seduce him, and she wanted George to record her doing it.

George really wasn't quite sure how seducing someone constituted revenge. Derek was going to enjoy that, having someone who was a million times out of his league flirting with him. And why the hell would George want to film it? He would rather be the one getting seduced.

Not that it would ever happen. He was a vertically challenged fifteen-year-old virgin, with ill-fitting glasses and a face full of pimples. The girl would never look at him in that way.

'Trust me,' she had assured him when he seemed reluctant. 'I have it all under control.'

George went along with her plan, partly out of curiosity, but mostly because he was enjoying being a part of something. He was used to being on the outside looking in and often that was worse, certainly more isolating, than when he was being bullied. The girl had asked for his help. She wanted him on her team. Even if he didn't approve of her plan, at least she was including him. Trusting him too.

At the start, she asked a lot of questions. Things about Derek, the type of girls he had dated, the places he liked to hang out, what kind of music he listened to and if he had any hobbies. It was all mundane stuff that forced George to focus on the person who caused him the most misery and he didn't really understand what the point of it was. Why would she care if Derek liked slutty girls and was obsessed with Nickelback?

He indulged her anyway, then, one Friday night, the girl told him it was time.

She had asked George to meet her in town and when she showed up at their meeting point, he didn't even recognise her. She was dressed completely differently, her skirt shorter and tighter and her cleavage on show. Her hair, which she generally wore tied back, fell loose around her shoulders, and her make-up was much heavier.

'What do you think?' she asked, grinning as she gave him a twirl. 'He's not going to be able to resist me.'

George cleared his throat. 'Wow, you look so different.'

'Just different?'

'In a good way,' he added, flustered, realising he was supposed to have complimented her. 'You look great.'

She was still pretty, but now she was sexy too, looking much older, and jealousy caught in his throat that Derek was going to be the one to enjoy her.

As they walked to the pub where his brother liked to hang out, she set out her seduction plan. When they arrived, George was to wait outside. She had handed him a video camera, showing him how to use it and telling him exactly what she wanted him to do.

'Stay out of sight. When we come out of the bar and head down to the park, I want you to follow us. Whatever happens, don't get too close and make sure you stay hidden. Start recording and no matter what you see happening, don't stop until it's over and I say I'm going to the police. That's your key word to stop filming. Police. Okay?'

He wasn't keen on her plan. It all sounded a bit risky. But what choice did he have?

When they reached the pub, the girl disappeared inside, and as he waited, George went from bored to paranoid to annoyed. Maybe the joke was on him. The girl had said she wanted to help him get revenge, but what if she had been lying? What if she had wanted all of that information about Derek because she fancied him and wanted to get to know him better? It seemed inconceivable to George that girls were actually attracted to his stepbrother. He was so bloody ugly, with his pointy nose, double chin, and eyes that were too close together. It had to be a confidence thing. Derek loved himself and knew how to flirt. He believed he was God's gift and he was good at convincing others he was too.

Or perhaps the girl wasn't interested in him and this was all part of a cruel joke. He could picture his stepbrother and his friends inside the pub laughing with the girl at George's expense. How they had managed to lure him here to sit in a car park all night.

He was bored and miserable and he was getting cold. Plus he needed a wee.

No one was about, so he nipped round the side of the pub, relieving himself in the bushes.

It was as he was buttoning his jeans that he realised just how close he had been to missing them.

He heard the peal of the girl's laughter and the sound of footsteps, and squinting into the darkness he could see she was with Derek and they were on the road, heading away from the pub.

George grabbed the video camera, then followed after them.

He tried to keep his distance as he trailed them down towards the park, not wanting Derek to glance back and spot him. As they reached the entrance, he could hear more laughter and a drunken belch from his stepbrother.

Street lights around the park, plus the almost full moon put him at greater risk of being seen and he kept a close eye on the pair of them as he crept behind the bushes, trying to find a position where he was able to see them but he was fairly certain he couldn't be spotted. They were both on the ground and kissing, and George could see in the silvery light that Derek's hand on the girl's breast.

Ignoring the stab of jealousy, he set the camera to record.

Nothing much happened for a few minutes and George's legs were aching from his crouched position, boredom setting in as again he questioned the point of this exercise.

The girl whispered something in Derek's ear and fresh paranoia crept up his spine, still worrying this could be a set-up.

What would be the worst that could happen if he walked away now?

Do not stop until I tell you to.

The girl's words played in his head. She had been insistent he keep recording regardless of what he witnessed and there was a little trigger warning in George's head that told him he would be wise not to let her down. That she was someone he didn't want to cross.

So he stayed where he was, tried to shuffle into a more comfortable position, and watched.

The girl's scream when it came almost shocked him into dropping the camera.

It was quickly muffled as Derek covered her mouth with his, making her wriggle as his hands pushed up her skirt. Her legs kicked out, her arms flailing, but he took no notice, yanking at her knickers.

'You like that, don't you, you little slut?'

The girl responded by raking her nails down his cheek, making him squeal.

'You fucking bitch. That hurt.' He slapped her across the face, the crack making George wince. 'Is that rough enough for you, you dirty whore?'

This was wrong. He wasn't supposed to hurt her. George had to stop him.

But how? He was no match for Derek.

Should he run and get help?

He lowered the camera, the scene before him sickening his stomach. It was then the girl looked over towards the bushes. Derek had his trousers and pants down now and he was thrusting into her, his white flabby arse caught in the light of the moon. She took no notice, though, her body just a vessel for him to pump his seed into. And although she said nothing, gave no acknowledgement that she had seen him, something in George's brain told him this was part of the plan.

He remembered her words.

Start recording and no matter what you see happening, don't stop.

She wanted this?

It had been her plan all along. She wanted it to look like he was raping her.

This was so extreme. She was fifteen years old. Why would she do this?

She looked away again, her face twisting in anguish and her hands pushing at Derek. 'Stop. Get off me. I said no!'

Although it was uncomfortable to watch, George kept recording.

As his brother eventually climbed off the girl, getting to his feet and yanking his jeans up, she started to sob, and for a moment George again wondered if he had made a mistake. Should he have tried to stop it?

He watched his stepbrother's confused reaction.

'What are you crying for? You got what you wanted.'

The girl was a mess, her skirt still bunched up around her waist and her make-up smeared all over her face. George could see her top had been ripped open at the cleavage.

'You raped me!' she hissed.

'What?' Derek's eyes bulged. 'No I didn't.'

'I told you to stop, but you wouldn't listen.'

'You enjoyed it, you dirty little bitch. Don't pretend you didn't.'

'You... forced me.'

She sounded hysterical now, stumbling around, looking for her ruined knickers.

Derek had his hands on his head, his eyes now filled with panic. 'I thought you liked it rough?'

'You should have stopped. You were hurting me. I'm only fifteen.'

'You're what?' Derek's eye bulged. 'I thought you were older.'

As the girl wiped at her eyes, she glanced towards the bushes. 'No, I'm fifteen. You're a filthy rapist and a danger to women,. Wait until I tell the police what you did.'

That was George's signal to stop. He did as asked, lowering the camera.

'You crazy bitch! You led me on. You said you were seventeen.'

The girl wasn't listening to Derek now, her eyes still on the bushes and when she spoke, it was to address George. 'You can come on out now.'

'What?' Derek sounded confused.

George's heart was pounding as he stepped out of the bushes.

Derek's eyes widened. 'What the fuck are you doing here?' he demanded.

'George had a very important job to do,' the girl said, taking the camera and glancing at the footage to make sure it had recorded okay.

'Why do you have that camera?' Derek sounded really worried now.

'Insurance policy.'

He was silent for a moment, processing her words. 'You set me up.'

The girl winked at George. 'I thought you said he was stupid. Seems like he's catching on pretty quickly to me.'

'You did this?' Derek turned on George, who was quick to take a step back, his anxiety levels going through the roof. He could see the red splotches in his stepbrother's cheeks and knew he was furious. He didn't want a beating.

'Stop right there,' the girl demanded, and although George shrivelled up a little inside, he was grateful when she moved to put herself between him and Derek.

'What do you want from me?'

Derek was eyeing the camera and George was scared he was going to snatch it.

The girl had noticed too. 'If you try to take it, I start screaming rape right now. There are plenty of houses nearby. How do you think it looks if you are caught with that footage on you? I will say you got one of your friends to record what you did to me.'

Her threat made him hesitate. 'And if I don't take it, what then? You said you're going to tell the police.'

'I guess that depends. I want some assurances from you.'

'Assurances for what?' He sounded wary.

'You walk away from here and you never tell anyone what happened tonight. You never hurt George again. You never call him names or make fun of him. You never tamper with his homework, you never let your friends touch him or poke fun at him, and if they do, then you make them stop. Do you understand?'

When Derek remained silent, staring at her, she took that as confirmation to continue.

'If you agree to that, I will never tell anyone what happened here tonight and no one will ever see this video. But if anything happens to George or if he tells me you've called him a name or even looked at him funny, I am going to go public that you raped me and I will make sure that everyone sees what is on this tape.'

'You're a fucking nutjob.' Derek was angry, but George heard the underlying panic in his tone.

The girl smirked. 'Do we have a deal?'

'Why him? Why the hell do you want to help this runt?'

'George and I are friends and I have his back.'

She did? George guessed she had just proven that it was true. And she had come through on her promise, even if her methods were extreme and unorthodox.

It played on his mind after Derek had left the park, his head hung low, either in shame or self-pity. George didn't really care which one. He was just glad his stepbrother had agreed to leave him alone. Though would he really keep up his end of the deal?

'I didn't like watching him hurt you,' he told the girl, as they made their way back to the road. 'We could have found another way to get him.'

The girl shrugged her shoulders, as if it was no big deal what had happened. 'It's just sex, George. And I told him to hit me and to make it rough. The stupid fool had no idea what trouble he was getting himself into.' She glanced over at him. 'See, I promised I would help you.'

She really had. 'Thank you.'

'So, I've helped you. Now I need to start plotting my own revenge.'

George had been so wrapped up in Derek, he had completely forgotten they had a deal. The girl hadn't yet told him who it was that she wanted to get her own back on and his stomach wobbled with nerves.

'I'm not sure what I can do to help. I can't pull off anything like what you just did.'

She must have noted the panic in his voice because she smiled reassuringly. 'Relax and don't worry. I know exactly what I need you to do.' Her eyes met his and she held his gaze as she spoke. 'I picked you to be my partner for a reason, George.'

39

Insisting he couldn't take Elise home with him, George had paid for her to stay in a guesthouse in Cromer for the rest of the night, promising he would come up with a plan.

Elise had been unimpressed with the basic and dated room she had found herself in, not buying his excuse that it had been difficult to find somewhere open that late at night Surely, he could have found her space in a proper hotel.

She was still seething about everything that had happened and held George solely responsible for her problems with the police. She repeatedly stressed that in the messages she kept sending him after he refused to answer her calls.

He needed to fix things. And fast.

She had lost everything and now had nothing to risk. It made her dangerous and she was quick to point that out to George when he finally called her later in the morning, telling him that he owed her and she intended to collect.

'Don't push me too far. You know how easy it would be for me to go to the police.'

It was a bluff, but he didn't know that. The Hamilton house had been her meal ticket and now it was gone. George wouldn't be able to compensate her if he was behind bars.

'There's no need for that,' he assured her, but she heard the hint of panic in his voice and knew she had him worried. Good.

'So what is your plan? You told me you would come up with one.'

'Don't worry. I have.'

'Well? Don't keep me in suspense. I refuse to spend another minute in this shithole and I want out of here now.'

'Give me half an hour and I'll pick up you. I'll explain on the way.'

'Way to where?'

George didn't elaborate. 'Half an hour. I'll meet you outside.'

When the line went dead, Elise threw her phone on the bed. She didn't appreciate being kept in the dark and wanted to know exactly what he was planning on doing to get her out of this mess.

Keen not to spend a moment longer than necessary in the guesthouse, Elise checked herself out and went to wait outside for George. Luckily, he didn't keep her waiting, arriving a couple of minutes before the agreed meet time.

He didn't get out of his van, though, the engine running as he beckoned her to get in, and Elise scowled at him, placing her hands on her hips. Was he seriously expecting her to load the suitcase herself?

'Come on, for Christ's sake. Just throw it in the back.'

'It's heavy!'

When she stubbornly refused to budge, he rolled his eyes at her and turned off the engine.

'You could do with learning some manners,' she grumbled at him as he climbed down from the van.

Ignoring her, he pulled open the side door, grabbing her case, and slung it inside.

'Be careful, dammit. All of my stuff is in there.'

George slammed the door shut and went back round to the driver's door. 'Get in the van, Elise. Now!'

Still muttering away under her breath, she did as told.

'So where the hell are we going?' she demanded, fastening her seatbelt as he pulled away from the kerb.

He didn't answer initially and she turned to look at him, could see he was working his jaw, either out of irritation or anxiety. It did nothing to help relax her.

'George? Where are we going?'

'To see a friend.'

'What friend?'

'Someone who is going to help fix this.'

That all sounded rather vague. Elise was going to need more information.

'Who is this friend and how do they plan to fix it? I want specifics.'

When George didn't answer, intently focusing on the road ahead, she decided to threaten him again. So far, using the leverage she had seemed to be the only way to get results.

'Can you please drop me off at the nearest police station? I'm going to hand myself in and confess to everything, including what you made me do.'

'You don't need to do that. The situation is in hand.'

'In hand how?'

'Fucking hell, Elise. Will you please just shut up?' His raised tone had her eyes widening in shock. George wasn't a yeller. Even when he had blackmailed her, he had done it in such a calm and laidback manner, it had been difficult to fully absorb his threats. 'You're a real piece of work. How the hell Ollie Hamilton managed to put up with you I have no idea.'

'How fucking dare you?'

'I said, SHUT UP! I was talking and I hadn't finished. We're going to see a friend who is going to help. That is all you need to know. Now you're not going to call or go to the police. You are caught up in something far bigger than you realise and if you turn me in, I promise I will find a way to take you down with me. So lay off the threats and the haughty attitude, and just concentrate on keeping that big whiny mouth of yours shut.'

He gave her such a vicious look, it actually made her want to cower.

As he turned his attention back to the road, Elise's mouth flapped open and shut, completely unsure how to react to his outburst. This was new territory for her and she wasn't used to being spoken to this way.

Sensing that George was a timebomb ready to explode and it was wisest not to call his bluff, she sank down in her seat, still smarting from his words.

They drove for a few miles, then George pulled off the main carriageway and onto a narrow side road. After half a mile, he indicated, turning into a secluded car park backing onto woodland. There was only one other vehicle present and as he drew the van to a halt beside it, Elise, for the first time, shivered with unease.

She had been so desperate to get out of the guesthouse and have George fix things, she hadn't really considered how safe this situation was.

'Why have we stopped here?' she asked, but with none of the belligerence of her earlier tone. Even to her own ears, she sounded nervous.

'I already told you; we're meeting someone.'

As George spoke, the door of the other car opened.

Elise realised she knew the driver who got out and her stomach knotted further.

Just what the hell was going on?

40

Lana wasn't quite sure what she thought yet of this new alliance between Ollie and Xav. On the one hand, she was relieved that they appeared to have buried their hatchet, but it seemed they now had a common goal to wrap her up in cotton wool.

She understood their concerns, she really did. First the hit-and-run and then what had happened last night. It had them scared and understandably so. She didn't consider herself to be a stupid woman and she knew the threats against her were real. She was fearful herself and intended to take precautions. Until the police made an arrest or until she returned home, whichever happened first, she would be doing her very best not to place herself in any vulnerable situations.

Unlike Ollie, who appeared to have become a private investigator overnight.

His idea about snooping around Bree McCarthy's workshop was stupid and dangerous. For starters, even though he had Xav's key, surely it would still be classed as breaking in, which she couldn't seem to get through his thick head was a crime, and if he was right and Bree had been responsible for the things that had happened to

Lana, possibly even for Camille's murder, what was to stop her trying to hurt Ollie if she realised he was on to her?

'You're the one we need to worry about,' he told her now, dismissing her concerns. 'I can take care of myself.'

That was her brother, full of ridiculous bravado.

'Like Bree took care of you last night?' she muttered sarcastically.

Her comment had him scowling as he reached to his nose, fingers smoothing over the plaster. 'That was different. Besides, she won't be there. Xav is going to preoccupy her.'

He looked to Xav now, who gave an apologetic smile to Lana.

'I can't believe he has you caught up in this stupid idea too,' she grumbled.

They had already told her they didn't want her staying at Mead House alone, having apparently already decided that she could wait for them at Xav's. Lana didn't appreciate them making decisions about what was best for her behind her back. It would only be for a couple of hours though, so she didn't complain too much. She had been attacked once in the house, and while she reasoned she would be okay if all the doors and windows were locked, perhaps she would be safer at Xav's.

He had already called Bree, asking if he could stop by to clear the air, and offering to pick up her favourite takeout on the way.

Never one to hold on to a grudge, Xav told Lana, Bree had been sheepish, welcoming his call and apologising for her part, which in turn had him feeling guilty about duping her.

'Neither of you have to go through with this,' Lana reminded him now, as the two of them drove over to his house. 'I've already told you I think it's a bad idea, but that's Ollie all over. He never thinks through the consequences.'

'He's just looking out for you.'

He was, and she did appreciate it. 'I get that, but he needs to go to the police. Let them speak to Bree. If the evidence is there, they can arrest her, and if it isn't, then you don't have to feel guilty about betraying your friend.'

Xav gave her a quick smile but was resolute in following Ollie's plan. 'Let him do this, okay? If he doesn't find anything, I promise I will make him go to the police.'

Xav and Ollie. They had been each other's shadow when they were kids. Ollie and Lana were the twins, but sometimes she had felt second fiddle to his friendship with Xav. Then, of course, things had changed. In that last year before Camille's death, it had been Lana attracting more of Xav's attention, and at times she had wondered if Ollie was a little jealous.

Now the three of them were together again and settling into their old roles. She had her brother back, truly back, for the first time in what seemed like forever, and she didn't want to lose that. As for what was happening between her and Xav, they hadn't discussed what the future held for them or even if it could work. For now, Lana was taking things a day at a time.

When Xav pulled up outside his house, her stomach began churning with nerves, and as she followed him inside, the newness of what was happening between them hit home. They had reconnected crazily fast and now he was putting himself into a potentially dangerous situation to help her. Okay, Ollie was taking the biggest risk, but if Bree was responsible for the attempts on Lana's life and she figured out that Xav had betrayed her, how would she react? He had always been a crappy liar. What if he slipped up?

She stressed over it while he fussed over his fat tabby cat, who had charged down the stairs to greet them. For food, not affection, Xav was quick to point out, filling up his dish. Hector was governed by his belly.

After he had fed the cat, he showed her the alarm system and where the cameras were, then said to make herself at home, but to stay out of his studio.

He had his serious face on when he told her that and had Lana not been so worried, she might have laughed.

'What's going on in there?' he questioned, tugging her round to face him and tapping a finger against her forehead. She had been quiet as she followed him round the house, but it was her lack of enthusiasm when he showed her how to work his fancy entertainment system that finally had him twigging that something was wrong.

'I'm scared, Xav.'

His expression immediately softened and he pulled her into his arms, soothingly rubbing her back. 'I promise you that you'll be safe here. And it's only for an hour or so.'

Lana pushed him away. 'No, you stupid idiot. I'm not scared for me. Trust me, I know I'm safe here. This place has more locks, alarms and cameras than Buckingham Palace. Makes me wonder who you're scared might try to break in.' She managed a grin and watched him pout a little in indignance.

'Nothing wrong with having a decent security system,' he huffed.

'Says the man who leaves his front door unlocked while he's upstairs painting,' Lana pointed out, remembering how he had let her wander in unannounced.

'That's different,' he argued. 'I was at home.' He studied her face. 'So if you feel safe here, then why are you scared?'

'Because I don't like this hare-brained plan of Ollie's. I don't want anything to happen to him... or to you. I've only just got you back.'

Green eyes locked on hers, finally understanding. 'Nothing is going to happen. I promise you. Ollie will be fine because Bree will be with me, and I don't have to do anything other than eat lunch. You're overthinking this.'

'Am I? If Ollie is right, she's dangerous, Xav. If she figures out you know—'

His burst of laughter was unexpected and a little annoying. 'What do you think she's going to do? Stab me with her fork?'

Lana shoved at his shoulder. 'Sorry for being concerned.'

'Don't be. I think it's very sweet that you are,' Xav told her, catching hold of her hand and bringing it to his mouth, sending a storm of butterflies fluttering inside her belly as he locked eyes with her again, watching her reaction carefully as he slowly grazed his mouth across her knuckles.

Her annoyance melted away, but she still made a final dig. 'We both know you don't have the best track record against girls.' She smiled slyly, pulling her hand free and reaching out to trace her finger along the crook of his nose.

Xav grinned and pulled her in close, kissing her. 'Well, hopefully Bree won't have a rounders bat hiding under the table.'

He was joking around, perhaps hoping to ease Lana's tension, but it soared again as he got in his car, ready to go for his lunch date.

'Lock the door,' he reminded her, as he wound the window down. 'And remember I just fed the cat. Don't let him guilt you into giving him anything else.'

She watched him leave, then went back inside the house, twisting the key and pulling the bolt across as instructed.

Hector had settled himself down on the arm of one of the sofas and was watching her with lazy interest.

'Guess you're stuck with me until he gets back,' she told him, wandering over to scratch behind his ears.

The cat tolerated it for maybe twenty seconds before deciding that was enough interaction, jumping down and sauntering back up the stairs. Lana watched him go, already bored and restless. Deciding to make a coffee, more for something to do than actually wanting the drink, she wandered into Xav's spotless kitchen, hunting through cupboards for mugs, then figuring out how his fancy coffee machine worked. While she waited for the water to heat, she looked out of the window at the view.

He really had picked a stunning location, the surrounding trees in the garden parting to reveal open fields that stretched right down to the main village and the coastline.

A flicker of something closer to the house caught her attention and she double blinked, certain it had been a figure moving between the trees.

Was it her imagination playing tricks? The house was in a remote spot with no nearby properties. There was no need for anyone to be out here.

Tension rippled through her, even as she told herself she was overreacting, and she drew in a deep breath, instructing herself to relax. It was a moment of paranoia, being here alone in an unfamiliar place, that was all.

The sound of a car engine starting had her head whipping round.

Lana stared at the locked door. No one had knocked, so who was there?

She rushed back into the living room and to the nearest front window, parting the blind just in time to see the split-second flash of the back of a car before it fully disappeared behind the hedgerow.

A black car, she thought, or maybe dark grey, though it had been so instant, she couldn't be sure.

Who had stopped at the house and what had they wanted? Why had they sped off like that?

She moved to another window which gave her a better view of

the front porch, just in case it had been a delivery driver who hadn't bothered to knock, but there was nothing on the front step.

Maybe she should message Xav.

No. He was with Bree and she didn't want to mess anything up there.

Okay, so it was a little odd what had just happened, but it didn't mean anything sinister was going on, and whoever it was had gone. No harm had been done.

Still, as she went back to finish making her drink, then settled down on one of the sofas with her Kindle, she couldn't shake the ominous feeling that something wasn't quite right.

41

Adrenaline buzzed through Ollie as he parked across the road from Bree's workshop, waiting for Xav's message to confirm he had arrived at her flat.

Their plan was fool-proof and Lana was safe. As Ollie had repeatedly reassured her, nothing was going to go wrong.

His phone pinged and he read Xav's text.

Now going in.

He sent a thumbs up emoji back, slipping his phone into his pocket and fishing out the key Xav had given him.

'Let's do this,' he muttered to himself, crossing the road to her workshop, glancing around the street, just to be certain there was no one about. It shouldn't look suspicious, unlocking the door and going inside, but even so, he would rather he wasn't seen.

The coast remained clear and he stepped into the dark room, fumbling for the light and closing the door shut behind him, before looking for the alarm that had started to beep. He had memorised the code Xav had told him and quickly punched it in, disabling the system.

He glanced around the room, a neat, but unfussy space with a desk and filing cabinet.

Adjusting the window blind so no one could see inside, he moved to sit down in her chair as he started to go through her stuff. There was nothing much of interest on the desk itself. A phone, card reader and a pot of pens, plus one filing tray that looked to contain invoices. Ollie flicked through them, but no names stood out and nothing looked suspicious.

He tried the two drawers, pleased to find them unlocked, but they only contained keys and packet of antibacterial wipes.

Swinging round in the chair, he looked at the filing cabinet. Would there be anything of interest in there?

As he rooted through the drawers, it occurred to him that while he had come here with a plan to search the place, he wasn't actually sure what it was he was looking for.

Anything suspicious. That was what he had repeatedly told Xav and Lana, but now he was actually here, he realised just how vague that was.

The cabinet was crammed full of more paperwork. Utility and rental bills for the property and more invoices, from what he could see. Leafing through half of the top drawer was taking forever and Ollie, who didn't have the greatest attention span, was growing bored.

After a while, he decided he would move on, certain he wasn't missing anything.

An internal door at the back of the room led into a narrow corridor with two further doors. One was the bathroom, a tiny, but practical space that smelt of bleach and pinecones, the other led into a garage area, which was where Bree worked on her clients' vehicles.

There were a couple of cars in various states of repair, and the only shelves and units in there were used to house the day-to-day tools she needed.

There were two garage doors: one that led out front, the other to the back of the property and that was the one Ollie went to try, irritated when he found it locked. He glanced around the room again, saw keys hanging on wall hooks and went through them, trying each of them until he found the one that worked.

Pushing open the garage door took him outside into a decent-sized area under a canopy roof and surrounded by a high fence. There were half a dozen cars out here, all looked in good condition and some of them had price tags on the windscreens. They were mostly smaller hatchbacks, but a retro Fiesta and a dark SUV made up the numbers. Ollie hadn't realised that Bree sold cars too, though he was sure he recalled Xav saying that she tended to buy in vehicles on the cheap, usually ones which had been written off in accidents or their owners had given up on. He had assumed they were just personal projects, but guessed it made sense for her to make money on them.

His gaze moved to the large bin behind the cars. It was probably just loaded with rubbish, but while he was here, he should probably check it out.

As he passed between the cars, he noticed the SUV that was parked nearest to the bin. Unlike the other cars which were polished to a showroom standard, the wheels of this one looked grubby and there were a couple of marks on the edge of the bonnet. The side trim was coming away too. Moving between the cars, Ollie took hold of the end to push it back in place and out of his way, wiping at the rust that came off on his fingers as he let go. The rust surprised him. Unless it was something else. Crouching down for a closer look, he frowned.

Yeah, the wheels definitely needed a clean. Was that sand stuck in the tread? And what was the spatter along the edge of the silver trim? His mind started to work overtime.

The SUV was black. Lana had been hit by a dark car.

Was it possible that this was the vehicle, and if so, was it her blood on the trim?

Pulling out his phone, he took pictures, then he messaged Xav.

42

Trudy decided to close up shop early and work at home through the afternoon. She had been doing shorter hours most weekdays since her father's stroke, wanting to keep a close eye on him as he recovered, but Saturdays she generally stayed open longer, knowing it was a good day for trade. Today, though, she wasn't in the mood for customers.

Although Ollie Hamilton's misdirected hit hadn't done much damage, her face was sore and she was feeling sorry for herself. Xav's admission that he still had feelings for Lana had been unwelcome news and although he had been kind to Trudy last night, bringing her home and making sure she was okay, it had played on her mind for much of the night.

After making her father some lunch, which he pushed away, she tried to focus on paperwork. Leaving him sitting in the living room with the TV on, she made a cup of tea and took it through to the small third bedroom that she used as her office, settling down to work through invoices, in desperate need of the distraction.

She had only been in there a few minutes when the volume of the TV increased, loud enough that she could hear every word being spoken by the actors of whatever show her father was watching. Trying her best to ignore it, she sipped at her drink and concentrated on the numbers before her. Her head was already throbbing with the beginning of one of her tension migraines and she really wasn't in the right mindset for one of her father's games. If he thought it wasn't bothering her, then maybe he would stop.

Unfortunately it had the opposite effect and Trudy's shoulders slumped as the volume went higher.

Her temper snapping, she got up, storming through into the living room and snatching the remote control from his hand. As she turned the sound down, he grinned up at her.

'Sorry. Was I disturbing you?'

'You know you were.'

Instead of giving the remote control back, she placed it on top of the bookcase, earning herself a furious look.

'Give that back.'

'If you can't be trusted with it, you can't have it.'

'This is abuse. I am not a child!'

'Then stop behaving like one.' Trudy snapped out the words, turning on her heel and trying to block out the bitter complaints that followed her as she went back to her office.

Moments later, she heard the sound of her father's wheelchair on the wooden floors and gritted her teeth as he appeared in the doorway.

'What do you want, Dad?'

'You keep me trapped here like a bloody prisoner in this house.'

'You're not a prisoner,' Trudy pointed out wearily. 'I'm trying to look after you. You know I didn't put you in that chair.'

'No? You might as well have done. It's your fault your mother was a mess that night. She should never have been behind the wheel. She wasn't thinking straight.'

It wasn't the first time her father had made that accusation, but it didn't hurt any less.

'Don't say that. You know how much I miss her.'

Ignoring her, her father warmed to his theme. 'It was like giving her a loaded gun. She's dead and you were responsible. Just as you're responsible for me being in this chair.'

'Stop it!'

Her father's face twisted, his smile cruel and familiar, pulling her back to childhood, when she had been too small, too weak, to defend herself against his constant bullying. 'The truth hurts, doesn't it, darling daughter.' The last two words were spat with scathing sarcasm.

'It's not true. You were responsible. It was all *your* fault.'

To the outside world, Angus Palmer had been a friend and a doctor. Somehow he had been able to slip on a mask that made him seem kind and approachable, presenting himself as a quiet man with family values. How that world would laugh if they knew the truth about him. That behind closed doors he was constantly belittling Trudy and her mum, making them both feel unworthy of his love. That he preached a set of morals that he didn't follow himself. And that it only took the slightest provocation to make him use his fists, or often in Trudy's case, his belt.

You were talking at the dinner table. *Thwack!*

Your homework wasn't finished on time. *Thwack!*

Your clothes are dirty. *Thwack!*

For so long, she had feared him, but then she had learnt the truth about who he really was and it had changed everything. That was when Trudy had stopped being afraid and had started resisting. Now he was in the chair, her mother was dead, and she held all of the power.

Still, there were moments where she doubted herself, succumbing to weakness and, being her father, he knew how to manipulate them, how to spread his poison through the cracks, just as he was doing now.

'You might do your hair all fancy and put on your posh clothes, but don't forget, I know the truth about you and who you really are. I heard you last night, all simpering and flirting. Do you seriously believe that a man like Xavier Landry would be interested in someone like you?'

'Shut up!' She screamed the words, backhanding him hard across the face, the stone in the ring she wore that had once belonged to her mother, drawing blood.

Her father's eyes flashed in temper, but other than that he didn't react to the slap, as he continued to goad her.

'You're not pretty or classy like one of the Hamiltons. You're just a pathetic little girl trying to pretend you're something you're not.'

'I said, SHUT UP!' Trudy struck him again. This time harder.

'And all the slaps in the world won't hide how ugly you really are, because it's not just on the surface.' He leered at her, blood dripping from his lip. 'That ugliness runs deep.'

Trudy wasn't even aware that her fingers had closed around the pyramid crystal paperweight on her desk, even though it cooled her hot palm as she squeezed it tightly. Her father was ranting now, his words becoming a whir in her pounding head.

Bitch.

Repulsive.

Laughable.

Diseased.

The paperweight was raised, its point about to swing down into her father's skull when she realised what she was doing and her eyes widened in horror, a whimper escaping her lips.

Her father watched her, his smile widening and his eyes taunting. 'Go on, do it,' he goaded. 'Let's see if you have the balls to kill your own father.'

'Daddy, I'm sorry.'

The words came out as a whisper as her arm dropped to her side, fingers opening and letting the heavy paperweight drop to the floor. What had she almost just done? And she had hit him, made him bleed.

'I'm sorry,' she repeated. 'I didn't mean to.'

He was laughing at her now. 'You weak and useless girl. You can't even put me out of my misery.'

Trudy pushed past him, fleeing down the hallway and into her bedroom, slamming the door shut. She sucked in a deep breath and shoved her hands back in her hair as she tried to grasp the magnitude of what had just happened.

She had been about to kill her own father.

He had pushed and pushed at her, and she had snapped, almost losing control.

That scared the crap out of her.

She needed to pull herself together and fast. If anyone ever found out how close she had come to hitting him with the paperweight, they would take him away from her. Whatever happened, regardless of the awful things he had done and how badly she hated him, she could never allow that to happen.

43

'Is everything okay?'

When Xav glanced up, he saw Bree was studying him and he couldn't decide if it was with sympathy or suspicion.

He had never been a big texter and was certainly not someone who constantly looked at his phone when he had company, but today was different as he needed to keep in contact with Ollie. The messages he had received about the car in the workshop with what appeared to be blood spatter on the broken side trim were enough to distract him and he was now struggling to focus on his conversation with Bree.

'What? Yeah, of course. I'm fine.' He made an effort to put his phone down and forced a smile for her.

She had always been there for him and Seb, their mum too. Had it really all just been an act?

He thought back to when he had first returned to town and how she had been quick to seek him out, reminding him that she was there as a friend if he needed anything.

Separately, everything up to this point had felt like a grasp in the dark, but the photo Ollie had sent Xav of the SUV was more difficult to explain away. While he couldn't say for sure it had been the car that struck Lana, it was certainly similar.

Did Bree really hate Lana Hamilton that much that she wanted her dead?

And what about Camille? Was Bree the mysterious G that Camille had written about in her journal?

Until Ollie had suggested it, they had only been looking at men. Stupid really, as it was entirely plausible G could be a woman. But realising that it could possibly be Gabriella McCarthy, his closest friend...

It cut deep.

He felt a sense of loyalty to Bree. She had been there for him time and again. But if she had hurt Lana, it changed everything.

She was still studying him curiously as he struggled to rationalise that she might be responsible. 'You're acting a little weird, Xav. Are things definitely cool with us?'

He met her gaze. Honey-brown irises framed with thick, dark lashes that were staring right into him.

Jesus. Pull it together, you idiot.

He had brought fish and chips with him, and the birthday Scotch which Bree had failed to take after the brawl at the pub and had believed he was doing a pretty good job of acting normal, but maybe not.

His thoughts drifted to Lana waiting for him at home. She had been reluctant for him to come here because she knew what a shitty liar he was. Determined to prove her wrong, he tried to relax.

Lana and Ollie were counting on him, and Seb was too. The idea that his brother might be proven innocent after all this time had lit a glimmer of hope within Xav, though he was scared to get too excited.

'Sorry, yes. Things are cool with us. I was just checking in with Lana. I wanted to make sure she is okay... after last night.'

He left that to hang and held Bree's gaze, wanting to see her reaction. Other than her eyes narrowing slightly, there was no tell-tale giveaway.

'Last night?'

'She was attacked.'

'She was?'

Xav nodded.

If Bree knew about what had happened, she wasn't saying. She didn't seem surprised either and his spider sense started working overtime.

There was a lengthy pause before she asked, 'So what happened?'

He told her, sticking to the facts and working to keep any emotion out of his tone.

'Oh my God. Is she okay?'

She sounded genuine, but Xav wasn't sure he believed her.

'She's fine. Now. I know you're not a fan, but—'

'That doesn't mean I want to see her hurt, Xav.'

Really? He wasn't quite so sure.

'Did it take you long to walk home last night?' he asked, abruptly changing subject. 'I came back looking for you after I dropped Trudy off.'

It wasn't completely a lie. He had taken a longer way home, but he hadn't fully retraced the route he knew Bree would take.

She shrugged. 'Not long. I was glad to get home, though. How is Trudy?'

Another swift change of subject. Xav knew Bree wasn't going to admit to any wrongdoing, so he wasn't sure why it annoyed him so much.

He continued the charade of good friends, but Ollie's last message had changed everything and Xav found himself questioning every word coming out of Bree's mouth.

The moment he got confirmation from Ollie that he had left the workshop, he made his excuses that he needed to go.

After a stiff hug goodbye and a vague plan to catch up later, he was in his car and heading home, some of the tension lifting, though he knew worse was still to come.

He had agreed he would pick up Lana and they would meet Ollie back at Mead House. Decisions were then going to have to be made. Did they have enough to involve the police? How would they react to Ollie breaking and entering? How would Bree react when she learnt what had happened and knew Xav had betrayed her?

Those questions weighed heavily as he pulled into his driveway.

'Lana?' He called for her as soon as he walked through the door, his gaze skimming over the kitchen and living room and not seeing her anywhere.

When she didn't immediately respond, the tension returned and he called out again, pushing the door shut and crossing the room.

The only closed-off space was the cloakroom, but he could see that the door was open.

Was she upstairs or had something happened? He had promised her she would be safe here and she should be. Still, his heart was thumping as he took the stairs two at a time. He glanced briefly into his bedroom, then looked to his studio. The one room he had asked her to stay out of.

There she stood, looking at the canvas he was working on. Her own face staring back.

Relieved that she was safe, but irritated she had ignored his instruction, and more than a little self-conscious she was viewing a piece of work that wasn't yet finished – that he had never planned to show to her or anyone else – his temper snapped. 'What the hell are you doing in here?

Lana glanced over at him, but she didn't react to his anger. Her eyes were shining. 'This is me?'

'I told you to stay out of my studio.'

'Blame your cat. He was coughing up a furball, so I came up to check on him. He's fine, by the way.'

Xav glanced at Hector, who was snoozing contentedly on one of the sofas.

'You should have respected my wishes,' he grumbled, though his annoyance was already waning. He still sulked a little as Lana came over to him, linking her arms around his neck, refusing to return her hug.

She tilted her head to look up at him. 'You're painting me.' When he didn't react, her smile widened, her dark eyes locking onto his. 'And I love it. I love that you're all embarrassed about it too and—'

'I'm not embarrassed.'

'Yes, you are. And you're doing that pouty face you do, where you're trying to look annoyed. I had forgotten all about that.'

'I am annoyed,' he pointed out, even though it was no longer really true.

He had missed this, having Lana teasing him out of a bad mood. It was impossible to stay mad at her, and when her lips pressed against his, her body melting against him, he surrendered completely, pulling her into him as he kissed her deeply.

For a few moments, he was so caught up in her, he completely forgot the importance of what Ollie had found in Bree's workshop. Not being able to find Lana, then realising she had discovered his painting had distracted him and he needed to get his focus back. He reluctantly broke the kiss, easing out of her embrace.

'We need to talk. About Ollie and Bree,' he quickly added when she looked worried.

He could tell the painting had distracted her too, because he immediately had her attention.

'Did he find something? How was your lunch? Did she do it?'

She had a lot of questions, but they had to go meet Ollie. Xav caught hold of her hand, pulling her out of the room. 'Potentially. It was okay. And yes, it's looking likely. Come on. I'll update you in the car.'

* * *

It wasn't until they were almost back at Mead House that Lana remembered the car she had seen while she was at Xav's. The painting had shocked her so completely she had zoned out of everything, simply staring in wonderment for several minutes. She hadn't even registered when Xav had returned home, calling out to her. How long had he been working on this painting? Certainly days, maybe a week or longer.

No wonder he had tried to ban her from going into his studio. Had he ever planned to show her?

It was a question she had to put on hold, because he had reminded her there were more important things to deal with. She had known Bree was a potential suspect, but even so, it still shocked her when Xav explained what Ollie had found. Had the woman really been the one to run her off the road, and to knock her unconscious in the garage?

She fell quiet as she processed everything, felt the warm comforting weight of Xav's hand as he caught hold of hers.

'Are you okay?'

'Yeah. It's just a lot to take in. She really must hate me.'

'Or maybe you are in the way.'

Lana tried for irony. 'That's comforting.'

If Bree was G and she knew Lana had found the journal, then it made sense Lana was a threat. It didn't explain how Bree had managed to steal it from the house, though.

'We're on to her, Lana.' Xav squeezed her hand. 'We'll tell the police everything we know and leave it with them. You won't need to worry about her any more.'

He was right, but his comment had her thinking back to when he had left to meet Bree for lunch and the driver who had stopped by the house.

'What if it isn't her? Or if she had help.'

'What do you mean?'

'I think someone was snooping around outside the house while you were gone.'

It was a good job they were on a traffic-free lane, as Xav abruptly pulled to a halt in the middle of the road, turning to face Lana.

'Why are you only telling me this now?'

'Because I forgot. I was distracted with the painting and then you and your news.' Xav looked annoyed again, but it was with his stern and pissed-off face, and she knew better than to tease him this time. 'It might have been nothing,' she added, trying now to backtrack.

'Define snooping, Lana.'

Trying to downplay the incident, she told him what had happened: that she thought she had seen someone outside the kitchen window, then the car pulling away moments later.

'As I say, it was probably nothing.'

She could tell from his frown and the way he was grinding his jaw that he disagreed. 'Is there anything else you need to tell me?'

'Nope, that's it.'

When he didn't say anything in response, instead restarting the car, she tried again to smooth things over.

'Look, the car points to Bree and so does the cigarette. What happened earlier was probably just my imagination running wild. It's likely unconnected.'

'Let's hope so.'

Xav didn't sound convinced and Lana was regretting saying anything. Of course it was Bree. And why would she have had help?

As soon as they arrived at Mead House, she would persuade Ollie to call the police. The sooner Bree McCarthy was arrested, the easier they would all feel.

Hopefully they would find the journal and finally get some answers.

A few weeks had passed since George had videoed Derek and while he had been wary about whether the plan would work, his step-brother had left him alone. No pranks, no intimidation, and, if anything, going to pains to stay out of George's way.

The video had Derek worried and George noticed at the dinner table – one of the few places they couldn't avoid each other – that there were lines of stress and anger on his face that hadn't been there before. He was unusually subdued, shellshocked even, and he had barely looked at or spoken to George since.

George was actually a little ashamed at the relief that brought.

The girl had held up her end of the deal, but now he was worrying about what she wanted from him. She had told him she had picked him for a reason and knowing that had him both nervous and curious, as he really couldn't imagine how he would be of help to anyone.

When he received a note from her saying she wanted to meet and it was time to discuss part two, his belly had churned. He wasn't going to be capable of carrying out a revenge on the same scale as she had. How could he possibly help her?

The following day, he learnt her plan and finally understood

George's uncle was the gardener at Mead House and the girl knew George sometimes helped him. She wanted him to be her eyes and ears and she needed him to get the key to the summer house.

The person she wanted to get revenge on was Camille Hamilton.

45

Elise Gladstone was turning into a first-class pain in the arse and George was keen to sever ties with her.

He had needed her at first and, to her credit, she had come through for him, but now the police were involved and Ollie had kicked her out of Mead House, she had outlived her purpose.

Knowing he couldn't take her home and that he couldn't afford to keep paying for accommodation, he had reluctantly reached out to an old friend for help, conscious that he needed to buy some time while he figured out a solution.

Elise was spouting her mouth off with threats that he knew she would go through with if he refused to help her. She was also extremely unhappy with her new living arrangements, grumbling about the basic facilities, but there was very little he could do about that. She needed to stay hidden until he could figure a way out of the mess for both of them.

He glanced at the McDonald's bag on the seat beside him, certain that it was going to be one more thing to annoy her. She was already screwing up his plans for his Saturday off work and needs must. She had to eat and takeout was the easiest option.

Pulling off the main road, he followed the winding lane down to the secluded cottage. Once a much-loved holiday home, these days it was seldom used. It was the perfect place for her to stay out of the way.

The cottage had been in his friend's family for years, but as it now stood empty, it no longer had running water or electricity. Elise hadn't liked that one bit, especially when George had directed her to the stream out back where she could bathe.

He had tried to make the place as comfortable as he could for her, preparing the bed with clean linen and bringing her books and magazines, but there was only so much he could do. He had left her alone while he went to get the food and hoped she would be in a better mood now he was back.

Letting himself into the cottage, he was pleased to be met with silence. That was a good sign.

He placed the McDonald's bag on the table and went to find her.

Noise came from the bedroom, and as the door was open, he walked straight in, his mouth dropping open as he stared at the two women.

One lying dead on a sheet of plastic, blood oozing from a wound in her head, the other calmly wiping bloody spatter from her face, as if she were simply removing her makeup.

'What have you done? This was not part of the plan! Why do you always have to turn into a fucking psycho?'

George knelt over the body, checking for a pulse, but already he knew it was too late.

'I don't want us to be partners any more, George. I don't trust you.'

He hadn't realised she was standing so close behind him and as he started to turn, he caught a glimpse of metal. He put his hand up to shield the blow, but wasn't quite quick enough, and his last

thought before the blackness pulled him under was that he had
made a terrible mistake.

46

George was becoming a liability.

He had one job. Get the journal. And he screwed up badly.

Now I need to clean up the mess he has created and take care of any loose ends. That includes him.

Tonight, though, is about the Hamiltons and that is a clean-up job I am relishing, as it is personal, as well as necessary. At least where Lana is concerned.

Lana Hamilton has too many lives and should, by all accounts, already be dead.

I wasn't thinking straight that night I ploughed the car into her. I had followed her to the beach intending only to watch. It had been a split-second decision. She was lucky to walk away from that, and she certainly shouldn't have survived what I did to her last night. She won't escape me again.

Xavier Landry has been the common denominator. If he hadn't looked in his rear-view mirror that evening at the beach, and if he hadn't shown up last night, Lana would be dead and all of my problems would be solved. How ironic that Xav has been the flaw in my plan.

And now he appears to be back on good terms with both Lana and her odious brother, Ollie. All three of them are poking their noses in, questioning who was behind the attacks and, more worryingly, connecting the dots back to Camille Hamilton.

Thank fuck Camille only used an initial, or it would be game over.

Still, I don't like how high the stakes are and while I have read through the journal and know I am safe for now, it throws up too many questions and casts doubt on Sebastian Landry's guilt. The journal is in my possession now, but Lana has read it cover to cover. She has raised too many questions and there is only one way to guarantee her silence.

It was by chance I followed Sebastian the day of Camille's death. Along with many others, I had witnessed the fight between the pair of them, revelling in destroying their so-called picture-perfect little romance. All it had taken was an anonymous letter posted to Sebastian suggesting they weren't exclusive. It must have arrived that morning. It seemed Sebastian had been having doubts already, because their showdown was crass and dramatic, and so satisfying as they screamed at each other, Camille bursting into tears, then tearing the pendant from around her neck, the one Sebastian had given her, and hurling it at him. The timing was perfect.

She had stormed off after that, leaving the poor boy stunned and forlorn as he scooped the necklace up, sticking it in his pocket. How fortuitous that I happened to see him down on the beach later. He was standing by the water, staring at the necklace and looking terribly cut up about the fight. I watched him throw it into the sea, before wandering off, his shoulders slumped. As the tide spat it back out, I knew that I had to have it. A trophy for my meddling. It was the least I deserved.

I only took it for that reason, not realising the significance that the pendant would play until later that evening, that it would go on to destroy two lives, while setting me on a new path.

I am a firm believer in fate and know that everything happens for a reason. Sometimes, though, fate needs a helping hand.

The Hamiltons have been the pillars of this town for too many years, but now only two of them remain. After tonight, there will be none.

47

Lana couldn't settle; aware now the matter of Bree was in the hands of the police, there was nothing they could do but wait. It didn't help that the officer they had spoken to had given little away as to what action would be taken, only advising it would be followed up.

If anything, he had seemed more annoyed with Ollie for being in the workshop in the first place, pointing out he had been trespassing. Fortunately for her brother, he had just been given a slap on the wrist, probably because, as Xav had said afterwards, trespassing was a civil matter and there hadn't been any criminal damage.

Ollie had disappeared upstairs for a shower, while Xav had returned home to catch up on a few things and pack an overnight bag, having agreed to stay with Lana at Mead House. Alone, she needed a task to occupy her restless mind.

Deciding to make a start on her grandmother's office, she went down to the cosy, mustard-coloured room at the end of the hallway. Kitty had served on the committees of a number of charities and it was here in this room that she had dealt with all of her correspondence. Her polished mahogany desk was just as Lana remembered and the only change was the laptop that now sat in place of the typewriter, a sign that after years of nagging, her grandmother had finally embraced the times.

Lana tried to be methodical, but as with her sister's room, there were so many memories and it was difficult not to be distracted as she found personal documents among the charity correspondence. There were the cards and drawings she and her siblings had made, and photos of her grandmother and grandad, and of her parents on their wedding day, as well as school reports and certificates. This room was a treasure trove and she found herself scrutinising every document, not wanting to risk throwing away something that might be important.

She had just found an album of photos from one of her and Ollie's birthday parties when she heard the sound of footsteps on the stairs, then, moments later, Ollie poked his head round the door. He had changed into joggers and a clean T-shirt, his hair damp from his shower.

'What are you up to?' he asked.

'Trying to keep busy. It's frustrating not knowing what happens next.'

'We're gonna get her, Lana. She will pay for what she did to you.' Ollie's gaze drifted to the album and he wandered further into the room. 'Was that the year we did Disney fancy dress?' he asked, leaning over her.

'Yes.' Lana turned the page. 'You were Peter Pan and I was Tinkerbell.'

'And Xav was Aladdin.'

Lana thought back, recalling how annoyed she had been at the time because she wanted to be Jasmine so she could be Xav's girl-friend, but Kitty had thought it better she be Ollie's sidekick. She smiled at the pictures now. How young they all looked.

On the next page was Camille dressed as Ariel from *The Little*

Mermaid. An obvious choice with her red hair. Even though she must have only been thirteen or fourteen, she already had an ethereal elegance about her.

Ollie fell silent as they flicked through the album together and when he did speak as Lana closed the book, his voice was thick with emotion, which he quickly tried to cough down. 'I'm going to open a bottle of wine. Do you want a glass?'

Lana nodded, reflecting. 'Yes, I think I will. Thanks.' For all his bluster, she knew Camille's death still affected him more than he would let on.

He had said he wasn't bothered about having any photos, but as she put the album onto the keep pile, she decided this was one memento he should take.

She opened the next drawer, lifting out a shoebox and removing the lid, her chest tightening when she realised it contained cards and letters of condolence following Camille's death. She had no idea Kitty had kept these.

Was she really going to look through them now? If so, she was definitely going to need the wine.

Lana had lifted the top card out and was reading through the kind words inside, her eyes already dampening, when Ollie returned.

'What's that?' He set the glass down on the desk and as Lana glanced up to answer him, she saw his eyes widen with realisation.

'I'm going to go see what I can rustle up for dinner,' he said before she could answer him, beating a hasty retreat from the room.

Ollie wasn't ready to look through these cards. Was Lana?

She took a sip of the wine and pulled out the next offer of condolence. This one a letter from one of her grandmother's close friends and as she swiped at tears, she realised she was going to be a blubbering wreck by the time Xav returned.

There were so many well-wishers, so many people who cared.

She read lovely messages from friends and teachers, from the pupils at Camille's dance class and from the parents of the kids she had babysat for. A beautiful card embossed with gold writing and lilies expressed sadness on behalf of the Palmer family, the names Angus, Juliet and Trudy written beneath the words of sympathy. A folded sheet of notepaper was inside the card and Lana opened it, reading the personal letter Doctor Palmer had written to her grandmother. He spoke of shock and grief at the loss of a promising young woman, telling Kitty he would be there for her whenever she needed him.

This was the Doctor Palmer Lana remembered. Not the cantankerous man she had encountered a few days ago, who had barely spoken a word to her.

She traced her fingers over his familiar scruffy writing, a tear dripping onto the notepaper as she read to the end, where it was signed affectionately, *with love from your faithful friend, Gus.*

Lana had forgotten her grandmother sometimes referred to him by that nickname, but then she supposed to her, he would always be Doctor Palmer.

She finished going through the cards, before putting them back in the shoebox and replacing the lid. These would definitely be going on the keep pile.

It was as she was emptying the bottom drawer – a mundane job as it was mostly filled with stationery supplies and nothing of interest – that Lana realised the significance of Doctor Palmer's shortened name. It began with the initial G.

No, it was ridiculous to even consider that Angus Palmer had been her sister's lover and that he had shared late-night trysts with Camille in the summer house. He was at least twenty-five years older than her. Camille had been nineteen when she was murdered and the Doc had been maybe mid to late forties. And he had been married at the time. There was no way he was G. He had been her grandmother's friend. Besides, all of the evidence pointed to Bree.

Shaking the thought away, Lana finished packing the boxes, sealing them with packaging tape and writing the contents in marker pen on the top.

Taking another sip of her wine, she glanced around the room. It was now mostly bare, except for the desk and chair. Once all of the personal belonging had been packed, she would call the charity shop again and see if they were interested in the remaining furniture.

She glanced at her watch, saw it was gone seven-thirty. Xav would probably be back soon. Time to stop work for the day and have a shower.

As she passed the kitchen on her way upstairs, she could hear the clatter of pans, the enticing smell of basil and garlic clinging to the air. She hadn't thought she was hungry, the events of the day stealing her appetite, but as her belly rumbled, she realised she was wrong.

Tonight, she decided she was going to chill out and relax a bit. She would enjoy dinner, maybe have another glass of wine, then spend time with Xav. The pair of them had a lot of catching up to do. She needed to live in the moment and stop overthinking the things she had no control over.

Still, as Lana stepped into the bathroom and under the warm spray, she couldn't stop her mind from wandering back to that last summer with Camille. A long-forgotten memory surfaced, of hearing hushed whispers as she approached her grandmother's office. She had been looking for notepaper and knew Kitty kept a selection in the top drawer of her desk. She had assumed it was her grandmother in the room, but as she'd peered through the crack in the door, she realised it was Doctor Palmer talking to Camille. He had his hand on her arm as he leant in close.

At the time, Lana hadn't read anything into it. He was the family doctor and she assumed Camille was asking him for advice about something. She hadn't snooped, quickly leaving to give them both privacy and, to be honest, she hadn't given it a second thought.

Until now.

Now knowing that her sister had a secret lover that summer put the memory in a whole new light. Had she witnessed a doctor comforting his patient or two lovers stealing a moment together.

Was Doctor Palmer really G? Had he been the one to do all those vile sexual things to Camille? Biting and bruising her, treating her as his property and his own personal slut. Had he killed her? Tying her to the chair in the summer house, torturing and graffitiing her body, before strangling her with the ribbon on her pendant?

Lana thought she might be sick.

The doctor was in a wheelchair now, but he hadn't been at the time of Camille's death. His car accident had happened not long after her funeral. Juliet Palmer behind the wheel, driving too fast and losing control of the car. Had she known about the affair?

Did Trudy know?

Lana quickly dried herself, slipping on a loose cotton dress, her hands shaking as she fastened the buttons at the front.

The burden of the memory weighed her down and she went downstairs to find Ollie, keen to tell him what she had remembered.

The kitchen was empty, a half-sliced loaf of ciabatta on the counter and a pan of boiling pasta bubbling over. Frowning, she rushed over to the stove to turn it off. Where the hell was he? Lana couldn't believe he had been irresponsible enough to leave the pan on and disappear.

'Ollie? Where are you?'

It was then she spotted the blood spatter on the grey tiled floor. Fear and panic coiled in her gut.

Unsure if it had simply been an accident or if something more sinister had happened, she grabbed the bread knife he had been using as a precaution, every one of her nerve endings charged.

'Ollie?' Was this his blood? Was he hurt?

This time she heard her brother's voice. 'Lana, get out of the house. She has a knife.'

What? Who had a knife?

Was Bree in the house?

Lana spun around in the direction of where his voice had come from, her heart catching as shadows filled the doorway. Ollie, a trickle of blood on his forehead and his face pale, reluctantly shuffled forward into the room. Trudy Palmer was standing close behind him and she had one arm wrapped across his chest, the hand of her other holding one of Nana Kitty's fancy and extremely sharp kitchen knives to his throat.

Seeing Lana's look of shock, she smiled. 'I think it's time we had a chat.'

Trudy had suspected her father was having an affair for a while, and she knew her mother did too. There were too many tell-tale signs. The changes to his routine and the late-night drives he took, which he claimed, when pressed, were to his surgery to catch up on paperwork. Then there was the lingering scent of perfume that didn't belong to Trudy or her mother.

There was nothing on his phone. Trudy had checked it when he was in the shower one morning, sneaking into her parents' bedroom and going through her father's text messages and call log. It didn't deter her. She knew he was hiding something and decided to keep a close eye on him.

It was during a visit to Mead House that she realised her suspicions were right.

Angus had picked her up from school, saying he needed to call in on Kitty.

Trudy hadn't been to the house in a while and the thought of having to stop by and make polite small talk was mind-numbingly boring for a fifteen-year-old girl. She would rather be at home, where she could change out of her school uniform and chill.

She didn't argue with her father, though. No one disagreed with Angus.

It was just Kitty at home, the twins away at boarding school and Camille out with Sebastian and as the woman chatted with her father, Trudy was on the verge of drifting off. It was a relief when Kitty picked up on her boredom and suggested she take her lemonade and go have a look in the games room. There were books and games in there, she said, that Trudy might find more entertaining.

Truthfully, there wasn't much that interested her, but it was better than sitting with the adults and at least it helped to pass the time. She was a couple of chapters into a *Harry Potter* book when she heard footsteps and, hopeful it was her father coming to get her, she slipped the book back on the shelf and wandered to the doorway to find him.

It was her father, but he didn't appear to be looking for her, instead he stood further down the hallway in front of one of the big paintings and kept glancing back in the direction of the living room as though he didn't want to be seen.

Instead of going to him, instinct had Trudy hanging back. He was up to something; she was sure of it.

Seeming content that the coast was clear, Angus reached into his pocket and removed a folded piece of paper. Carefully, he pulled the bottom left corner of the painting forward, slipping the paper underneath. Making sure everything was back in place, he glanced around again, then quickly headed into the cloakroom opposite.

Why had he put a piece of paper behind the painting? And why hadn't he wanted anyone to see him do it?

The idea that her father was up to no good sat uncomfortably in the pit of Trudy's stomach. She wanted to go and look, to see what the paper was, but hearing the chain flush, she knew there wasn't time.

Instead she quickly grabbed her book and sat back down. And when her father poked his head through the door a few moments later, she managed to fake a smile.

'I'm just finishing my tea. Be ready to go in about ten minutes.'

'Okay.' She nodded, listening to his footsteps as he made his way back to the living room, then tiptoed into the hall, needing to see what the paper was.

She could hear her father and Kitty as they talked, knew they were both far enough away. Still, her heart thumped as she lifted the frame and removed the paper. She unfolded it and read the words, immediately wanting to be sick.

The summer house. Tonight at midnight.
  You've been a bad girl and need to be punished.
  G xxx

Who was the note meant for? Was her father having an affair with Kitty?

The woman was older than him, but maybe only by fifteen years. Still, the idea repulsed Trudy. And why would they meet in the summer house? Surely, they would go into Kitty's bedroom?

Her mind was working overtime as she returned the paper to its hiding place, knowing she had to find out what was going on.

Trudy was quiet on the ride home, unable to connect the strict father sitting beside her, who preached family values, with the man who had written the note.

That night, a short while before midnight, she snuck out of her bedroom window, for the first time disobeying her father's rules. She cycled the short distance to Mead House, leaving her bike behind the bushes on the edge of the treelined lane, then waited. When she heard a car approach, she ducked down out of sight. It slowed, but instead of turning into the driveway, the driver pulled into a layby just a little bit further along the road.

Trudy bit down on her bottom lip and tried to steady her breathing as she watched her father get out of the car and walk back to the driveway, passing perilously close to where she was hiding. She waited until he was a good few seconds ahead of her before following after him, trying to stick to the grass verge where she was more immersed by the darkness and the sound of her footsteps were muffled.

All of the lights were out in the main house, but instead of approaching the front door, he disappeared round the side of the building, following the path that led to the top lawn.

Trudy's heart thumped as she followed, aware of where he was going as he headed into the rose garden and then onto the path that led through the orchard.

Who was waiting for him in the summer house?

She held back, heard the sound of the door opening, then closing again, then spent a few minutes steadying herself, aware that whatever happened next, whatever she saw, she wouldn't be able to take it back.

Was she ready to learn the truth about her father?

Even as she considered the question, she knew she didn't have a choice. She had come too far now and she had to know.

As she made her way through the orchard, saw the flickering of light at the window as the summer house came into sight, a muffled scream cut through the air and she froze. The noise had come from ahead, but still she glanced back in the direction of Mead House.

Would it have woken anyone?

They were some distance away, though, and although the noise seemed loud, it was probably because it was so quiet out here.

Trudy stepped closer to the summer house, hearing her father now.

'Who do you belong to? Tell me? Whose whore are you?'

Trudy peered through the window. She could see a woman bent over a table, her arse exposed, Angus Palmer standing behind her, a scowl on his face as he repeatedly slapped her.

The sound cut through the air, making Trudy wince.

Why was he beating her?

She watched, horrified, disgusted, but unable to tear her gaze away as Angus caught hold of the woman's braid, yanking her head violently back and revealing her identity.

Camille Hamilton.

Her features were twisted in pain and although Trudy couldn't quite hear her, she saw Camille's lips form the word 'please', and understood she wanted him to stop.

Or did she?

Still yanking on her hair, Camille's white throat exposed, Angus leant forward, whispering something in her ear that made her smile.

Please.

Please.

Please.

She was repeating the word over and over, but it wasn't for him to stop. She was begging for more. She actually wanted this.

Trudy was so shocked; it took a second for her to realise her father's trousers had dropped. She watched him enter Camille from behind, his hands going from her braid to the throat, choking her as he pumped.

Enough!

She needed it to stop, but he would kill her if he found she was there.

Instead, she tore her gaze away from the window, going to the side of the summer house and vomiting into the bushes.

What had she just witnessed?

Camille was only nineteen. Less than half her father's age.

Still, Trudy's mind wandered back to the previous summer and a garden party Kitty had thrown. Everyone was there, including all three of her grandchildren. Camille had been wearing a striking red dress that dipped at the cleavage. Everyone's eyes had been on her. Especially Angus's. Trudy remembered glancing over and seeing him watching her, his leer grossing her out. It was rank seeing her father perv over her.

Trudy was shaking as she made her way back to the road, part of her wishing she had never pushed to find out what her father was up to, but also grateful to finally learn the truth about who he really was. He had ruled over her like a tyrant for too long. But it was over now. Trudy had lost all respect for him and would no longer bow to his law.

She could barely bring herself to look at him the next day, her thoughts with her mother, who had no idea about the man she had married. If she learnt the truth, how would she react? Would it break her?

Trudy was disgusted knowing she was a part of him. And with that disgust came rage. How dare he do this? And with a patient.

And how dare Camille involve herself with a married man, her father?

As her frustration grew, so did her fury. And it was easier to direct much of that at Camille. She was trying to break up Trudy's family by taking what wasn't hers. She needed to be taught a lesson. But how?

It was being thrown into detention with George Maddox, a kid whose uncle was the gardener at Mead House, that first gave her an idea. When she learnt that George sometimes helped his uncle and could access keys, it felt like fate.

After weeks of plotting, determined to make Camille pay, Trudy knew exactly how she was going to do it.

49

It wasn't until just as he was about to leave that Xav remembered Lana saying she thought there had been someone snooping around outside his house.

There had been so much going on over the last hour or so, and the idea of Bree's guilt was still weighing heavily on him. He wondered how she would react when she realised he had betrayed her. After speaking with the police, he had returned home briefly, throwing a few things into an overnight bag and putting down food for the cat.

This would be his second night staying at Mead House, but he reminded himself that it was only a temporary situation until Bree had been investigated, though there was no timeline for when that might be.

The police officer hadn't said what would happen next and Xav understood there were several factors involved. Unless Bree willingly allowed them to explore her workshop, they would need probable cause and warrants. The warrants took time and it was possible that Ollie's statement would not be enough to get one.

The officer had said it would be looked into and now they had to leave the police to do their job. Until Xav knew Lana was safe, though, he intended to stay close.

The snooper had slipped his mind, but now remembering, he decided to take a closer look. Lana had downplayed what had happened, even suggesting she may have been mistaken. It was possible, but he would be happier when he had checked for himself.

The footage linked to his phone but knowing he could view it clearer on a computer screen, he waited for his Mac to load. Clicking into the camera app, he forwarded slowly through the footage. He watched himself leave as he went to go and meet Bree for lunch, then a short while later, another car pulled up. He saw Trudy emerge from the driver's door, taking a few decisive steps towards the porch as if coming to knock on the door, then stop abruptly, her eyes widening as if she had seen something unexpected.

He switched cameras, watching as instead of approaching the house, she disappeared around the side of the property, peering through the kitchen window.

What the hell was she doing? Was she spying on Lana?

That must have been when Lana had realised someone was outside, because suddenly Trudy was bolting back to her car, the vehicle reversing back onto the road, then, moments later, speeding away.

It meant nothing. Xav told himself that, but still it sat uncomfortably. Something about the footage felt off.

Had it been one of Trudy's annoying impromptu visits?

But if she knew Lana was inside, why didn't she knock?

Before heading back to Mead House, Xav decided he would stop by to see her.

He had promised Lana he wouldn't be gone long, but it wasn't as if she was home alone. Ollie was with her. And the visit to Trudy wouldn't take long.

Logging off his Mac and shutting it down, he grabbed his overnight bag and let himself out of the house.

50

George knew the blow had been meant to kill him.

He had hit the ground hard and, reaching to his head, his hand came away sticky with blood, which had him questioning why he was still alive. His brain was throbbing in his skull and it was like he had the world's worst hangover.

He tried to stand, instead stumbled, his balance off, and realised he was going to need a moment. Collapsing onto the nearest chair, he sucked in deep breaths, his vision swimming and convinced that he was going to throw up.

Fucking bitch.

He hadn't wanted to go to Trudy for help, knowing she was a psycho, but Elise had left him with little choice. He desperately needed somewhere for her to stay, but he should have also known from history that anything involving Trudy Palmer would end badly.

She might come across as sweetness and light, the respected daughter of Doctor Palmer, with her successful art shop, but George knew what lurked under the surface and that she had a black soul. He had long ago witnessed what she was truly capable of and just how ruthless she really was. If Trudy perceived something to be a threat, she dealt with it.

He looked at Elise now, where her body was lying sprawled on her back on the plastic sheeting. She hadn't been as lucky as him and he suspected her smart mouth had been responsible for the frenzied beating she appeared to have suffered before her death. Her face was almost unrecognisable. So much for his attempt to try to resolve this situation without further blood being shed.

Perhaps it had been a mistake using Elise to get the journal, but George didn't see that he had any other choice. With three people living in Mead House, there was invariably always someone at home and it would have been too big a risk, even the night of the poker game, to sneak upstairs and try to find it himself.

He had seen Elise watching him and realised she liked what she saw. It hadn't been difficult to take advantage of the situation and seduce her. He knew her type.

Luring her to a hotel room in Sheringham had been easy and she had been quick to make up an excuse to Ollie, saying she was going to visit a friend in Norwich.

Instead of getting the night of passion with the mind-blowing orgasms he had promised her, though, she had ended up with a five-minute shag, while his well-positioned phone had recorded the whole encounter.

When he had started to get dressed and she had realised he was planning on leaving her unsatisfied, she had been furious, but when he had revealed he had videoed the whole thing, she had turned into a madwoman.

George had waited until she finished exploding before calmly explaining what he needed her to do.

'I can't go into Lana's room,' she had wailed. 'She'll kill me if she finds out.'

'I'm sure you'll find a way.'

'What is so damn special about a stupid journal anyway?'

'That's none of your business.' He was hardly going to tell her the truth. 'I just need you to get it for me.'

'No, I can't do it. I can't risk Nolly finding out.'

'Scared you might lose your cash cow?' He had grinned at her and when she'd glowered back, he'd dangled his phone in front of her. 'So you would rather he see this?' he'd asked, easily lifting it out of her reach when she'd tried to grab for it.

Elise's face had twisted in rage as she understood she had been played, her humiliation complete when he had suggested she make a night of it and enjoy the meagre facilities the cheap hotel room had to offer, knowing she couldn't return to Mead House until morning.

He had copped some shit that night for showing up late to the poker game, but it was worth it, knowing the reason why was because he had been fucking Ollie Hamilton's slutty fiancée.

It had taken a few days to get the journal, Lana's bump with the car meaning she was recuperating in the room where it was, but Elise had finally come through for him.

Except now she was dead and while part of him felt guilty for involving her in the first place, he couldn't help but believe this was all mostly her own doing. If she hadn't threatened to expose the truth about what had happened to the journal, she might still be alive.

George hadn't liked her, but he had still tried to protect her. He didn't know what had happened in the time he was gone from the cottage, hadn't even realised Trudy was planning to stop by. And he assumed she had done so because she figured Elise was a threat that needed to be eliminated.

He knew the only reason she hadn't tried to kill him before now was because he had been an accomplice in Camille Hamilton's murder. It had been Trudy's first kill and he had been there to witness it. He always got the impression she fed on knowing he had seen the true her. And that she basked in the knowledge that if he told on her, he would go down too.

Although it hadn't been his hands holding the ribbon that strangled Camille, he had been at the summer house that night to help Trudy get her revenge and he had played a part in the suffering Camille had endured prior to her death.

If he could take back that night, he would. Instead, the awful memory lived on inside of him and while it was his most bitter regret that he hadn't tried to stop Trudy, he also knew the secret of what happened could never come out, that his life would be over.

These days, he mostly tried to stay out of her way. But then Lana and Ollie Hamilton had come back to Mead House and all hell had broken loose. When Trudy had found out about the second journal's existence, then realised George already knew about it and hadn't told her, she had been furious.

'We are in this together,' she had raged, and he had been quick to assure her he had already taken care of the problem, not wanting any more blood to be spilt.

He had thought that once he handed the journal over to Trudy, their problems would be over. But then the whole Elise thing had blown up in his face and he had needed help.

All he had wanted was a place for Elise to stay for a few days while he figured a way out of this mess. Instead, Trudy had made things so much worse for him. If the police came looking for Elise, eyewitnesses would be able to connect him to her, especially as George had paid for her room last night. Suddenly, he had a whole lot more to worry about than covering his tracks over his involvement in Camille Hamilton's death, and it was also forcing him to look at the two attacks on Lana and accept that Trudy was probably behind them.

He had genuinely questioned the hit-and-run, as it had

happened before Trudy had learned of the journal, but the incident in the garage that the police had questioned Elise about was classic Trudy Palmer.

It seemed that even though she was now in possession of the journal, she was still eliminating any potential connections to her crime in that cold and calculating way of hers. The attempts on Lana's life, Elise's murder and now trying to silence George. She was out of control and he wasn't sure what to do.

If he stood by quietly and let her take care of things, he would have more deaths on his conscience, of that he was certain. Plus there was a good chance she might try to frame him.

The other option was to try to take her down. Although he feared her, she thought he was dead. That gave him an advantage.

One thing was for certain. He no longer trusted he was safe, and not for the first time, he was wishing their paths had never crossed that fateful Wednesday in detention.

51

'What the bloody hell are you doing?'

'Put the knife down, Lana.'

Trudy spoke calmly, but her gaze was steel and there was a quiet determination to her words that suggested she was being deadly serious.

Ignoring her, just as she was trying her best to ignore that the blade at Ollie's throat was pressed firmly enough to draw the first spurts of blood, Lana tightened her grip on the breadknife and locked eyes with Trudy. Her heart thumped, with anger as much as fear.

What the fuck was the woman playing at? Was this because of what had happened last night? Lana was livid with Ollie about his misdirected punch, but it didn't warrant pulling a knife on him.

She could see now that his arms were pulled behind his back, tied somehow, and there was blood on his forehead. Had Trudy hit him with something? What kind of twisted game was she playing?

'Let my brother go!' She enunciated every word as an order, relieved her voice wasn't trembling, even though she was quaking inside.

Whatever this was, whatever the hell Trudy was up to, Lana would not plead. She sensed the woman wanted her meekness, but to hell with her if she thought she would get it. How bloody dare she burst in here like this?

Lana took a step towards her, raising the knife instead of dropping it, hoping to get her to back down. Instead, Trudy nicked the blade deeper, earning a wince of pain from Ollie, and Lana froze.

'I will kill him.' Trudy's tone was void of emotion and the sickness churning in Lana's gut warned her that the threat was also a promise. The first flutter of fear dropped in her stomach. 'I'm going to ask you again. Put the knife down.'

'Don't listen to her, Lana.'

Ollie was trying to be brave, but Lana recognised the tell-tale signs that he was scared. His nostrils were flaring and his eyes wide.

'Why are you doing this?' she demanded, trying her best to stay calm, though it was increasingly difficult, knowing that one slip of the blade and her brother would be dead.

'I think you know why.' Trudy smiled cruelly. 'You're in my way.'

In her way? That threw Lana. How in the hell was she in Trudy Palmer's way? Their families went way back.

That thought had her remembering why she had come downstairs to find Ollie. Doctor Palmer and Camille, and the moment she had witnessed when they had been together in the study. Did Trudy know?

'Your dad was having an affair with my sister.' She blurted the words, watching her reaction. Other than the tightening of her mouth, Trudy gave little away. She didn't look surprised.

Ollie did, though. 'What?'

Lana ignored him, focusing on Trudy. 'You knew.'

'That Camille was a dirty slut who went after a married man? That they used to fuck each other in your grandmother's summer house? Of course I did. And so did my mother before she died. It broke her heart.' Trudy snapped out the words. 'Your sister disgusted me. She deserved everything that happened to her.'

Lana's hand tightened around the handle of the breadknife, rage heating her veins. How dare Trudy say that? 'And what about your dad?' she reasoned, more calmly than she felt. 'Yes, Camille should have known better, but he was Kitty's friend, and her doctor, respected in the community. He took advantage of my sister.' Knowing the truth sickened her.

'He hardly took advantage. *She* was old enough to understand the games they played. I made sure she knew the consequences of her actions before I strangled her.'

What?

Lana blinked in shock as the words registered and for a second, she struggled to breathe.

She was aware of a keening guttural sound from Ollie. Trudy's admission catching both of them off guard.

'You hadn't worked that bit out, had you?' Trudy seemed amused. 'Seems the second journal didn't quite have all of the answers you'd hoped for.'

Had Trudy been the one to steal it? Lana was about to ask, but then another thought occurred to her as she remembered back to the night of the hit-and-run, then how she had been locked in the car boot.

'But you tried to kill me anyway,' she murmured, still taking everything in. 'It *was* you, wasn't it, at the beach and in the garage?'

'You're a loose end. You and this pathetic excuse of a brother of yours. It's nothing personal, Lana. Well, not entirely personal.'

'What's that supposed to mean?'

'I did warn you to stay away from Xav Landry.'

'What has Xav got to do with this? Does he know?'

Although she didn't want to doubt him, Trudy's revelation had her reeling and now questioning everything.

'About your slutty sister?' The bubble of Trudy's laughter was so
girlish, it only added to the surrealness of this nightmare. 'Good
lord, no. And he's not going to. As far as Xav is concerned, his
brother is guilty. He had come to terms with that until you showed
up and started poking your nose around, putting ideas into his
head.' She smirked at Lana. 'I'm sure he'll be upset when you're
gone, but I'll help him deal with the loss.'

It seemed implausible that this mild-mannered woman had
murdered Camille. She had been little more than a child at the
time. But it was clear she wanted Lana out of the way. Ollie too.
Sever any loose ends that could tie her to the murder.

If she put down the knife as asked, Trudy was going to kill Ollie
anyway. Lana couldn't relinquish her only weapon. She willed
herself to think of a solution, a way to outwit her.

'You won't get away with this.'

Another shrill of laughter. This time revealing the madness that
had until now been well hidden. 'Of course I will. I've been getting
away with it for years, you stupid bitch. Do you really think your
sister is the only person I've killed? She was my first, probably my
most memorable too, so I suppose it's quite fitting we've come full
circle, back to where it started.'

'You're crazy,' Ollie managed to choke out a laugh of his own.
There was no humour in it and Lana could see he was as shocked
as she was, and no doubt even more conscious of the blade against
his throat.

Had she really killed others or was she bluffing?

'No, Ollie, you useless and ineffective piece of shit. I am definitely not crazy. Psychotic perhaps, but all of my ducks are lined up.
Now, tell your sister to drop that knife or I will cut off your slimy
head.'

Trudy raised her eyebrows at Lana as Ollie looked to the ceiling and appeared to mutter a silent prayer. Lana knew he was struggling to hold it together.

'Let him go. Please.'

'The knife, Lana.'

When she didn't oblige, Trudy tutted.

'Okay, let me tell you how this is going to work. I'm going to count to three. If by the time I reach three, your knife isn't on the ground, I am going to slit your brother's throat, then come after you. I am faster, I am smarter, and I've done this before. All of the doors are locked and I have taken the keys. You won't get away. If you want to call my bluff, though, go ahead.'

Lana didn't and although she was angry, she was also scared. Trudy had already stolen Camille from her. She couldn't let her hurt Ollie.

'Don't do this, Trudy. We will leave town. I promise we won't say anything, not even to Xav.'

'One.'

'Please. There are other ways to deal with this.'

'Two. The knife, Lana, now.'

It was pointless trying to reason with her. She wasn't going to listen. Lana was desperate to keep hold of the weapon, but Ollie's life wasn't worth the risk.

'Okay. Stop.'

Reluctantly, she bent to place it on the ground.

'Stand back up and kick it over to me.'

Lana hesitated but did as told. She kept a close watch on Trudy, terrified in case she still went through with her threat to slit Ollie's throat.

'What are you going to do to us?'

'That depends entirely on you. There are a lot of ways I can hurt you and your brother. I can make things quick and painless for you, or if you upset me I can take my time. So how is it going to be? Are you going to do as you're told?'

When Lana scowled, refusing to answer, Trudy gave an exaggerated sigh.

As if to make a point, she sliced the blade of her knife down Ollie's cheek, making him scream.

'Okay, stop! I'll do what you ask. Just please don't cut him again.'

'Better.'

Not really, but what choice did she have? Trudy had always seemed so normal. Polite, nice even. How the fuck had Lana missed that she was a total raving psycho?

She hissed out a breath, determined to steady herself. If her and Ollie were going to get through this alive, she needed to keep her wits about her and her brain engaged.

'Okay, you've got what you wanted. So, what now?' Lana tried hard to keep her tone authoritative, hating not having the upper hand.

Trudy's smile was twisted as she pushed Ollie forward, the knife still too close to his throat. 'Now we take this back to where it all started. The summer house.'

52

Lana Hamilton had been my only target, but then she went and involved her useless brother, and I am going to enjoy ending his life too.

I always intended to keep a close eye on the pair of them when they returned — there are too many secrets hidden in Mead House — but initially I had no plans to hurt anyone. I might hate the Hamiltons, but they were only back to sell the place and that was good with me. Finally the town was going to be free of them.

If only it had been that simple. And if only Lana had kept her distance from Xav Landry.

What is happening to her now is her own fault. She should have stayed out of my way.

Xav is off limits. He is mine and I refuse to share.

Our paths hadn't crossed that often when we were kids. He was in the year above me at school and I often wonder if he even realised I existed. I had friends, but I wasn't popular like he was, and I guess it wasn't until that last summer, before my final year of school, that I finally learnt to rebel. To shake off that straightlaced and studious tag I had been forced to live with for so long.

He may not have noticed me, but I knew exactly who he was. The *beautiful dark-haired boy with the wide, green eyes and the faintest hint of French accent.*

Even back then, he had turned heads, but what was always charming about Xav was the slight self-doubt he had about himself. Yes, he was confident, but it never spilled over into arrogance, because he never believed he was better than anyone else.

It was unfortunate that his brother ended up as collateral damage. I hadn't set it up that way, but Camille's necklace had been in my pocket the night she died and in the heat of the moment when I lost control, everything just fell into place.

I remember seeing Xav after his brother's arrest and realising I had broken him. I don't often experience guilt or remorse, but he looked haunted and in shock as he carried the weight of his brother's alleged crime on his shoulders. Because of Camille and the chain of events she had set in motion, he had lost everything.

I never forgot that look and it stayed with me, even after he had moved away.

Over the years, I followed his journey. At first by stalking his social media accounts, then, as he grew successful, through his art. Through the news articles, interviews and critiques. Even though we lived miles apart, it was as if we had some deep, emotional connection. When I heard he was returning to Norfolk, planning to set up home close to his mother, I knew I had to be a part of his life.

I was his guardian angel. I wanted to watch over him, protect him and have him for myself. He needed friends, so it was easy to find a way in, and a little alcohol had already helped pull down the barriers so we could consummate our relationship. Although it was a while since that night when we had made love, I was laying the groundwork and working on fully gaining Xav's trust. It was going well. At least it had been. Until Lana had come back and confused him.

I have been keeping tabs on her and the dimwit brother. It had been easy enough to slip AirTags into their cars. Those things are a godsend at tracking people. There is one in Xav's car too. I like to know where my beloved is at all times.

My blood had boiled when I realised Lana had headed down to the beach at Salthouse. Straight towards where Xav's car was parked.

Had they planned this? I needed to know.

I borrowed a car from Bree McCarthy's garage to drive to the beach. She has come in useful over the last year and it's handy her garage is just a couple of roads away from where I live. I have never regretted taking the spare key she entrusted to Xav and having a copy cut. Of course he doesn't know I have it and neither does Bree.

I initially wanted it so I could keep a close eye on her. I didn't like or trust her friendship with Xav, and at first I had suspected she wanted him for herself. If that turned out to be the case, I wanted to know what I was dealing with.

Luckily, Bree hadn't posed a threat. I don't approve of her closeness with Xav, but I am smart enough to know I can't remove everyone from his life. I have to pick and choose my battles, so I don't raise suspicion.

Bree is an irritant I can deal with. Lana, however, is a different story.

I was keeping an eye on her and Ollie out of caution. I didn't know she was going to try and rekindle things with Xav. Although I am aware of their history, I had seen the way Xav had dismissed her in my shop. I thought he wanted nothing to do with her. So why had they arranged to meet at the beach?

I watched through binoculars as Lana approached him, the knot of fury in my gut twisting tighter. How fucking dare she?

My mind had worked overtime as I plotted my next move. I needed to scare her, to find a way to make her back off, to understand that she had to stay away from him.

My plans went out of the window as I watched them return from the beach, the rage taking over as I aimed the car at her. A momentary loss of control. I hadn't acted on instinct since Camille. I couldn't afford for her sister to be my undoing. Even as I drove back to Bree's workshop to return *the car, I realised I had just taken a huge and potentially terrible risk in hitting Lana. There was a witness.*

Xav had stopped. He should have left and I should have made sure he was gone before acting, but instead I had been irrational and he had seen what I had done. Even as I sped past him that night, I had no idea that I had just managed the reverse of what I had hoped to achieve. I had pushed Lana and Xav closer together.

I covered my tracks as best I could and played the concerned friend, taking Lana flowers, but my actions had consequences and I knew even as I warned her to leave him alone that my words were falling on deaf ears. This was all my fault and I needed to fix it.

The hit-and-run could be explained as a random encounter and I knew I couldn't risk attacking her again. It would be too suspicious. But then I learnt about the second journal and how Lana was beginning to question whether Sebastian was innocent, and my rulebook went out of the window. The night I went to Mead House and attacked her in the garage, I fully intended for her to die.

Lana Hamilton has proven to be more trouble than she's worth.

I saw her through the window at Xav's place earlier today when I stopped by on my way home from work, swanning around as if she belonged there. This has to end tonight.

I look at her now, her head held high in defiance and hatred in her eyes as she tosses a look back at me. She doesn't seem fearful, at least not for her own safety., Seeming only concerned for the wellbeing of her useless brother.

Although I am keeping him close, Lana walking ahead as per my instructions, I have no need to subdue Ollie. It's his sister I don't trust and I know her concern that I might hurt him is the only thing keeping her compliant right now.

Ollie doesn't want to go to the summer house, and it's becoming clear from Lana's attempts to reassure him it will be okay that he hasn't been down there since finding poor Camille's body. He is trembling against me, seeming more afraid of returning there than of the knife in my hand. I didn't realise quite how badly it had scarred him. Knowing this sparks an idea and a slight change in my plan.

I had intended to kill Ollie first, the anticipation of ending the snivelling weasel's life fizzing through my veins. Once he was dead, it would allow me to give Lana my full attention and punish her for trying to steal Xav from me. What is it with these Hamilton women, thinking they can take what isn't theirs? Camille thought it was okay to fuck my father and now Lana is trying to steal the man I love.

Ollie hasn't taken anything from me, but he is an entitled, arrogant piece of shit. I haven't forgotten how he hit me last night, even if it was an accident, and I know the only reason I have his attention now is because of the knife I am holding to his throat. There is a better way for him, I realise. The ultimate torment. I want him to have to watch as he loses a second sister. I could even stage it to look as if he was responsible.

'You're not going to get away with this,' Lana hisses as we enter the orchard.

She keeps making threats and, while amusing at first, they are now getting tiresome. I need a quiet moment to mull over my new plan. I only get to kill the Hamilton twins once and I want to make sure it's memorable.

When I don't respond, she stops walking, looking back at me again, and I am aware of the anger bouncing off her. I am bigger and stronger, but I suspect that if I wasn't holding a knife to her brother's throat, she would try to take me down in a heartbeat.

I raise the knife to Ollie's cheek again. Time to remind Lana she needs to do as she is told. 'Keep walking,' I snarl.

When she hesitates, I press the blade against his skin, but catch myself, stopping before it cuts into flesh. I need to think this through. If I am going to frame Ollie for his sister's murder, how to explain away the cuts to his face?

Fortunately, the threat seems to have worked and she starts walking again.

A fight. That's how I will make it look. Ollie attacks his sister and Lana fights back before he manages to overpower her. People will believe that. I can make it look like he takes his own life after ending hers. They will even start to question whether he murdered poor Camille.

Perfect.

We are almost at the summer house now. Where it first started with Camille and tonight it will end with Lana and Ollie.

Lana acts as if she isn't afraid of me, but before I am through with her she will experience true fear. And before she dies, she is going to understand that she should never have gone after what is mine.

53

2005

It wasn't until late in the summer that the second revenge took place.

Trudy didn't want anything to get in the way of her plan to punish Camille Hamilton, plotting everything out in great detail. And as she plotted, her hatred towards Camille grew.

How dare the bitch think it was okay to have an affair with her father? What right did she think she had to try to break up their family?

Juliet Palmer might have a few suspicions about her husband's infidelity, but she remained blissfully unaware of the nature of Angus's relationship with Camille, of his obsession with a woman so many years younger than her, and of the disgusting and perverted games they liked to play.

If her mother knew, it would break her, so Trudy kept what she had seen to herself. It was a heavy burden to carry alone and the anger and injustice of what she had seen twisted and coiled inside of her until it was all she could think about.

She had lost all respect for her father and she started to rebel.

Drinking alcohol, sleeping with boys, smoking. All of the things she knew would disgust him.

As for Camille, all she could think about was getting revenge, and nothing was going to get in her way.

Of course she hadn't planned to kill the girl. The idea had been to scare her and humiliate her, to teach her a lesson.

George had come through for her, managing to get hold of his uncle's keys and they had taken a copy of the one for the summer house. They would lure Camille there, then once she was secured to the chair, Trudy would reveal herself and make sure she never went near Angus again.

Trudy had copied her father's handwriting as she'd penned the first note.

Wait for me in the summer house. Midnight.
Wear your red dress. And don't put on any underwear.
G xxx

The request for the red dress and no underwear had been a whim. She had seen how Camille was with Angus and it sounded like the kind of request he would make. Besides, it was fitting that Camille should be punished in her whorish dress.

There was a second note too, that gave instructions of what Camille should do when she arrived at the summer house. They would leave that one on the chair.

But the first note? How was she going to get it into Mead House and behind the picture?

Eventually, it was the fictional wizard, Harry Potter, who helped her and a phone call to Kitty Hamilton, asking if it was possible to borrow the books.

As Trudy suspected, the woman was more than obliging, inviting Trudy to stop by and pick them up.

The plan was in motion and the day of reckoning finally arrived.

Angus was going fishing. Something he generally did once a month and Trudy was confident that Camille would not know this. They were hardly likely to discuss his schedule while they were fucking each other's brains out.

Slipping her backpack onto her shoulders, Trudy cycled over to Mead House, taking up Kitty's offer of a glass of lemonade, before making her excuses to use the toilet.

Camille was out somewhere with Sebastian and through the window she could see Lana and Ollie were messing around in the pool with Xavier Landry. Kitty had invited her to join them, but she had declined. For one thing, she didn't have her swimming costume, plus she knew she had to get the note in place. Part of her wished she could be outside with Xavier, and she hated knowing that Lana had him all to herself, but there was no time to dwell on that now.

Her palms were sweating as she pulled the frame forward, sliding the paper behind it. As she repositioned the picture, she took a step away. The older woman in the portrait had thin lips and dark eyes that seemed to follow her every movement, which had her gut tightening.

It was okay. It was just a picture, she reminded herself. No one knew what she had just done.

'That was my mother-in-law.'

Trudy jumped at the voice, realising Kitty was in the hall watching her.

Had she seen?

No, if she had, Kitty would say. She was always fairly direct.

'She was a lovely-looking lady,' Trudy lied, which brought a smile to Kitty's face. There was nothing pretty about the woman in the portrait.

'How about we get you those books?' Kitty suggested, leading her away from the picture and into the games room.

As she cycled away from the house, Trudy felt a strange sense of achievement, as well as the heavy weight of the knowledge that the plan was now in place. It was too late to back out.

Well, of course, she could simply not show. Camille would go to the empty summer house and would no doubt ask questions when Angus wasn't there. They would realise someone knew their secret, even if they couldn't prove who. And perhaps that would be enough to make them stop.

It would mean Camille would go without punishment, though, and Trudy couldn't bear the thought of that. No, she wanted to make Camille pay.

The sun was beating down on her, the day warm, and rather than heading home, Trudy decided to cycle down the beach. First though, she would stop in town and pick up a couple of cans of Coke to take with her.

It was as she was coming out of the shop that she saw Camille with Sebastian Landry.

The pair of them were fighting and it was heated. Maybe Sebastian had finally learned the truth about his slut of a girlfriend. A small crowd had gathered as the pair of them raised their voices, before Camille ripped off the pendant around her neck, throwing it at Sebastian, then storming off. Trudy watched him slip it in his pocket. As he disappeared back to his car, the group of onlookers dispersed and she grabbed her bike, her heart thumping and excited by what she had just witnessed. It was satisfying to see that Camille's life wasn't perfect.

She cycled down to Salthouse, surprised when she spotted Sebastian's car. It was empty and she spotted him down on the beach looking out to the sea. When she watched him toss the pendant away, she knew she had to have it.

Later that night, she met up with George, both of them dressed in black and disguised as best as possible, just on the off chance they were seen. Trudy's hair was hidden under a cap, the dark jacket she was wearing far too warm for the hot summer night, but bulking out her frame. Along with her height, she was confident that anyone who saw her at a distance would think she was male. She had even dabbed on some of her father's aftershave before leaving the house, knowing it would fool Camille.

She sent George down to the summer house to unlock the door and set everything up.

'Is it done?' she asked anxiously when he re-joined her in the bushes to the side of the house. 'You put the note on the chair and lit the lamp? And you remembered the scarf?'

He looked a little nervous as he nodded and she tried to quash down the jitters in her own belly as they both settled down to wait.

Despite all their efforts, Trudy didn't know how often Camille checked behind the portrait and couldn't be certain her plan would work, so when shortly before midnight, Camille emerged from the house, her blood heated in excitement. A fizz of anticipation burning through her when she realised the barefoot girl was wearing the red dress as instructed.

It was then that George almost lost his bottle.

'What if this goes wrong? What if she realises it's us before we get her tied up?'

'She won't,' Trudy hissed, not liking the panic in his tone.

'But what if she tells people what we did? We'll be in trouble.'

'She won't be telling anyone. We will take videos and make her admit to what she's done. She won't want anyone knowing about what she's been up to or what happens here tonight. I promise you.'

When George still seemed uncertain, she reminded him of their deal.

'I helped you, remember? I had sex with your pig ugly stepbrother to get him to leave you alone. What I'm asking you to do is nothing in comparison. Once we have her tied to the chair, you can wait outside if you like. Be the lookout. But you're doing this, George. You owe me. And you don't want me to give that video we have to Derek, do you?'

Trudy could see from his alarmed expression that he didn't and her own worries calmed a little. She was so close to settling the score with Camille. Nothing was going to get in her way now.

She glanced at her watch, saw it had been about ten minutes since Camille left the house.

'Come on.' She gave George a nudge. 'It's time.'

Excitement and nerves jumped about in her belly as they made their way across the lawns and into the orchard. Up ahead, she could see the glow of orange in the window of the summer house, exactly the same as the last time she had been here. This time, though, Angus was away and Camille had no idea that her night was about to take a turn for the worse.

'Wait here,' Trudy whispered, removing her backpack and taking out the sections of rope she had brought with her. Her hands were hot in the latex gloves both she and George wore, her fingers trembling with anticipation, eager to punish.

She peered through the window, saw Camille sat on the chair, the skirt of her red dress spilling around her and the blindfold knotted at the back of her head. She was so still as she waited; no doubt excited for what was to come. As Trudy entered the summer house, closing the door behind her and locking it, the older girl tensed and Trudy heard her draw in a breath.

Realising Camille was nervous too helped build up her confidence.

Trudy took her time, drawing the curtains, then circling her prey, liking that with each recognisable noise Camille was reacting, biting into her lip, clenching and unclenching her hands, not knowing what was coming next. She flinched when Trudy touched her, her breath coming quicker when she realised her hands were being bound, though she didn't resist until she realised she was tied to the chair, whimpering as she struggled against ropes that were cutting into her flesh.

'Please stop, you're hurting me.'

She was frightened now. Good.

Trudy moved to the door, unlocking and opening it, beckoning George inside, but putting a finger to her lips, warning him to be quiet. His eyes widened as he took in Camille, and together they watched as she struggled to free herself.

'I want to stop,' she begged, realising she was not alone. 'I don't like this game.'

George was trembling and Trudy could see he was about to lose his nerve again. Time to reveal the truth to Camille and get George in too deep so he knew he couldn't back out.

She moved behind the girl, leaning in close, her mouth against her ear. 'This isn't a game.'

Her revelation was followed by a moment of stillness as the words sank in and Camille realised it wasn't Angus, then violent struggling as she tried to break free.

Ignoring her efforts, Trudy removed the blindfold and calmly pulled up another chair, sitting down in front of her.

'What do you want? Untie me, please.' Camille was looking frantically at Trudy, then at George.

'You've been fucking my dad.'

Trudy was expecting either a brazen admission or a blatant denial. She got neither.

Instead, a brief silence was followed by tears. 'I'm sorry.'

Camille honestly thought she was going to cry her way out of this situation. The fury grew, along with the need to punish.

'Maybe we should let her go.'

George sounded unsure, and Trudy wanted to slap him, to remind him of why they were here, of the sacrifices she had made for him. She wasn't sure if she was angriest with him for falling for this pathetic pity act or with Camille for trying to fool him.

'Get me the scissors,' she snapped, grabbing his backpack from him when he didn't comply.

Camille's eyes went wide when she saw the silver blades. 'What are you going to do?'

'I'm going to make sure you never go near my father ever again.'

'Please. I won't. I promise. Don't hurt me.'

The rage took over then as Trudy started cutting, then tearing at the red dress. She was aware of Camille frantically struggling. Pleading with George as he looked on in stunned silence. The red scarf was retied, this time across her mouth when the begging turned to screaming, and Trudy grabbed a permanent marker pen, using it to tattoo Camille's body with vile words.

Slut. Whore. Slapper. Tramp.

That night, it was as if she had stepped outside of herself, punishing, threatening and torturing, persuading George to join in as she grew more sadistic in her torment, bruising and cutting the girl, then forcing him to record Camille's degradation.

The whore was a mess, both physically and emotionally, as she tried to plead with Trudy to stop, and at some point she had lost control of both her bladder and bowels. The place stank, her humiliation complete, but still it wasn't enough.

Tonight was never going to satisfy the need for revenge, Trudy realised. She wanted more.

Her fingers closed over the pendant in her pocket, the one she had watched Camille throw back at Sebastian earlier that day, and as she wrapped it around the older girl's neck, she wasn't entirely sure what her intention was. The ribbon was thick and wouldn't tear and she pulled it tight across Camille's throat, initially just wanting to scare her.

When Camille started thrashing in the chair, her eyes widening, Trudy pulled tighter, refusing to let go. Time seemed to blur and she had no idea how long had passed, but when she came to her senses, Camille was limp in the chair and George was looking on, stunned.

'She's just unconscious,' Trudy told him.

'You... killed... her.' He looked in shock, struggling to speak.

Had she? Camille's eyes were wide open, staring sightlessly ahead and there was a deep, dark mark around her neck where the ribbon had cut deep into her skin. It looked crude against her pale throat.

Trudy looked at the pendant still in her hands. Flinching as she realised she didn't want to touch it any more, she threw it to the floor. Needing to cover the strangulation mark, she removed the scarf from Camille's mouth and retied it in a bow around her neck.

She had just killed someone. Why did she not feel any kind of remorse?

'Come on, we need to go.'

She pushed George out of the summer house, leaving Camille tied to the chair.

Later that night, after she had parted ways with him, reminding him they were partners and that he was as deeply involved in everything that had happened as she was, Trudy lay in bed, waiting for emotion to hit.

She had punished Camille, but she hadn't meant to kill her. It had just happened.

She waited for guilt, then for tears, for fear that she might get caught.

The only thing she felt, though, was satisfaction.

For so long, all of her energy had been channelled into getting revenge on Camille Hamilton and finally it was over.

Her only regret was that she hadn't taken the necklace before they left the summer house, a trophy to remind her of what she had done. Little did she know, though, that it would go on to play a part in Sebastian Landry's arrest.

When Trudy rose the next morning, when gossip started to drip through that Camille Hamilton was dead, a rush of power took over. She had done this. She had dealt with a problem that had been in her way. If she could deal with a bitch like Camille, then she could handle anything.

54

It was Doctor Palmer who eventually opened the door, rolling back his wheelchair to let Xav enter the house.

'What do you want?' he grumbled in that typically direct way of his.

Xav had known the Doc for long enough to let his bluntness wash over him. He wasn't about to tell him he was here to confront Trudy about snooping around his house. Whatever her reasons were, he wouldn't cause further conflict between her and her father. He already knew Angus wasn't the easiest man to deal with.

'What happened to you?' he asked, ignoring the question as he frowned at the man's fat lip and the crusted blood on his face. 'You look like someone hit you.'

'None of your business if they did, you nosey bastard.'

'Guess it must have been that charming mouth of yours,' Xav commented dryly.

'Did you just come round here to insult me? Or are you looking for that pathetic excuse of a daughter of mine, because she's not here.'

'She's hardly pathetic, Angus. You should be grateful she looks after you and puts up with your shit.'

'She looks after me? Is that what she tells you?' The Doc shook his head. 'She has you all fooled.'

What was that supposed to mean?

He was about to ask, but the Doc was already spinning his chair around and wheeling down the hallway to the kitchen.

Xav followed. 'So where is she?'

'Don't know. Don't care. As long as she stays the hell away from me.'

'What would you rather she do? Put you in a home?'

'They'd probably treat me better.' Angus's eyes narrowed, the hint of a smirk on his swollen mouth. 'How do you think I got this, Xavier? I didn't do it to myself.'

What exactly was he insinuating?

'If you're trying to suggest Trudy hit you, I don't believe you.'

Xav knew Trudy, and while he didn't want her in his life in a romantic capacity, she was a good person. When Angus had suffered his stroke, she had dedicated much of her time to caring for him.

Angus considered him for a moment. 'Maybe she's right.'

'About what?'

'She does have you wrapped around her finger. You poor fool. And there was me wasting my breath, telling her you would never love her back. I thought you had better taste.'

Xav's temper rose a notch. It wasn't the insults. Those were like water off a duck's back. But the riddles the old man was talking in were getting annoying. 'Can you just spell it out, Angus? If you have something to tell me, then say it.'

The Doc considered him for a moment. 'Why do you think she insists on the pair of us living here together?' he asked. 'Are you really stupid enough to believe she does it because she's my daughter and she loves me? We hate each other.'

Xav didn't buy that, but still he remained quiet, waiting for the man to continue.

'She keeps me here to punish me, because she knows I can't do fuck all about it. It's mostly mind games. Or she'll serve me food I hate or leave me to shit myself. She likes knowing I rely on her. Today she took it a step further and hit me.'

'Why haven't you told anyone this before?' It was a reasonable question, one Xav was certain would prove the Doc was lying. 'You've had plenty of opportunity over the years.'

'We've always kept each other's secrets. She knows what I did and she's been holding it over me, threatening that she'll expose me, saying that even though she did it, no one can prove it and they will still blame me.'

'Blame you for what? What did you do?'

'I'm not playing her games any more. They say I have three months left if I'm lucky.'

'Three months?' Xav repeated. Was he dying? He knew Angus had suffered the stroke, that there had been several weeks where he had barely been able to communicate, but Xav thought he had been getting better.

'I have nothing to lose and I want everyone to know who she really is before I die. I told her that. Just as I told Kitty Hamilton the truth when she came to see me.'

'What truth?' Xav's heart was thumping, his mouth dry. While he wanted to believe this was just the rambling of a bitter old man, there was a quiet acceptance now in the Doc's words that made it hard to dismiss them.

Angus looked up at him, his eyes focused and seeming more controlled than Xav had even seen him. 'That Trudy killed her granddaughter.'

Xav was silent, initially disbelieving. Angus was wrong. Trudy didn't have it in her to kill anyone. And back when Camille died, what would she have been? Fifteen? Camille hadn't been killed by a fifteen-year-old girl. It was ridiculous.

'You don't believe me, do you?' Angus shook his head. 'Kitty didn't either. In fact, she was angrier with me for having an affair with her granddaughter.'

'You were Camille's lover?' Xav's tone was flat, every part of him numb with shock. If this was really true, it was all too much to process. But then why would the man have any reason to lie?

Angus Palmer. The good doctor.

Gus.

'Trudy came home early,' the Doc continued, keen now to get his story out. 'She heard Kitty shouting at me. It didn't take much for her to realise what we had been talking about. After Kitty left, I told that bitch daughter of mine it was over, that now her secret was out, the police would be coming for her. I didn't expect her to go after Kitty.'

Was Xav hearing this right? Angus was now claiming Trudy had killed Kitty as well as Camille? It seemed implausible. Kitty's death had been ruled as an accident, but she had been in the house alone when she had suffered her fall. Was it possible Angus was telling the truth and Trudy had been there?

His thoughts went to his brother in prison. Sebastian had always protested his innocence, but the evidence had been stacked against him. All of this time, Trudy had played the good friend, yet had she really let Sebastian take the fall for her crime?

'Why now?' he demanded, anger replacing shock as it hissed through his veins. He struggled to keep his tone calm. 'Why wait until now to finally admit the truth?'

'I told you. I'm dying. If my life is over, I want hers to be finished too. I didn't expect Trudy to kill Kitty. The doctors said it was my tumour that caused the stroke, but I think the shock played a part. That darling daughter of mine couldn't wait to get me home so she could nurse me in private, make sure that there would be no one for me to expose her secrets too. But here you are.'

Was this true? Thinking back, Xav realised he hadn't really seen Angus alone since his stroke. Trudy was always present, hovering over him, and Xav knew she had cancelled the carer who used to visit, saying she wanted to tend to her father herself. He had believed she was acting in kindness, but Angus's revelations put a whole new slant on things. Horror and disgust twisted in his gut.

He needed to talk to Lana. To tell her about Trudy, and about what had happened with her sister and grandmother.

Lana.

The hit-and-run, then the incident in the garage.

Bree was guilty. Wasn't she? It had been her car and her pink roll-up they had found.

Unless she had been set up.

Xav's heart began to thump.

'Do you know if Trudy left the house last night after I dropped her off?'

If Angus was curious about the question, he didn't say. 'She went out about five minutes after you. I wanted to go to bed, but she left me sat in the living room. She does that a lot'

'And she didn't say where she was going?'

'Nope. But I imagine it has to do with the other Hamilton girl, the one you left her for.'

'What?' Xav demanded. 'I didn't leave Trudy. We were never together.'

'That's not how she sees it. I heard her muttering to herself when she came home earlier. She had stopped by your place, found Lana there, and she was in a foul mood. I had a lot of fun pushing her buttons.'

'And you think that's where she is now? Mead House?'

The Doc's mouth twisted into a humourless smile. 'I don't know. She said something about tying up loose ends. Your guess is as good as mine.'

Xav felt sick. Lana was with Ollie. She was safe. Even so, he pulled out his phone, dialling her number, needing the reassurance. When it went to voicemail, he cursed and tried Ollie.

Damn it. Why the fuck were neither of them answering? He was getting scared now.

'Are you calling the police?' Angus asked, seeming unfazed. 'Tell them I have quite a story for them and they should stop by to see me.'

Xav didn't bother with goodbyes, barely sparing the Doc a parting glance as he left, eager only to get back to his car and over to Mead House.

He was overreacting, he told himself. Lana was fine. Ollie was fine.

But even so, until he had seen that for himself, he wasn't going to settle.

55

Even after I strangled that bitch, Camille, she continued to blight my life and I remember being shocked at the level of grief my father displayed at her death.

The bastard even cried.

In all of my years, I had never seen him show any other emotion apart from anger. He never had any tears or even concern for me or for Mother. Not when I fell off my bike and broke my leg, not when Mother miscarried my younger brother, and I hated him for it.

I couldn't stand it and I realised Mother deserved to know the truth about the affair, to understand what kind of man my father really was. Maybe we could leave and start afresh.

When I told her about what I had seen that night in the summer house, she didn't believe me at first.

'Your father's a good man, Trudy. Why are you making up these lies?'

It wasn't until I insisted, telling her in detail what I had seen, that her face had finally crumpled. I wanted to hug her, to say I was sorry, but to my horror she screamed at me to get out. As I fled to my room, tears choking my throat, I wondered, had I just made a terrible mistake?

She confronted Father when he arrived home, but his denials quickly *turned to rage.*

The screaming was awful and I covered my ears to try to block it out. I feared this wasn't going to end well, but little did I realise it was about to destroy my life.

Mother had been drinking, and in her rage she stormed out to the car, getting behind the wheel. Father followed, managing to clamber into the passenger seat before she roared out of the driveway.

The crash that happened twenty minutes later changed everything.

My mother died and my darling Daddy, the good doctor, ended up with a broken spine. He hasn't walked since.

At the time, I blamed myself. I had told Mother and in doing so I lost the one person I truly loved. I should have kept my mouth shut. Why hadn't my father died? He was the one at fault.

It wasn't until later that I realised I had been handed an opportunity. He needed me now, and our relationship was going to be all on my terms.

For years, I have been the one in charge and we have lived by my rules. When he received news about the brain tumour and I learnt he was going to die, I thought it would be a fitting end for him. Little did I know that he intended to use his remaining time to try to ruin my life.

I didn't plan to kill Kitty Hamilton, but he left me no choice. When my father told me what he had done, that he had revealed my secret. I knew I had to bury it again before Kitty went to the police.

She had looked shocked as she opened the door to me, reluctant to let me in, and in a way I had felt a little sorry for her. She hadn't asked to be burdened with the truth. I made her death as quick as possible, disguising it to look like a fall.

My father has a lot to answer for and I enjoyed making him return to Mead House that day we went to meet Lana, where the memories of his good friend Kitty and his precious Camille lingered.

Death is too good for Daddy Dearest. I want him to suffer until he has drawn his last breath.

Lana and Ollie, though, are a different story. I'm going to enjoy this.

56

Back when they were children, the summer house had been used as a play den and for birthday parties. Kitty would put colourful banners up on the walls and balloons on the door. There would be crisps and pizza slices, bottles of fizz and cake.

By the time Camille, Lana and Ollie were all in their teens, it had fallen out of favour, standing empty and neglected as they preferred going into town to hang out with their friends.

It had been Camille who had eventually decided to spruce it up, putting in new accessories, and making curtains for the windows and covers for the cushions on the sofa. It became her sanctuary. A place she could escape the noisy chatter of her younger siblings to do her homework or read in peace, then, later on, where she could be alone with Sebastian and, eventually, when her tastes turned darker, with Doctor Angus Palmer.

Since Camille's death, it had been abandoned, a soulless place with tragic memories, and a musty smell clung to the air. Lana had been down here just the once, Ollie not at all since finding Camille's body, and although it was difficult for both of them being back here, Lana understood it was harder for him.

He hadn't said much since Trudy had appeared with the knife held at his throat, but even though the knife had now gone, he offered little resistance as she pushed him down on to the floor and bound his ankles together with rope. His face was pale and his eyes downcast and it seemed he had retreated into himself, unable to deal with what was happening.

Lana had no idea what Trudy was planning for them both, but she didn't intend to die without a fight. While Trudy was focused on her brother, she concentrated on the knots tying her to the chair, trying to ignore that she was sat in the same spot as where Camille had died.

Seriously, how had they all missed the signs with Trudy? Or had there really not been any? She was a year younger than Lana and Ollie, the quiet daughter of the doctor. Lana hadn't taken much notice of her back then. Sure, she was friendly if their paths crossed, but Trudy always seemed to blend into the background.

Things had been different since their return to town. Trudy had grown in confidence, but still, it was difficult to accept that this warm and seemingly professional woman, who cared for her disabled father, was actually a cold-blooded killer.

Lana watched her now as she moved away from Ollie, pulling a box of matches from her pocket and lighting candles. What was she doing? The candles hadn't been here when she had come down to the summer house before, had they?

The candlelight softened the neglect of the room, but it was also a little unnerving, adding another level of weirdness to this awful situation they were in. When Trudy moved to the windows, drawing what remained of the curtains across them, a sense of claustrophobia set in. This flickering nightmare was now far too real.

Lana had no idea what the time was, but the fact there was still some light outside told her it must be before 9 p.m. Why wasn't Xav here yet? Or was he up at the house wondering where the hell they were?

Right now, he was their only real hope out of this situation.

She looked at Ollie, willing him to make eye contact. They needed to stick together, figure out some kind of plan. Escape didn't seem an option right now, given how tightly the knots were tied, but if they could somehow distract Trudy, at least until Xav returned, then perhaps they had a chance.

When Trudy stepped between them, blocking Ollie from view, Lana tensed. She tried not to react when she laid eyes on the knife.

Don't show her any fear.

Easier said than done, but still Lana raised her chin in defiance.

'Dress it up any way you want to. My sister having an affair with your dad does not justify what you did to her.' When Trudy scowled, but said nothing, she pressed on. 'And look at what you're doing to us now. We've done nothing to deserve this.'

'Wrong!' The venom in that one word had Lana flinching. 'You Hamiltons think you're so fucking special. You show up back in town and think everything is yours for the taking. He was mine!'

What?

Lana must have looked confused, because Trudy decided to elaborate, going on a rant.

'He didn't need you coming here. You broke his heart once. Do you have any idea of the torment you put him through? How difficult it was for him to see you again?'

Was she talking about Xav?

'He had me and we were doing fine. He doesn't need you. You're bad for him.'

Was she insane? For a moment, Lana forgot about the knife. 'You killed my sister,' she snapped. 'And you let Xav believe his brother did it. You have the nerve to call yourself his friend?'

The blade flashed before her, the sharp point suddenly

digging into her jaw, and Lana froze, her eyes widening at the pain, hating that she was trembling. Somehow she managed to hold Trudy's stare, determined not to show her how scared she was.

'Camille deserved what we did to her,' Trudy snapped. 'And Xav and I are lovers. Not friends.'

What the fuck? Was she deluded? And who was 'we'?

'He loved me. Did love me. Until you showed up.'

The point of the knife pressed deeper and Lana jerked against the rope, refusing to let go of the scream that was ripping through her. She couldn't stop the tears springing to her eyes, though, or hide the fact that she was now shaking badly, and she had an awful feeling Trudy was going to feed on it.

A crunch of what sounded like a boot against gravel came from outside, the noise echoing through the summer house, and Trudy paused as she looked back towards the door.

Was someone outside? Lana wanted to scream for help, but with the blade so close to her throat, she didn't dare.

Several seconds ticked by and she was aware of her thumping heartbeat in the otherwise silent room.

Another crunch came, and it sounded closer.

This time, Trudy withdrew the knife and as she moved to the window, Lana sensed she was rattled.

Please let it be someone coming to help us.

She watched the woman open the door and peer outside, then, without another word, she left the summer house.

As soon as she was gone, Lana tried to get her brother's attention. 'Are you okay? We need to get free before she comes back.' When he didn't respond, his gaze on the door as he watched, looking terrified that Trudy would be back at any second, she tried again. 'Ollie? Is there any slack in your rope?'

She tugged at her own wrists and knew she couldn't pull them free. She needed him to help her. They didn't have much time and Lana dreaded to think what would happen when Trudy returned.

She thought back to Camille and the torture she had endured, and that was when the emotion hit, hot tears running down her cheeks. She didn't want to give Trudy any kind of edge, but she couldn't help it, she was scared.

'Ollie, please. I can't do this alone.'

He looked at her then and she watched as he fought to pull his arms free. 'The rope's too tight,' he muttered, sounding defeated.

Footsteps had her tensing, her head turning sharply as a figure entered the summer house.

She blinked when she realised it wasn't Trudy. Instead, George Maddox stood in the doorway. Lana was so relieved to see him, she didn't question why he was here.

'Please help us,' she begged. 'Before she comes back.'

He glanced between the pair of them before going to Lana, working at the knots binding her wrists to the spindles in the back of the chair.

'Do you know where she is?' she demanded, wriggling in impatience, desperate to be free. George didn't seem at all surprised finding them here, so she assumed he knew Trudy had done this.

'Shh!' he urged. 'We don't have much time. I managed to hide, but she's outside looking for me.'

Lana glanced at the door as another shadow filled the doorway, and panic clawed its way up her throat.

'You bastard!' Trudy cried, as Lana screamed, watching as the woman pounced at George, the knife in her hand.

'NO!'

It was too late and as the blade disappeared into George's back, blood instantly spurted. His expression was one of shock as he gasped, trying to reach for the blade, and he stared at Lana, his eyes wide, before collapsing. After a moment of twitching, he stilled, but

Trudy wasn't done yet, wrenching the blade from his back, then stabbing him again.

Ollie watched in pure horror, while Lana looked away, unable to bear what was happening. Trudy was crazy. She couldn't be reasoned with and it didn't matter how brave they were, it wouldn't make any difference. They were going to die.

As fresh tears spilled, Lana made another attempt to undo the knots binding her to the chair. Her wrists were looser now, but not enough to free herself. There was definitely some movement in the knot though, and she pulled at it frantically, trying her best to keep her grip steady as she worked.

Realising Trudy had finished with George, Lana looked up. The woman was covered in blood, a slow, sadistic smile widening on her face.

'Please let us go. You don't have to do this.'

Trudy was moving towards her now, the knife in her hand glinting in the candlelight.

'Leave her alone! Don't touch her.'

Ollie had found his voice, but it wasn't going to help. Trudy was focused, like a cat closing in on its prey.

'Please don't—'

'Lana?'

Her last plea cut short by a new voice. Lana realised Xav had entered the summer house, looking horrified as he took in the scene before him. While part of her wanted to beg him to help her, she couldn't risk putting him in danger.

'Xav. Run. She has a knife.'

He wasn't listening, his gaze now moving to Trudy as she turned to face him.

'I was hoping you wouldn't come here.' She sounded disappointed and Lana watched in terror.

Go, Xav. Leave now.

He had no idea of the danger he was in.

'What the hell are you doing?' he demanded.

'You weren't supposed to see this. Now you've ruined everything.'

She sounded petulant, like a child.

Xav was silent for a moment and then his tone changed, softening. 'Why? Don't you want me to see the real you?'

'What? What are you talking about?' Although Trudy was still clinging to the knife, her tone was curious.

'This, what you're doing here.'

'What about it?'

'It's for me, right?'

Lana was holding her breath, watching the pair of them, and she could see Ollie was doing the same.

Xav took no notice of either of them, his gaze fixed on Trudy. 'I didn't realise you cared about me so much.'

'I've always loved you. But you chose her.' She stabbed the knife in Lana's direction. Xav was losing her.

'Because I didn't realise. I didn't know how far you were prepared to go for me.'

Now Trudy was looking genuinely confused. Lana could see she wanted to believe what Xav was saying, but she was still sceptical.

'You must really love me,' he pressed on. 'I get that now.'

'You do?'

'I do. I've never had anyone prepared to go to such great lengths for me before.'

Trudy cocked her head on one side as she looked at him. She was still unsure, but Lana realised she was processing what Xav was telling her and giving it consideration.

He sounded convincing. Lana had known and trusted him for over half of her life, but even so, the teeniest sliver of unease had crept into her belly.

She cursed herself for her moment of doubt. Xav was on her side.

'Do you want to watch me kill her?'

She tensed at Trudy's words and tugged again at the rope. This time, it was looser and she managed to pull one of her hands partly free.

'I have a better idea,' Xav proposed.

'You do?' Trudy sounded hopeful. Excited, even.

'Let me do it.'

What?

'You fucking prick. What the hell are you playing at?' Ollie was twisting on his side now as he yelled the words, frantically trying to break free, clearly buying into Xav's performance.

Xav ignored him. 'If this is going to work, we need to be able to trust each other. I know your secrets. This way you can keep mine too.' He took another step closer to her. 'Let me do this for you.'

Lana managed to wrench her hand free, just in time to see Xav kiss a stunned-looking Trudy. As he stepped back, Lana realised he had taken the knife from her. She wanted to weep with relief.

There was a moment of hesitation as he glanced down at George's body and it seemed it was enough to rattle Trudy.

'Do it then!' she demanded. She was impatient now, sounding annoyed.

What happened next was so fast, Lana could barely register it.

Xav finally turned to look at her and from the subtle nod he gave her, Lana understood this was all part of a plan. Unfortunately, Trudy saw the exchange too. One moment she was weapon-free, the next second she had pulled out a pocketknife.

The blade gleamed as she flicked it open, and Lana screamed.

'Xav! Watch out.'

As the blade tore through the air towards him, the word, 'Liar,' on Trudy's lips, Lana managed to free her other hand. With her ankles still bound to the front legs of the chair, her leap towards Trudy was clumsy, but it achieved the desired result, knocking the blade from Trudy's grip, before she could stab it into Xav, and causing Trudy to lose her balance. She toppled to the ground, knocking one of the candles as she fell, and her head cracked hard against the floor, a gurgled gasp escaping her lips.

Lana landed on top of her, the chair snapping, and with her hands now free, she started to pummel the woman, hitting her again and again. For Camille and for everything Trudy had put her and Ollie through, and for Sebastian, who had taken the fall for her crime.

She was vaguely aware of flames rising but continued to lash out until arms wrapped around her, lifting her back. It was only then she realised Trudy was already gone. That she had landed on her own knife. The puddle of blood beneath her head and eyes wide open telling Lana that she hadn't felt a single blow.

'It's over. She's dead.' Xav had hold of Lana, pulling her into him and holding onto her as though he was scared to let go. 'We need to get out of here before this place burns down.'

Lana's eyes widened as she realised the fire had taken hold and was spreading quickly, the curtains and the furniture already alight. She glanced at her brother in panic as he tried to shuffle away from the flames. 'I'm fine. Help Ollie,' she protested, as Xav dragged her out of the summer house.

She worked at the knots binding her ankles as he disappeared back inside, frantically trying to free herself so she could help.

Even out here, she was coughing with the smoke, the intensity of the fire heating her skin. In the distance, she heard sirens wailing and realised they were growing closer.

When Xav emerged, half dragging, half carrying Ollie, Lana choked back a sob of relief. The two people she loved the most in the world were safe.

As her brother collapsed to the floor beside her, Xav glanced back at the summer house.

'George is still inside,' he commented.

Lana finished untying Ollie's wrists. 'Don't you dare go back in there.'

'We can't just leave him.'

'I'm pretty sure he's dead. The police are nearly here. Please just wait.'

'But what if he isn't? There's not enough time.'

'Xav, no!'

It was too late. He wasn't listening and had disappeared back into the flames before she was even on her feet,

'Lana!' Ollie was yelling at her, as she tried to follow after him. 'Stay outside.'

She didn't have a choice, the heat from the flames beating her back.

'Xav!' She sobbed his name. After everything they had been through, and the suffering they had both endured, she couldn't lose him again.

The whole building was alight, the roof about to collapse. He didn't stand a chance.

'Lana, get back over here.' Ollie's tone was frantic, and knowing there was nothing she could do, she went to him, tears falling as he held her.

'Jesus.'

Suddenly, Ollie was pushing her to one side and scrambling to his feet, and Lana looked on shocked as two blackened figures stumbled from the summer house, her heartbeat quickening.

'Xav?'

George was either dead or unconscious, dropping heavily to the ground, as Xav choked and spluttered, trying to catch his breath.

Lana didn't give him a chance, launching herself into his arms.

'I don't know whether to kiss you or kill you,' she sobbed against his ear, breathing in the smoke clinging to his damp hair.

As the sirens grew closer, she stared over his shoulder at what remained of the summer house. It was the place where her sister had died. How fitting, it had now taken the life of Camille's killer.

57

EIGHT WEEKS LATER

As far as George Maddox was concerned, he had been a victim too, and although he had been coerced into the attack and subsequent murder of Camille Hamilton, he figured he had absolved himself of any guilt by trying to rescue Lana and Ollie.

The doctors told him he was lucky to be alive, but it didn't feel like it, and after a couple of weeks in the hospital, he was finally released.

Initially, he had been touted as something of a hero, putting his life on the line to stop Trudy Palmer from claiming any more victims. But when the police delved deeper, there were questions asked that started to expose the holes in his story.

George clung to denial.

Elise's body had been found in the holiday cottage and his prints were there, plus he had been seen with her the previous day.

They couldn't prove fuck all, though, and they certainly knew nothing of his past history.

He was a good person these days. Well, mostly. And he had a family who needed him. He would do whatever it took to protect them.

* * *

It was a tenacious detective who was his undoing.

DS Finn Murphy became the thorn in George's side, determined to take him down.

He knew the man's story didn't hold up, though there wasn't enough evidence to tie him to Elise Gladstone's murder or connect him to Trudy Palmer. And he had spoken with all of George's friends and family, but other than his stepbrother, Derek, who was cagier than George, shutting down completely when questioned, Finn was struggling to get to the truth. He suspected George had been an accessory to Elise Gladstone's murder, possibly Camille Hamilton's too, but when the payoff came, it was bigger than expected.

Unlike George, Angus Palmer had been more than willing to assist the police, seeming more interested in helping to tarnish his daughter's name than to do right by her victims.

Finn wasn't a fan.

It helped that Angus was compliant, though, agreeing with any requests for interviews and searches, and it was during a return visit to the man's house that Finn struck gold.

He found the bicycle in the cluttered garage. It was at the back of the room, partly hidden behind an old pasting table. A girl's bike with red bodywork and a basket on the front. There was a blanket folded in the basket and beneath it was Camille Hamilton's missing journal, the one Lana Hamilton said had been stolen, along with a cassette.

It took a little while to reveal the contents, Finn having to go to a video specialist to have the tape converted, but what the footage revealed was worth waiting for, even if it hadn't been easy to watch. The shaky footage playing the last minutes of Camille Hamilton's life as she tried to plead with Trudy Palmer.

Finn understood serial killers, the constant tweak of pain in his side a reminder of the bullet he had taken while trying to stop one, and he recognised the dead look in Trudy's eyes as she casually tortured Camille, displaying no emotion or mercy.

Eventually, she turned to her partner, the person responsible for the jerky camerawork. 'Come on, George. It's your go.'

He had needed a little persuasion, but eventually their places had switched, and Finn recognised the small boy with glasses from the photographs he had seen in the living room of George's mother's house.

When George had finished, he faced the camera, giving Trudy the thumbs up as he smiled.

Gotcha.

* * *

Lana was shocked by George Maddox's arrest, especially after he had tried to save her and Ollie, but she was also relieved. She hadn't missed Trudy's words that last awful night in the summer house when she had referred to a 'we', suggesting there had been another person there with Camille the night she was murdered.

It wasn't Bree McCarthy, who had been investigated and cleared after Trudy's prints had been found in the car that was used for the hit and run. Bree was still being a little testy with Xav for doubting her, though she was slowly coming around. So who had it been?

Finally learning the truth, that it had been Trudy and George she had heard outside the night of Camille's murder, meant Lana was able to put it behind her and now George understood he was going down, he had decided to talk, in turn giving her full closure. The story came out about how he and Trudy had first met in detention all those years ago, and how she had coerced him into helping her.

George claimed he hadn't killed Elise and there was nothing to link him to Kitty. He insisted he and Trudy had parted ways following Camille's death.

The revelation about Kitty had been one of the hardest to take in, and it was news that had shocked the local community. Knowing that Trudy had killed her grandmother made the remaining time at Mead House all the more poignant and difficult to bear, and remembering the phone calls she had missed, Lana couldn't help wonder if the outcome would have been different had she answered.

Doctor Palmer was never able to shed any light on things. Just a few days after the discovery of the video and the second journal, he had suffered a second stroke, this time fatal. Lana didn't feel any sadness at his death. Okay, so he hadn't killed anyone, but he had abused his position of power and betrayed her grandmother's friendship in seducing Camille, and he had kept Trudy's dark secret for all of these years, instead of giving the family closure. She tried not to let the anger overwhelm her, but equally she wouldn't mourn the man.

She had wondered why Trudy had kept hold of the evidence that could have put her away. She had gone to such lengths to get the journal and without that and the video, there was no conclusive proof of her guilt.

DS Murphy had told them Trudy was a narcissist and it was highly likely she thought herself above the law. The tape and then the journal were more than likely her trophies, though it was also possible she had kept the tape as blackmail against George.

With Mead House eventually emptied and ready to go on the market, Ollie prepared to return to London. Before he left, he and Lana took a trip to the church in Holt to lay flowers at both Camille's and Kitty's graves. She hugged her brother tightly as they said their goodbyes, more aware than ever that he was the only family she had left.

'Are you going to be okay going back to the house by yourself?' he questioned, easing away. 'I can hold off for a couple of hours until you're ready.'

He had been like a changed man these last few weeks and the terrible night which could have ended with both of them being murdered had bonded them closer together. He had already been in shock about Elise's betrayal, especially when he learnt she had cheated on him with George, and her murder had shaken him. Lana had helped him to deal with it as best as she could and knew Ollie was unlikely to trust so easily again.

'I'll be fine. I haven't got much to pack and Xav will be over soon. You're good to go.'

She planned to move in with Xav temporarily. She had been working remotely for the last couple of weeks and her boss had agreed she could continue to do so. It would give her time to decide what came next, though she knew whatever future plans she made would involve Xav. She had loved him for nearly all of her life and they had too much catching up to do. The painting of her that he had now finished, where he had poured his passion onto the canvas, told her that he felt the same.

She didn't intend to come back to Mead House at all unless there was a problem, and the keys were now with the estate agent. They had told her recent events might hamper the sale, but Lana and Ollie had decided they would drop the price if they had to. It was time for a fresh start.

Ollie nodded, climbing in his car.

'Make sure you call me,' Lana told him as he started the engine, reminding him of their pact to stay in touch this time.

He gave her his cheeky trademark grin, though she didn't miss it was a little tighter than usual, saluting her as he pulled away, and she knew they both had to learn to heal again.

Ollie remained on her mind as she returned to the house, dragging her luggage downstairs, then taking a final walk through the place where she had grown up. It was a warm evening and the sun was low in the sky, beaming through the wide windows and illuminating the now empty rooms. It was a peaceful moment she took for herself to savour the happier memories and to try to steady her nerves for what came next.

When she opened the door to Xav a short while later, she must have looked a little anxious, because he frowned, eyes narrowing as he studied her face.

'You okay?'

'Yeah, I will be.'

When he didn't look convinced, Lana reached up, linking her arms around his neck.

'I'm fine, honestly.' she tried to assure him, moulding her body to his.

She suspected he knew better, but he took the hint anyway, pushing her into the house and kicking the door shut, then turning her round and pressing her up against it as he kissed her deeply.

As far as distractions went, it worked.

Later, after Lana had locked the door for the last time and they had loaded her bags into the car, he caught hold of her hand, giving it a squeeze.

'You ready to do this?'

Her nod was decisive, and her smile relaxed as she looked up at him.

She had experienced both sad and happy times at Mead House, but it was time to close the door on this part of her life. The memories of those she had loved would always be with her, but she wanted to start living in the present and make new ones with Xav.

Before she could start on that, there was one more thing she had
to do.

She squeezed his hand back, ignoring the swarm of butterflies
in her belly. 'I'm ready.'

* * *

Xav had been the one to propose the meeting.

Lana had kept a low profile since Sebastian's release, but for
things to be right between them, Xav knew that could only be
temporary. He loved Lana and he loved his mother and brother too.
Somehow this would have to work.

Joanna Landry had been reluctant, conflicted over the girl she
had once loved who had played a part in her son being wrongfully
convicted, but she had eventually agreed. Sebastian had initially
given a resounding no.

Xav had been shocked by the changes in his brother. Prison had
aged him and Seb was more reserved than he remembered. Reflec-
tive too. It was going to take a while for him to adjust to life in the
outside world. He hadn't pushed, knowing that they would have to
do this on his brother's terms when he was ready, but he was
relieved when that happened sooner rather than later.

They had agreed to meet at the beach, Xav taking Lana's hand
as they crossed the stony ridge. The tide was out and he spotted his
mother and Sebastian standing by the shore, watching the waves as
they talked.

The sky was now a moody hue of deep blues and purples, as the
sun prepared to set, and along with the sound of the thrashing
waves hitting the shoreline, it added unwanted tension to the
moment. As though sensing their approach, Sebastian turned to
look at them, his eyes locking with Lana's.

Aware of the nerves that were bouncing off her, Xav sought to give her reassurance. 'It's going to be okay, I promise.'

She didn't look convinced, but he could see the determination in her eyes as she glanced up at him, and understood this moment was important to her too.

It wasn't going to be easy, and there may be some bumps in the road ahead, but together they would deal with them.

Tightening her grip on Xav's hand, Lana took the first step down onto the beach.

ACKNOWLEDGMENTS

Some books you write, others reach deep inside of you and squeeze at your heart. *The Summer House* was one of those for me, and I fell in love with Lana and Xav while telling their story. I hope you enjoyed reading their tale as much as I enjoyed bringing it to life.

My thanks go to the brilliant Boldwood Books team. To my fab editor, Caroline, to Jade, Emily, Amanda, Nia, Claire, Jenna and Ben, and anyone working behind the scenes who I may have missed. Thank you for everything you do to help our books shine.

To all of my reader and blogger friends. There are so many of you and I am always scared of missing someone. Please know you are all awesome.

Writers get writers, and I am lucky to have some lovely ones I chat with. Just a few who need singling out – Nathan 'NJ' Moss, Heather Fitt, Valerie Keogh, Diane Saxon, and of course, Patricia Dixon. Trish's support is unwavering and she calms me when I have a wobble, picks me up if I am down, and helps me fix those pesky plot holes when I panic. Thank you, mate, for everything you do.

Thank you also to Jo Bilton, who has been my beta reader since day one, and to Tina Jackson, who has just joined my beta team, reading alongside Jo and Trish. Tina, your beta experience and brilliant feedback makes me wish I had asked you much sooner. Thank you.

The name Mead House was suggested to me by another writer friend, AJ Griffiths Jones. Thank you, AJ.

Finally to my family and friends. To Mum, Holly, Paul, Nicki and all the furry kids. To Paula, Ness, Andrea, Caroline, Shell, Hannah, The Smervs, etc, etc. Sorry again for anyone I've missed. I love you all.

MORE FROM KERI BEEVIS

We hope you enjoyed reading *The Summer House*. If you did, please leave a review.

If you'd like to gift a copy, this book is also available as an ebook, large print, hardback, digital audio download and audiobook CD.

Sign up to Keri Beevis' mailing list for news, competitions and updates on future books.

https://bit.ly/KeriBeevisnews

The Sleepover, another twisty psychological thriller from Keri Beevis, is available now...

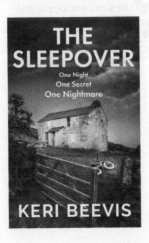

ABOUT THE AUTHOR

Keri Beevis is the internationally bestselling author of several psychological thrillers and romantic suspense mysteries, including the very successful *Dying to Tell*, published by Bloodhound. She sets many of her books in the county of Norfolk, where she was born and still lives and which provides much of her inspiration.

Visit Keri's website: http://www.keribeevis.com/

Follow Keri on social media:

 twitter.com/keribeevis

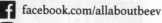 facebook.com/allaboutbeev

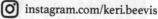 instagram.com/keri.beevis

THE

Murder

LIST

**THE MURDER LIST IS A NEWSLETTER
DEDICATED TO SPINE-CHILLING FICTION
AND GRIPPING PAGE-TURNERS!**

**SIGN UP TO MAKE SURE YOU'RE ON OUR
HIT LIST FOR EXCLUSIVE DEALS, AUTHOR
CONTENT, AND COMPETITIONS.**

SIGN UP TO OUR NEWSLETTER

BIT.LY/THEMURDERLISTNEWS

Boldwood

Boldwood Books is an award-winning fiction publishing company seeking out the best stories from around the world.

Find out more at www.boldwoodbooks.com

Join our reader community for brilliant books, competitions and offers!

Follow us

@BoldwoodBooks

@BookandTonic

Sign up to our weekly deals newsletter

https://bit.ly/BoldwoodBNewsletter

9 781804 151327